JUST STAB ME NOW

Just Stab Me Now

JILL BEARUP

SWORD LADY BOOKS

PUBLISHED BY SWORD LADY BOOKS

Copyright © 2024 Jill Bearup

Edited by Stephanie Gail Eagleson, eaglesonediting.com
Typesetting by Libris Simas Ferraz, oncapublishing.com
Cover by Scott A. Perry, artforhire.com

ISBNS:
978-1-7394319-0-7 (eBook),
978-1-7394319-1-4 (paperback),
978-1-7394319-2-1 (hardcover).

For my mother, who always wanted me to be a novelist,
for my viewers, who made me write this book,
and for my husband and daughter, who put up with me while I did.

Table of Contents

Chapter 1

'I CAN'T BELIEVE IT!'

Lady Rosamund Hawkhurst had lived through worse days than this, but not many. 'A trip to Abrenia with one guard would be risky even in peacetime.' A pair of long hose flew through the air to land precisely on top of a set of saddlebags at the foot of her four-poster bed. 'Why is Queen Eudosia willing to send me thus while we're still at war?' She pulled an undershirt from a drawer, shook a stray caladrius feather out of the sleeve, and folded the garment roughly before dropping it on a saddlebag and flopping onto the bed. 'Hasn't Hawkhurst given her enough already?'

The distant tap of the mourning drum came flooding back, as sharp as the day she'd heard it eleven months ago. The black-robed messengers had been all-too-visible out of the window, and when she'd seen them, she'd slumped against the wall, shaking.

Sir Hugo Hawkhurst was dead. Killed in the war between her home country — Abrenia — and Bevoria, where she had lived for the last sixteen years.

But grief was a luxury afforded to those who didn't have an estate to look after, so Rosamund had straightened her dress, wiped her eyes, and marched wordlessly downstairs to face a future without her husband in it. At the funeral, she'd hugged her sobbing daughter and stared up at the ceiling to keep her own tears in check. Her son hadn't spoken for

1

the entire day. Both of her children had vanished as soon as the ceremony concluded, and Rosamund was grateful that they, at least, had been able to mourn in private.

But somehow, that day had passed, as even the worst ones must, and they had all been learning to cope. Until last month, when Baron Mabry, their liege lord, had come to visit. He'd complained at length about a shortage of caladrius salve for his men (despite having claimed most of the stock delivered to the front lines a mere fortnight prior) before beginning to pontificate upon the Hawkhurst estate's lack of martial leadership.

'As long as the war continues, I simply must have a Hawkhurst knight to lead the soldiers at the front. Perhaps Edmund will be free to assume the duty soon, despite his tender years.'

Rosamund had demurred as politely as possible. Edmund was barely fifteen, she had argued; surely there could be no reason to let an untried youth lead troops into battle. But Mabry had kept up the pressure ever since; she needed a more effective deterrent, and that meant she needed to curry favour with the Bevorian Crown. She needed Eudosia to intervene.

When news of King Adelric's death and the ascension of his son Roland to the Abrenian throne arrived at Hawkhurst, Rosamund kissed her children goodbye and made haste to Veleria, the Bevorian capital, to offer her services to the queen. The last thing she wanted was for her family to get more involved in the war—but better her than Edmund. And given her personal connection to King Roland, Rosamund was sure that Eudosia would be eager to make use of her.

But Rosamund's audience with the queen had not gone as anticipated, and now she was back in the palace's guest quarters, packing for a trip that might as well have been a suicide mission. She drew a deep, shuddering breath. 'Have I offended the Crown in some way? Does Eudosia not *want* to make peace with Abrenia?' She hauled herself into a sitting position, too agitated to stay still. 'And where did I put my green knife?'

×

Sudden, absolute silence fell, the normal noises of the palace abruptly cutting off. Rosamund jumped to her feet and ran to the window. Outside, everything had frozen in place — the queen's pet phoenix perched on a flagpole in the courtyard, golden tail feathers glittering; guards clad in blue and gold paused mid-step; a nobleman stood with one arm suspended in the middle of an expansive gesture.

A woman appeared. Not through the door, nor the window, no: she simply blinked into existence at Rosamund's elbow. Her outfit was incongruously modern: a striped blue shirt, blue-framed glasses, and tightly-bunned red hair with a rollerball pen stuck through it. She and Rosamund were otherwise almost identical. And as the second woman appeared, the truth of the matter dropped into Rosamund's brain like a stone into a pond: *I am the main character in this woman's story.*

And her author looked peeved.

'Lady Rosamund Hawkhurst,' Caroline said testily, 'you really need to calm down. The details regarding your trip to Abrenia aren't that important; I was going to fill them in later!'

Rosamund sat back down on the bed. 'It's *not that important* that I'm taking a week-long trip to my homeland in a time of war?' She knotted her hands in her lap, willing herself to patience. 'Caroline, I

3

heard rumours that Queen Eudosia was considering a peace treaty with King Roland, so I came to offer my services as an envoy.'

'A bold and risky move,' said Caroline, as if this hadn't been her idea in the first place. 'But it makes perfect sense, seeing as' — she produced a worn, leather-bound notebook from thin air and flipped it open to a page entitled *Family Tree* — 'while you live in Bevoria now, you're King Roland's sister-in-law, and originally from Abrenia! And won't it be nice to see your little sister again? And call her "Your Majesty"?'

'Yes, it'll be lovely to see Cat again,' said Rosamund, ignoring the "Your Majesty" part, 'but the queen has decided to send me to Abrenia with a Declaration of Truce and *one guard*. Not even an attendant! Is she trying to enrage King Roland by putting me in mortal peril? Is Eudosia running mad? Is this a trap? Does she secretly hate me?'

Rosamund had not been a frequent visitor to either court in the years since her marriage. Neither she nor Hugo had been social butterflies, and court gossip was dull as ditchwater. She'd never thought much of her absences from the mainstays of the social calendar, but perhaps it had offended the Bevorian Crown in some way?

'Of course not!' Caroline plopped down next to Rosamund on the bed. 'But you have to understand, I — she — couldn't send you with a maidservant and an entire contingent of guards; that's not how the trope works at all!' She slanted a sly smile at her heroine. 'This is an enemies-to-lovers story! You and your Hot Enemy have to be alone together, in close quarters, dependent on each other, building trust and covertly eyeing each other and trading heated barbs and . . .' She flapped her hands, causing several stray scraps of paper to fall out of the notebook. 'It's just how these things work!'

Rosamund's mouth fell open. 'It's just not reasonable that I'm being sent with a *single guard* —'

'Very single,' Caroline interrupted. 'Your Hot Enemy is neither married nor involved with anyone else.'

Rosamund sighed, pinching the bridge of her nose between thumb and forefinger. 'No attendants at all? What about my maidservant Sally and my own guard from home? They accompanied me here.'

'There's been a terrible bout of, um, highly contagious fever. Or maybe infectious, I'll have to check what the difference is. Most of the servants at the palace have caught it, including Sally and Jones, and those who haven't are being run off their feet.' Caroline shrugged, still cheery. 'Your mission is too urgent to delay, so you and your Hot Enemy will just have to cope.'

Rosamund gave up arguing. For now. 'Does this Hot Enemy have a name?'

'Captain Collins, of the Queen's Guard.'

'A first name?'

Caroline wrinkled her nose. 'Working on it.'

Rosamund nodded stiffly, took a deep breath, and stood up again. 'Fine.'

She could survive this. She could facilitate peace and end the war. She could get home to Edmund and Charlotte without being killed by the dangers of the road or Captain Whatever-His-Name-Was Collins. If she was careful. If she was wise. And if she gave Caroline enough of the things she wanted. 'Then let us continue.'

Caroline beamed. 'Great! Time to crack on with the preparation scene!' She consulted a list on another page of her notebook. 'Oh, one quick note: you are planning to pack either a knife or an ornately decorated dagger, yes?'

'Of course I'm planning to pack a knife,' Rosamund replied, befuddled. As if she'd go anywhere without one.

Caroline marked an item on her checklist with an ostentatious tick. 'To threaten your Hot Enemy in the middle of the night?'

Rosamund rolled her eyes. 'The knife is for eating.' She gave Caroline a flat look. 'Though I suppose I could stab someone with it if sufficiently motivated.'

Caroline either didn't notice the threat or ignored it, instead scribbling something on another page of her book. Indeed, Rosamund's author seemed to have a talent for ignoring things that didn't fit in with her bizarre and often clichéd plans. Take this "Hot Enemy" business, for example: Caroline seemed to be under the impression that the fantasy story she had placed Rosamund in was some kind of . . . *romance*.

Truthfully, Rosamund should have known something was amiss from their very first meeting. It had taken place in a spartan, white-walled room, where Caroline willed Rosamund into being and then started criticising her appearance.

'Why do you look like me? And why are you so *old*?'

'I'm thirty-six!' Rosamund had retorted, bewildered by this strange, bespectacled goddess who had complete power over her existence while remaining maddeningly vague on details.

'Yes, I see. Can you handle a sword?'

'Yes. What kind?'

'You know, a sword! Pointy end goes in the other man, weighs about' — Caroline frowned — 'four-and-a-half kilos?'

Rosamund wasn't sure what system of measurement her world used, but she was very sure that wasn't a reasonable weight for a sword by any standard. But Caroline was uninterested in specifics unless they related to the multiple attractive men she was planning to introduce. Men whose attention Rosamund was supposed to both desire and agonise over.

'Love triangles are perennially popular for a reason, Rosamund!'

Rosamund, whose grief for Hugo still caught her by surprise at odd moments, was not impressed by this. Especially now that she was preparing to embark on a dangerous mission. The reason she had come to the palace had nothing to do with romance and everything to do with the safety of her children — children of a wonderful marriage to an irreplaceable man. But it was no use trying to make this point to Caroline.

'I assume that you're packing travelling clothes?' Caroline enquired, making another note.

'Yes.'

'And your most beautiful gown?'

Rosamund's eyes drifted to the saddlebags and the items jumbled atop them. Before she left the Hawkhurst estate five days ago, she had packed two court-appropriate changes of clothing: the green velvet underdress and surcoat she was currently wearing, and another dress . . . the details of which currently escaped her.

Caroline, still bent over the notebook, folded over the corner of a page and scribbled something that Rosamund interpreted as — *wobbly dress*? 'I haven't made up my mind about your other gown yet,' Caroline said, snapping the book shut and looking up, 'but I'm making a note that you're packing it!'

Rosamund pressed her fingers to her temples. She felt a headache coming on. 'Lovely. Could you please leave me in peace to finish this?'

Caroline faded out of view, and Rosamund forgot that the other woman had ever been there.

But she remembered that her green knife was in the third drawer.

×

Caroline Lindley was rather enjoying her new story. It did require an awful lot of Internet research about subjects ranging from the difference between woods and forests to the probable weight of a sword, but she had to admit it was creatively refreshing. Definitely better than attending useless meetings and serving as wildly overqualified tech support for Crossguard Solutions' Chief Finance Officer.

Database administration, Caroline's actual job, lagged a distant third behind doodling in her notebook while her colleagues debated minutiae and (more recently) playing the part of George Radley's pet IT monkey. So for the past few years, Caroline had turned to writing fanfiction, slotting characters from large movie franchises into coffee shop romances. This had garnered her a small but enthusiastic audience who had subsequently demanded the stories as actual books. That endeavour had required a number of name changes (and the alteration of the more obvious parallels), but it wasn't a great deal more work. It had even made her a little bit of money, especially once she'd found an editor to help smooth the rough edges.

Then her fifth coffee shop romance had achieved . . . *popularity*. Or to be more accurate, popularity on a certain section of social media. This had meant (what felt like) every single Internet denizen suddenly had Opinions, which hadn't been great for Caroline's self-esteem. She didn't consider herself the world's best writer by any means, but the acidity of a few of those reviews had left a mark.

After a particularly well-known commenter had opined, 'One wonders what C. S. Lindley would do if she didn't have ready-made characters with which to populate her tedious, derivative modern "romances",' Caroline decided she'd had quite enough of people besmirching her abilities: she was going to write something *original*.

She had called her usual editor and told him so — omitting the part where she was about to create an entire work of fiction out of spite. She also expressed, at some considerable length, her frustrations with her current book series and half-threatened to end it in a spectacular fashion.

Henry Walker, who had been working for her on a freelance basis since her second self-published book, wasn't impressed.

'Your *Moonbeans Coffee Shop* series actually sells, Caroline. It would be a terrible business decision to kill off half the characters and close the place down in the next book just because you're a bit sick of it right now!' He paused, mouth set, and the image of his face was still for long enough that Caroline checked the Wi-Fi strength in the corner of her laptop screen. The tiny cafe she wrote in at lunchtimes was not known for its connection speed.

Henry's face fast-forwarded into his next remark: 'Also, calling it *Lethal Flat White* might get you into legal trouble.'

She scowled into the camera at him, and he gave her a sympathetic half-smile, pushing his hair out of his face. *His stupid, thick, wavy blond hair that always falls perfectly, and . . .*

Caroline realised she was staring. She blinked and resumed scowling. She really did *not* want to go there. It was embarrassing enough to have a crush on someone who technically worked for her; she didn't need him noticing.

He was still talking. Caroline tried to pay attention.

'—good idea for you to take a break from the series and write something completely different,' Henry said. 'Even if it is just an experiment.'

Caroline sighed, more relieved than was really appropriate. 'Yes, but I've never written fantasy before, so if you're willing to do a bit of extra hand-holding on this manuscript, I'd appreciate it.' She felt her face heating up and rushed on, 'I know it's not your usual way of working, but I'm sure we can—'

'Not a problem,' he said.

But then Caroline's laptop pinged ("George Radley has sent you a message"), and she'd had to go.

Henry's support of the project notwithstanding, the germ of an idea for a fantasy romance had brought with it Lady Rosamund Hawkhurst, and from the start Caroline had sensed that she wasn't going to be a cooperative character. Rosamund was positively ancient compared to Caroline's usual parade of late teen and twenty-somethings; she seemed to have very Henry-like opinions on the appropriate kind of sword to use; and she came complete with two living children and one dead husband.

The Hot Enemy, Captain Collins, would probably be a little easier to work with, and Caroline had a charming character she'd originally been working on for a different story to cast as the Hot Childhood Best Friend—but Rosamund?

Rosamund was clearly Trouble.

And yet . . . Henry had seemed keen on the idea. That counted for something.

An alarm sounded on her phone, and Caroline pulled herself back to the present, swept the lid of her laptop closed and shoved it into her bag. She had to leave now if she wanted to catch the early bus to work. Maybe she could cram in a little extra writing on the journey. And maybe in her office, before the day officially started. But one thing at a time.

×

Across the table of the palace dining hall, Robin Waverley surveyed his oldest friend and worried.

Rosamund had appeared at court for the first time in years the previous evening, without so much as a messenger bird to precede her arrival. This morning she had waited in silence among her peers for three hours until the queen had called upon her for a private audience. She had spoken to Robin in passing upon her return to the Great Hall, but not since. Now they were at table in Queen Eudosia's uncharacteristically quiet banqueting hall—the fever had taken its toll on nobles and commoners alike—and though she was smiling and nodding as her immediate neighbours spoke to her, the dark smudges under her eyes and the stiffness of her posture made his stomach turn. Was she sick? Or was something else going on?

Robin wasn't surprised when Rosamund left dinner early, but staying to hear the end of Countess Linnivar's longwinded tale of border skirmishes meant it took him a few moments to follow suit. He caught up with Rosamund as she exited the hall, snagging her arm at the base of the sweeping staircase that led up towards the guest quarters. She didn't quite jump when he touched her, but she did relax when she saw who it was.

'Rosy!' Robin said, trying to keep his voice light. 'May I be so bold as to say it's wonderful to see you?'

'It's been half a year since you last saw me,' said Rosamund, 'so that would be an appropriate comment.'

She'd written to him a few times, but it was true, Robin realised with chagrin—he'd only seen her twice, and that briefly, since Hugo's body had been committed to the flames. At the funeral she had moved through the crowds like a ghost, bowing, making small talk, attempting to smile; and her current manner retained that distant, careful quality, even now they were alone. The crease in Robin's brow deepened. He had not anticipated the degree to which grief still shadowed her.

A Bevorian himself, Robin had attended boarding school with Rosamund in the neighbouring country of Calter. Both the school and the country had retained absolute neutrality regardless of which nearby sovereign states went to war, over what, and with whom, ensuring that Calter itself was never the object of hostilities. Robin missed the simplicity and quiet of that country sometimes; but hope sprang eternal that he could go back one day. Rosamund, as the eldest daughter of Abrenian paper merchants who had bought their patents of nobility, had retained absolute unconcern with the dictates of politics or status. They'd become fast friends, keeping up a correspondence even after they went their separate ways.

Robin had been delighted when Rosamund married Sir Hugo Hawkhurst as part of the previous Abrenian–Bevorian peace agreement. This had brought her to the Hawkhurst estate in northeastern Bevoria, and for much of their twenties they had seen each other fairly regularly. Robin had been particularly pleased to see how well Rosy and Hugo got on and took special pleasure in regaling Sir Hugo with stories of Lady Hawkhurst's school days.

But then the realities of Robin's own private obligations had intervened, and he had visited less often than he should have. Especially since Hugo's death last year. And both of the times Robin had seen Rosamund since the funeral, he had been on official business, hurrying off again as quickly as he had arrived. A pang of guilt twisted in his stomach. He should have written more. 'May I also mention that it's less than wonderful to see you looking so ill?'

Rosamund raised an eyebrow. 'Such flattery,' she retorted, but there was a hint of a smile on her face.

'You look like you ran all the way from the Hawkhurst estate,' Robin ventured, and Rosamund shrugged.

'I was in a hurry.'

'Why?'

Rosamund stopped at the top of the stairs and leaned on the banister. 'Robin, I know you don't enjoy politics—'

If only she knew.

'—but with King Adelric's death and King Roland's coronation, there's been a definite shift in military deployments on both sides. The knight who sought Hawkhurst's hospitality two weeks ago told us that Roland seems to be taking a less aggressive posture, and we know his farms will be suffering as much as ours in this drought. He needs labourers, not soldiers. I came to see if I could get the queen to—I came to see if I could be of any assistance to

Her Majesty.' She pushed herself upright again and started to walk away, but Robin matched her pace.

'I'm sure you're very helpful,' he offered, after a short silence.

Rosamund gave him a wry smile, though the set of her shoulders belied it. 'I am a model of helpfulness. But also a dire warning as to why one shouldn't skimp on sleep when travelling. Good evening, Robin.'

And before he could think of a reason to detain her further, she reached the door to her rooms and disappeared.

Robin frowned. That Rosamund had come all the way to court after years of absence was a clear sign that something was amiss at Hawkhurst. Both Abrenia and Bevoria strenuously insisted that the resumption of hostilities was the other side's fault, but regardless of how the conflict had started, it had dragged on for more than two years, casualties were mounting, and Rosamund was right: the lack of rain was now affecting harvests on both sides of the Grenalla River, making a bad situation worse. As an estate near the border, Hawkhurst had been expected to provide more than its fair share of manpower and resources. Perhaps that was why she had come. Perhaps he should urge Queen Eudosia to consider a peace treaty.

Perhaps he should have done a lot of things.

×

'That was excellent, Robin, well done!' said Caroline, and Robin started as the world froze around him. 'Very supportive but also just a *little* ambiguous, perfect for the Hot Childhood Best Friend role. I knew I could count on you.'

Robin decided to say nothing, though in a book not written by Caroline he might have had more words to choose from. The author had some bizarre ideas about what he should be doing—including pining over his widowed best friend, apparently—and he wasn't sure what to make of it yet.

He had a feeling he'd have fit better in the merchant sailor/ nobleman romance for which she'd originally created him, but the author's word was law.

At least . . . most of the time.

Chapter 2

THERE WAS A VOICE from outside the stables. 'Your Ladyship?'

Inside the stall Rosamund finished digging the stone from her horse's hoof. Only one groom had escaped the fever, and he was nowhere to be seen, so she'd taken care of readying Willow for the road by herself. She straightened up and squinted at the figure who had just addressed her.

Her escort loomed outside the door. Rosamund tried not to take offence. Captain Collins was a tall, broad-shouldered man; he might not have been looming on purpose. And while she wasn't inclined to be charitable, it wouldn't be sensible to be unfriendly to her only protection for the next few weeks. Rosamund was still baffled at Queen Eudosia's apparent disregard for the diplomatic mission. One widowed noblewoman and a single guard? But speculation changed nothing. She had a task to complete.

'Good morning, Captain Collins.' She waited for him to say something else, but he didn't. 'Was there something you needed?'

He looked over Willow's tack, a faint crease between his brows. 'Do you intend to bring a sword, Your Ladyship?'

She nodded and pulled back a piece of cloth on her saddle to reveal the scabbard concealed there. She also decided against providing him with an inventory of all her other weapons. Not least because he might ask to see those as well, and several of them would require her to root around in the back of her riding doublet.

The captain inclined his head. 'I intend for us to leave within the hour. Is that convenient?'

'Certainly, Captain. Shall I meet you at the main gate?'

He nodded, turned on his heel, and strode off.

Rosamund watched him go, thinking hard. She'd expected a captain to be older, but he looked thirty, if that. And she didn't like the way he'd looked at her. Part suspicion, part resignation, and part something else she couldn't quite place.

She'd felt the suspicion before. Hugo had died in an ambush in Abrenia, and Rosamund, an Abrenian by birth, had been left to administer his estate. *Wasn't that convenient?* certain members of the court had whispered. *And she visited him on the front lines only a week before his death . . .*

Rosamund shook herself. There was no reason to suspect that the queen gave any credence to those ridiculous rumours. She was being silly. Captain Collins was a trained soldier. His uniform was well-kept, his hair neatly contained at the nape of his neck with a black ribbon, and she'd watched his green eyes sweep the stables with professional detachment before settling on her. She couldn't accuse him of anything other than professional alertness.

×

Willow froze as Caroline appeared in the stall. 'Well,' chirped Caroline, 'he's a beautiful blond grump, isn't he?'

'He has just been ordered to escort the sister-in-law of the king of a hostile nation to the capital of said nation,' replied Rosamund, running her fingers under Willow's noseband and ignoring the "beautiful" part. 'There are a dizzying number of ways this could go wrong for him.' She shook her head. 'If he's tense, I can't blame him. I'm tense too, but there's no sense dwelling on it. The sooner we leave, the better.'

×

Rosamund and her escort set off promptly at ten of the clock, she on Willow, he riding a heavyset bay called Scout. The road out of the city was—

×

Caroline stared at the carefully annotated pages, then at the struck-through paragraphs, and ground her teeth to keep from shouting. 'Really? You think I should remove *all* the description?'

Henry looked up at the camera, giving the disconcerting impression that his deep green eyes were actually on hers. 'No. But remember your audience. It may be a fantasy romance, but they're really just there for the romance part. Paragraphs of route mapping are going to make them skim at best and put the book down at worst.'

He was probably right. Dress details were fine, but nine paragraphs on the scenery that Rosamund and Captain Collins (he did have a first name, it just hadn't settled yet) were passing? Not so much. But Caroline had spent a good hour researching what kind of trees there would be and coming up with a plausible map for the journey, even if it did look like it had been drawn by a toddler with a broken crayon. Bad form or no, she wanted to show her work. 'Fine. Any other notes?'

Henry shrugged. 'I didn't want to get too much into the weeds. It'll need an extensive rewrite regardless.'

Not an encouraging statement. But given Caroline's drafting process, also not an inaccurate one. She bade Henry farewell and had just started to prune her thicket of description when her laptop pinged.

George. Again. For the third time that hour—and it was Saturday. She ignored it.

✕

The road out of the city was straight and well maintained, though the recent drought meant that the ground had baked hard. Given the risk of spraining the horses' fetlocks, Rosamund and Captain Collins kept the animals to a walk until they entered the woods. Here the summer sunlight filtered through a canopy of oak and ash leaves, and they rode comfortably side-by-side for the next few hours. Neither of them had much to say.

✕

Caroline frowned and took a sip of her tea. It had long since gone cold. Grimacing, she moved it from the desk to the windowsill and reached for her water instead, wondering how best to finesse this. Captain Collins was meant to be the strong, silent type, but she'd hoped she could at least rely on him for flirtatious banter. Maybe she should have sent Rosamund on the trip with Robin instead; he was a talker.

Still, she could work with this.

✕

The scene around the captain froze as Caroline inserted herself into his world. 'Good day, Captain Collins!'

He said nothing, wondering what she wanted. He hoped it would be less ambiguous than her previous request, which had been, 'Could you maybe . . . *smoulder* a bit more?' Caroline tended to pop up at very inconvenient moments, and nothing she said ever quite made sense.

'Now would be an excellent time for an internal monologue from your point of view,' Caroline said. 'Perhaps with a grudging note that your travelling companion is pretty?'

Captain Collins, who wasn't sure that he had a first name, frowned and continued to say nothing. First, because it was obvious that Lady Hawkhurst and Caroline had the same face, and the implications of that disturbed him. Second, because he had the feeling that arguing with the actual creator of his world might get him in worse trouble than arguing with his monarch.

'All right,' said Caroline, 'maybe Lady Rosamund isn't actually *beautiful*, but . . . something about her has caught your attention, surely? Her pretty red hair? Her intense blue eyes? Her adorable . . .' Caroline gestured weakly at her own face.

'Dimples?' he offered.

'I was going to say "freckles",' said Caroline, smiling like a shark, 'but "dimples" will do nicely.'

His ears burned. He should have stuck with silence.

×

Captain Collins risked a longer glance at his travelling companion and tried not to frown. Queen Eudosia's instructions had been simple, but not easy. And while her faith in his abilities was substantial, right now he feared it had been misplaced.

'We *need* to make peace, Collins,' the queen had told him, 'and Lady Rosamund is the perfect envoy to show that we're serious about it. Getting her to Quayforth with the declaration is the priority, and I will do everything in my power to make sure it happens. But with the fever I am severely short-handed. I hope that by travelling as a pair you will attract less attention, but walk wary. And there's still the matter of Sir Hugo's death. The lady might have information we do not, so while you are on the road with her, see if you can find out what she knows.'

Given the circumstances of Hawkhurst's demise, Collins was anxious to discover what had gone wrong. But prying into whatever knowledge Hugo's widow might have about his death was a delicate business, and he hardly knew where to begin. Perhaps the lady might open up when she grew used to his company. He could only hope.

Their first two days on the road were uneventful, for which Rosamund was grateful. The horses kept a steady pace along bone-dry roads, raising dust with every step, and the stillness of the air muted the jingle of bits and the creak of leather.

Captain Collins was an undemanding travel companion. His near silence initially made Rosamund worry that she had offended him in some way, but by the second day she decided that he just didn't like talking. It was oddly soothing. When her children were at home — *as they are now, alone*, she thought with a pang of homesickness — noise and silence both could be a comfort. But when Edmund and Charlotte were away at school, attempts at quiet from the household staff served only to remind her of Hugo's effortless, wordless presence, and how much she missed it. The captain offered her silence without strings, without pity, without judgement. Even if she sometimes wished for a little conversation, she'd missed that kind of peaceful companionship more than she'd realised.

The road was often busy, and since Captain Collins insisted they regularly dismount and walk to stretch their own legs and give the animals a break, Rosamund took the opportunity to distract herself from her anxious thoughts by making polite conversation with amenable fellow travellers.

✕

Rosamund's discussion with a pedlar froze mid-sentence.

'Shouldn't you talk to Captain Collins rather than random strangers?'

Rosamund didn't bother to look at Caroline. 'Why?'

'Banter is an important component of an enemies-to-lovers romance!'

Rosamund, her eyes still fixed on the road ahead, set her jaw and did not reply.

×

The Bevorian nobles in whose homes they stayed seemed very aware of who Rosamund was, which made her uncomfortable. She was used to a certain level of deference as the liege lady of her estate, but to receive the fawning attention of aristocrats who far exceeded her station was unsettling.

Not many people had previously paid attention to the foreign wife of a minor border lord, especially one who avoided court so assiduously. But despite the covert nature of her mission, her hosts were not stupid. A lady who lived in north-eastern Bevoria travelling up the country's western side from the capital? With one of the Queen's Guard in tow? That said *diplomacy*, for all that Rosamund politely deflected questions about her eventual destination.

Captain Collins, for his part, received precious little respect from their hosts, which was irritating. He was risking his life on this ridiculous mission to Abrenia too. Even if the lords didn't know that, there was no need to be so dismissive.

'Lady Rosamund.' Lord Stanley's words brought her back to the present. 'How have you found the journey so far?'

They sat at a long, polished table laden with game, bread, and (Rosamund counted) eight kinds of pastries. Lord Stanley himself, resplendent in his estate's yellow, obviously had a sweet tooth. Among his other vices.

'It has exceeded all my expectations, my lord,' Rosamund said, trying not to stare at the hairs sprouting from his red nose. 'Though I imagine much of that has been due to Captain Collins.'

Collins started. He had remained silent for the entire meal, and no one had addressed him directly.

'I am very grateful that Her Majesty could spare him,' Rosamund continued. 'I'm sure his regular unit is missing him.'

Lord Stanley, realising that he hadn't spoken more than three words to one of the supposedly honoured guests in his house, turned to her travelling companion.

'Captain Collins, have you found —'

Rosamund returned her attention to her dinner.

Captain Collins, for his part, was unsurprised by how the aristocrats tried to ingratiate themselves with Lady Hawkhurst. What did surprise him was how discomfited she appeared by the whole experience. The nobles whose homes in which they stayed fell over themselves to offer hospitality, to entertain their guest, to engage her in court gossip. But Lady Hawkhurst, while gracious, held herself at a distance that he could not understand. These were her peers, and yet she seemed less comfortable around them than she was alone on the road with him.

Her treatment of him had been another surprise. Of course, he deferred to her under most circumstances, given their difference in rank and the queen's orders to get the lady to Quayforth by any means necessary. But she shared, or at least respected, his preference for silence; she uncomplainingly assisted with the menial chores attendant to travel on horseback; she was, all told, an easy travel companion. Not at all what he had expected from a noble-woman. One of his few friends at court knew the lady and had assured Captain Collins that he would not find escorting her home too troublesome.

If only that had been their destination.

However, after two days on the road, Lady Hawkhurst's apparent patience ran out, and whenever they found them-selves in a crowd, she would converse with their fellow travellers. From this the captain discovered that she had two children, Edmund and Charlotte. But company dwindled as they neared the border, and Lady Hawkhurst began to cast about for subjects to engage his interest. He couldn't tell if this meant she had relaxed around him or grown restless.

'Is it usual that heads of households treat you as if you're invisible, Captain Collins?' she said on the third morning as they ambled through a small market town.

Collins looked over at her sharply, but he saw none of the slyness that usually preceded a verbal trap from a superior. He decided to be diplomatic. 'Many lords prefer to preserve the distinctions of rank, Your Ladyship.'

She snorted. 'Oh, I'm sure.'

'You disapprove?'

'I think it's wise to seek perspective from anyone willing to give it.' She glanced over at him, eyes thoughtful. 'I sup-pose there is such a thing as overfamiliarity with the people over whom one has power.' Then her mouth twisted. 'For example, Lord Stanley's villages house more than a few children who are the direct result of his overfamiliarity with his servants.' She sniffed derisively, glancing back the way they came, and fell silent again.

Captain Collins was not a talker by nature, and with practice, he had learned how to turn this to his advantage:

if he didn't say anything for long enough, people either assumed he was stupid or forgot he was there and so didn't watch their words. But this would not work with Lady Hawkhurst. She was either too considerate of him or too watchful of her own words, and when she did speak, she always waited pointedly for him to reciprocate. If he wanted her to divulge confidences or suspicions worth reporting to the queen, he would have to say something back. Something substantial even.

'I once had a leader who insisted on referring to everyone by their first names, to improve morale,' he offered.

That got her attention. 'Did it work?'

'No, Your Ladyship, because he kept getting them wrong. I was "Landon" for my entire time there, and he kept asking me if my wife was well.'

Lady Rosamund unsuccessfully attempted to smother a smile. 'I take it your name isn't actually Landon?'

He couldn't help but smile back. 'No, Your Ladyship. It's Leo. And I've never been married, either.'

✕

Three hours after she'd emailed Henry the first paragraphs of her revised travel chapter, Caroline's phone pinged.

> **Henry**
> So you finally picked a name for him then?

> **Caroline**
> Did you doubt me?

The reply was near instantaneous.

> **Henry**
> Remember when you wrote "English Breakfast at Tiffany's"?

> **Henry**
> And the love interest didn't actually get named until the third draft?

> **Caroline**
> His name wasn't that important anyway.

> **Henry**
> No, just his manly abs.

The words *Envy isn't pretty, Henry* were on the tip of her tongue (and the tips of her fingers). But no, that was a little too close for comfort.

> **Caroline**
> I know what the people want! :)

> **Henry**
> If you say so.

✕

A few hours later the travellers walked beside the horses in the shade of the trees, looking for somewhere to stop for luncheon. It was almost midday, and Leo watched Lady Hawkhurst as she judged the position of the sun. She had recited the Litany for the Dead at midday every day of their journey so far. Considering Hawkhurst had been dead almost a year now, this was an unusual display of piety, but it seemed a harmless one.

That said, it had almost got him into trouble on the second day. Lady Hawkhurst had begun as usual, murmuring the words to herself, but her diction had been clear enough that he was able to hear.

'We bring nothing into the world, and we carry nothing out,' she said, staring straight ahead. 'The Wisdoms give us life, and all our days are numbered. Deliver us from darkness, that we may rise to Light.'

'Deliver us,' Leo had echoed, distracted by his own thoughts on the dead man and momentarily forgetting himself. Lady Hawkhurst had started at his interruption, but when she looked over at him, Leo saw a glimmer of sympathy on her face, and she had carried on without comment.

He was wondering whether or not to join in properly today when there was a noise ahead.

Rosamund squinted overhead at the sun, trying to judge if it was close enough to midday to begin the litany. As Hugo's widow, she would be expected to lead the recitation at his Feast of Remembrance, and she was in the middle of calculating the precise number of days left before that anniversary when Captain Collins tensed beside her.

What? she mouthed. His eyes flicked forward, then over her shoulder past her horse. Rosamund edged closer to Willow and reached under the saddlebags in a gesture she hoped appeared absent-minded—but her hand closed on the hilt of her concealed sword. It slipped out of the scabbard with barely a sound, and just in time.

A stocky man dressed in grey darted out from a thicket before her, sword upraised; at the same moment a second assailant yanked Willow's reins out of Rosamund's hand. The horse reared in fright and tried to bolt from the stranger. But Rosamund's eyes were fixed on the man in the grey tunic. His sword bore down on her head like a club.

Amateur. Or is he just trying to scare me? No matter. She stepped in to parry and let the force of his blow slide her sword down his until the steel bit into his neck.

He didn't have time to scream.

Rosamund turned to see what had happened to Captain Collins, but she barely caught a glimpse of him fighting a third man when the second bandit, a bearded man in a brown cloak, dropped Willow's reins and tackled her from behind. They hit the gravel hard, and Rosamund rolled onto her back, trying to scramble out of reach while keeping her assailant in view, but he knocked her sword out of her hand and pinned her to the ground.

He was too strong. His hands were around her throat, she couldn't breathe, there were spots before her eyes, she was going to—

Abruptly the pressure eased and Rosamund gasped, pushing herself away from her attacker, hands protesting as they scraped across the stones. Her vision returned to reveal Captain Collins seizing the man by the scruff of the neck. He slammed the bandit into the nearest tree; the man bounced head-first off the trunk and landed in a sprawl on the ground. Brown Cloak stumbled to his hands and knees, turned tail, and bolted.

Rosamund coughed and tried to stand, but her throat ached, and a wave of dizziness washed over her. She pushed herself to her knees and cast around desperately. Where was her sword?

A choked cry of pain arrested her thoughts. Rosamund whirled to see a fourth bandit in bright green pull a dagger from the captain's calf. Collins fell towards her but twisted onto his back to drag Green Tunic after him. They hit the ground with a thud, grappling.

Rosamund reached for the green-handled knife hidden in her boot, drawing a pained breath; when the bandit glanced up at her, she saw her chance. 'Leo, stay down!'

The knife flew straight and struck true, lodging in the fourth bandit's throat. He clutched at his neck, choking, and Captain Collins was up on one knee in a flash. He rolled the man onto his back and pulled out the knife.

Rosamund closed her eyes at the sound of metal on bone, willing herself not to be sick.

The captain staggered to his feet, wincing.

'Where's the other one?' he demanded.

Rosamund opened her eyes again, uncertain. 'I don't know.'

He scowled, retrieved his sword, and propped himself against a tree to assess his injuries.

Rosamund pushed herself to her feet, feeling her neck. Swallowing felt like her throat was full of dry bread, and it hurt to turn her head. Captain Collins still had her knife, so she recovered her sword and went to catch Willow, who had fled some distance away. The mare was well-trained enough not to abandon them entirely, and while she was sweating and rolling her eyes, she was also, Wisdoms be praised, unharmed. Rosamund coaxed Willow over to the captain and hurried off again to retrieve Scout. By the time she had returned with the gelding, Captain Collins had managed to bind a piece of cloth around his bleeding left leg. He grunted in pain when he mounted up but otherwise maintained his quintessential silence.

Rosamund winced in sympathy. Her head pounded, her body ached, and breathing was uncomfortable at best, but at least she wasn't bleeding. Collins had saved her life and, by doing so, opened himself up to attack from behind. His injury probably wasn't life-threatening if treated promptly, but she couldn't help being impressed by his stoicism.

However, regardless of how much pain he was in, they needed to leave. Now. Three dead bodies lay in the road, but the bearded man in the brown cloak had disappeared without a trace. Rosamund mounted, all thoughts of food forgotten, and she and Captain Collins set off at a canter. The trees flashed past, and Rosamund's neck throbbed as they laboured to put as much distance between themselves and the site of the ambush as possible before Brown Cloak returned with friends.

✕

'On first-name terms with Captain Collins now, are we?' Caroline looked smug. 'Well, I suppose you did just save his life.'

Rosamund didn't even have it in her to glare. It hurt to breathe. It hurt to swallow. Captain Collins was injured. And he still had her knife.

'And now you have to find a safe place to stay and patch up his injuries!' Caroline crowed. 'Which will give you plenty of time to have a Meaningful Conversation!'

Rosamund grimaced at the capital letters in the author's voice. 'Oh. Goody.' She sighed. 'Is,' she whispered, then coughed again, 'is the hidden knife going to be an issue? I didn't deliberately keep it from him, you know. He asked if I was bringing a sword, and I was, so I said yes.'

'Failing to mention it rather makes it look like you don't trust him,' said Caroline, and Rosamund was not comforted to hear that she sounded pleased about that too.

Chapter 3

A HEAVY FIST assaulted Caroline's office door at nine-thirty in the morning. 'Christine! I have a job for you!'

The day had not subsequently improved.

'I need you to fix this!' George barked, waving his very expensive laptop in Caroline's face and knocking over her desk lamp.

'That's your *personal* computer, sir,' said Caroline, but George slapped it down on her desk, right on top of her keyboard. Caroline had once spent an entire afternoon fixing a problem caused by him dropping a sheaf of files onto her keyboard. Nowadays, she reflexively locked the screen when anyone opened the office door, but that didn't make it less nerve-wracking.

'Chop chop, Christine! I need it fixed by this afternoon!'

'I don't even know what's wrong with it! And it's Caroline —'

But he had gone.

Caroline cleared a space for the CFO's ostentatious personal device (complete with four-colour backlit keyboard, unnecessarily shiny case, and — were those go-faster stripes on the sides? Probably, knowing George) and rued the day she had first come to his attention. It was over a year ago that she had been on her way to yet another pointless employee development seminar when George had burst out of the main conference room with —

'Come on then, IT girl, we haven't got all day!'

— and dragged her by the arm into his presentation of accounts to the board.

Or rather, the complete lack of presentation. Caroline fixed the problem in five minutes, but George had insisted that she stay for the whole hour to deal with any other technical issues that might arise. Eunice Wood, the CEO, had smiled and thanked her.

George Radley had decided that from that day forward, Caroline was his go-to tech support. It was maddening. Not only was he a condescending bully, but since he was head of her department, no one was prepared to risk his wrath by telling him they needed Caroline to do her actual job. The last person to argue with the CFO about anything had been summarily dismissed.

Caroline still missed Nick. He had been fun.

And while she had previously enjoyed her work very much, the constant walking on eggshells and task interruption that indulging George entailed had put an end to that.

Caroline made a mental note to check if her CV was current before tapping in George's password (which he hadn't told her, but he used the same one for everything) and trying to work out what he'd done to his machine.

George's security settings, such as they weren't, nearly gave her a heart attack. Caroline had to wonder how he had attained the lofty heights of executive status when he clicked on every random link in his email inbox. Since it would take at least twenty minutes before the scans finished running and she was able to tell exactly how much malware he'd managed to install on his personal laptop (upon which, she soon discovered, he was doing company work), she pulled out her notebook to write Rosamund's next scene. She was, technically, still complying with the needs of her superiors. But she could multitask.

Now, where would they have stopped for the night?

✕

Rosamund and Captain Collins travelled for hours without finding anywhere safe to rest, but eventually salvation appeared on the horizon. The serious expression on the face of the dark-haired woman who opened the farmhouse door turned to horror when they told her about the bandit attack, and she immediately offered them the hospitality of her hearth.

The household, which included the woman, her two daughters, and a young son, cleared the main room for their guests with almost unseemly haste. Rosamund found herself alone with a grey-faced Captain Collins, a pot of stew, and a few basic medical supplies. The farmhouse itself was of solid construction and neatly kept, with carefully whitewashed walls and thick rugs on the floor; this helped reassure her that their hosts were unlikely to be in straits desperate enough to induce pickpocketing, despite their proximity to the front. It was also an unlikely spot to find an envoy of the queen. They should be safe for now.

Rosamund had asked for—

×

Caroline pushed George's computer to the back of her desk before pulling up her messages to Henry, ignoring for the moment the text from her mother about her cousin's wedding plans.

Caroline
What sort of antiseptic would be available in a Renaissance-ish setting? Preferably one that stings?

Henry
Vinegar, or maybe salt and hot water?

Caroline
Ta!

Caroline
Unrelated reminder: never click on links from people
you don't know. Or from people you haven't seen in
a while. Or from people purporting to know about
Hot Ladies Waiting For Your Call.

Henry
Noted?

✕

—vinegar, and now she poured it into one of the rough
blue bowls on the table that the farmer had filled with
boiling water.

The steam wavered in front of Rosamund's eyes. She
blinked away the tang of the fumes, the rough white walls
and carefully but inexpertly carved wooden furniture drift-
ing out of focus as the full implications of the fight sank in.

They'd been *attacked*.

They could have died.

Her children might have been orphaned.

But Leo Collins had saved her life.

Although, she told herself firmly, that was just as well for
the both of them. Otherwise, how would she have saved his?

✕

Caroline grinned knowingly. 'Are you ready to patch up and ogle your
Hot, Shirtless Enemy? Perhaps while experiencing rising feelings of
admiration for his manly pain tolerance? And maybe a desire to ease
his discomfort?'

Rosamund stared at her, mouth hanging open. 'First, his leg is
injured, there is no need for him to remove his shirt. Second, he's not
my enemy.' She frowned. 'Or probably not, anyway, given that he just

saved my life. Third, if he can't ride tomorrow, we are sitting ducks. He needs medical care, and our hosts, while generous in their hospitality, obviously do not wish to entangle themselves in the political intrigue implied by a noblewoman and guard travelling alone through border territory. Frankly, I don't blame them, I wouldn't want to get involved either.' She turned away.

Caroline raised an eyebrow. 'Noted.'

✕

Leo had propped his injured leg onto a stool. Rosamund winced in spite of herself as he gingerly pried off his boot. Even if the thick leather had taken the brunt of the dagger blow, she wasn't sure how the captain had stayed upright, let alone ridden for the entire afternoon. His trouser leg was soaked in blood, and she now noticed blood from quite a few cuts seeping into his torn shirt as well. Rosamund recalled the thorn bushes by the side of the road and wondered if they were the cause.

Captain Collins dipped a rag into the bowl she brought him and wrung out the steaming cloth, but then stopped. At first, she wondered if he was waiting for the water to cool, but the utter exhaustion on his face tugged at her heart. 'Would you like some help, Captain?'

Leo looked up, eyes unfocused. After a moment, he nodded. 'Thank you, Your Ladyship.'

Rosamund knelt on the floor and took stock. 'We need to roll up that trouser leg, Captain Collins.'

It took some time. The sturdy blue fabric was saturated with blood and clung tenaciously to his leg. Rosamund peeled it away as gently as she could, using her own scissors to snip at the ragged sections.

She looked up at the captain every time her ministrations pulled at his torn skin, but he bore his obvious
discomfort in silence — *of course*, she thought, allowing herself a small, wry smile — and stayed perfectly still.

But even as Rosamund worked, she worried. She
couldn't shake the feeling that their encounter had been
more than a random wayside robbery. Had they been followed from Lord Stanley's estates? If so, had their host
known about it? Her thoughts spun in her head, but she
tried to push them aside. One problem at a time.

✕

'Shouldn't you be making conversation that borders on flirtatious,
which is only stopped by a well-timed application of something that's
going to sting?' said Caroline.

Rosamund pursed her lips, annoyed by the interruption and
Caroline's inability to understand any of her characters. Leo —
Captain Collins — was injured, exhausted, and tense. Even if he had
been flirtatious by nature (which he obviously wasn't), these were
hardly ideal circumstances for a lighthearted chat.

On the other hand, Rosamund had a feeling that this was a point
on which Caroline would be particularly stubborn. If she couldn't
be persuaded to keep quiet and let her characters concentrate,
Rosamund was concerned that there would be blood.

She sighed. 'Will you stop —' She cleared her still-aching throat.
'Will you stop bothering me if I do?'

✕

'Would conversation ease the passage of time, Captain
Collins?' Rosamund said, setting a large cloth and an empty
grey bowl beneath his leg.

He was silent for a long moment. She had just decided that he didn't want to talk, and that she didn't have the heart to press him, when he said, 'You seem very calm.'

His words were quiet. Casual, almost. Yet Rosamund had the unnerving impression that she was walking on pond ice and listening for a cracking sound under her feet. Her hands started to shake as she stood up and crossed the room to retrieve a jar from her saddlebag. 'I assumed that hysterics would be unhelpful,' she said, her voice steadier than she felt. She returned to his side, set down the jar, and tested the temperature of the solution in the blue bowl. Probably cool enough to rinse the wound.

'Was this your first . . . armed conflict, Your Ladyship?'

Is this the first time you've killed someone?

Rosamund shook her head, the motion stiff. 'No. But it's been a long time.'

A pause. And then—almost gently—'What happened?'

She swallowed, touching a hand to her neck as if the bruises had caused the sudden tightness in her throat. 'Hugo and I went to Abrenia to visit my parents when Edmund was a baby.' She looked down. 'We were attacked. Three of them distracted the guards; a fourth broke the carriage door open. He tried to grab Edmund, presumably to take him for ransom.'

Rosamund fell silent as the scene came back to her: the shouts of the men outside, Hugo among them; the sound of the door breaking; the smell of the grim-faced man, his eyes adjusting to the interior, his gloved hand reaching out . . .

'What did you do?'

Rosamund jolted back to the present. Leo was looking at her with an expression she couldn't quite categorise. 'He was threatening my son. I had a knife.' She paused. 'I did what I had to do.'

And she poured half of the still-hot liquid over his leg. He yelped in pain and nearly fell off the seat.

'Sorry. But we don't want that wound to fester, do we?'

Leo scowled; whether from pain or anger, Rosamund couldn't tell. Probably both. She decided to ignore him, patting the uninjured portion of his leg dry with a clean cloth. 'At least I can glue the edges together for you. And if I put bandages on top, it should hold for riding.'

Leo looked startled. 'Glue?'

Rosamund waved at the jar on the table, relieved to change the subject. 'Caladrius glue. We keep the birds on the Hawkhurst estate.' She reached for it and noted that the contents had started to separate: white at the bottom, pearly and translucent at the top. 'They're dreadfully moody and astonishingly picky about their living quarters, but they're also invaluable, especially in wartime. You're familiar with caladrius salve, I assume?'

'Yes, Your Ladyship. Shimmery white stuff. Good for wounds. You make it from the bird's tears, I believe?'

She nodded, pleased, and held up the jar to examine the contents more closely. 'We've been experimenting with mixing it with glue to seal the skin while preventing infection. We're hoping that it keeps better, too. Transporting the salve to the front lines has always been a risky business.'

Rosamund dabbed at the wound with a cloth, and Leo flinched again. He settled himself, slightly shamefaced, when it became clear that she was going to be gentle. She gave the jar a shake before peering at it again. 'But if you'd prefer stitches . . . ?' She let the question hang in the air.

'No, thank you.'

Rosamund got to work. 'You'll need to wait for it to dry, but we can deal with your other injuries while it does, so long as you don't move around too much.' She considered his leg again and dabbed on a little more glue, determined to seal the wound completely. 'You were lucky.'

'I'm aware, ma'am.'

While the glue dried, Rosamund made quick work of cleaning the ground-in mud and dirt out of the scrapes on the captain's neck and hands before asking, 'Would you mind removing your shirt, please? There are some cuts on your back that I don't think you can reach.'

He complied wordlessly, and Rosamund was disinclined to break the silence while she cleaned the cuts on his back. She didn't want any more questions about how many men she'd killed. The last thing she needed was for the captain to consider her a threat. If he had heard the rumours at court about her — if Eudosia really did suspect Rosamund of being complicit in Hugo's death . . . no, she wouldn't think about it. One crisis at a time.

Caroline threw up her hands in despair. They'd just undergone a life-threatening experience, but were they willing to let their guards down? Of course not.

Where was the chemistry? The banter? The flirtation and the heat generated by forced proximity? Neither of them had noticed each other's bodies, and there had been no bitten lips and barely *any* heavy breathing.

Useless, the pair of them.

Once Rosamund finished dressing the captain's leg, she retreated to a chair by the fire to see to her own cuts and scrapes. She had been unreasonably fortunate: her only real injury was to her neck. She touched it gingerly with her fingers once again, wincing. There would be some very pretty bruises by the morning.

'Let me see.' Captain Collins sat down heavily in the chair beside hers, and she gave him a look of polite enquiry. 'Your neck, Your Ladyship.' He made a sideways gesture with his hand. Rosamund raised her eyebrows but turned her head in the direction indicated.

✕

The world froze as Caroline appeared behind Leo to scowl at Rosamund. 'No! You were supposed to object! And then after a brief, heated exchange, he could take your chin in his hand and turn your head! In a surprisingly gentle fashion!'

Rosamund rolled her eyes.

✕

'How's your breathing, Your Ladyship?' Leo narrowed his eyes, concerned. She'd been clearing her throat every couple of minutes.

'It's—' Lady Hawkhurst broke off to cough, then smiled wryly. 'Breathing isn't a problem,' she croaked. 'But I may have been overly optimistic regarding speech. I'm fine.'

Well, a quiet meal wouldn't bother him. After they ate—though he cringed a little at how slow and painful the process was for her—she addressed him again. 'Given our recent encounter, I think we should keep a watch tonight. Just to be sure we weren't followed.'

'Agreed, Your Ladyship.'

'I'm happy to take the first watch. I . . .' She shrugged. 'I don't think I could sleep just now anyway.' She looked down at the floor.

Leo wondered if he should say something . . . comforting? They'd both had an interesting day, but the kind of interesting that he had more experience dealing with than she did.

He put the kettle on.

×

Henry noticed a comment on the word *kettle*.

> **CSLindley:** I'll have you know that the earliest example of a kettle is from 3000 BC!

He couldn't help but smile.

×

Leo set the unchipped mug of thornapple tea in front of Lady Rosamund and suppressed a frown. He shouldn't have asked her if she'd ever killed anyone before, however obliquely he'd tried to word it. Now she was going to be suspicious of him, which wouldn't do at all, given the circumstances. She'd patched him up, after all, and used caladrius glue to do it. The difficulties attendant on caring for the pearlescent birds and harvesting their healing tears were nearly as well-known as the caladrius themselves, and the Hawkhurst estate was one of precious few places in Bevoria that managed to keep a breeding flock. Leo could only imagine how much even the small amount of glue applied to his leg would fetch at market — or how profitable its invention might have made the war for Hawkhurst. That alone might be reason enough to suspect foul play, but he couldn't let the lady know that. A peace offering seemed to be in order, but what?

Her knife. He'd been so distracted by his injuries (though the thornapple tea was taking the edge off) that he'd forgotten to return it.

It took some time for him to complete his usual chores, but once everything was in order he retrieved the knife from his saddlebag. He had wiped it in haste after the bandit attack, but now he took the time to thoroughly clean the blade and the deep green handle before offering it back to her.

Lady Rosamund took it with a small smile. 'Thank you.'

He shrugged and lay down on his bedroll, not meeting her eyes. 'You might need it. Goodnight.'

✕

'I still can't believe you gave her that knife back,' Caroline huffed. 'I had a whole scene planned where you would catch her trying to sneak it out of your bag when you were asleep! You were going to pin her to the wall in a threatening manner and everything! But what do you do?' She threw her hands up in disgust. 'You just hand the thing over with nary a qualm!'

Leo, who had, in fact, harboured several qualms on the subject, said nothing.

✕

As exhausted as he was, it took him some time to fall asleep. The farmhouse floor didn't bother him; he'd stayed in many a worse place. The tiny, leaky barn he'd once sought shelter in during a thunderstorm hadn't been pleasant, but his least favourite was when he'd had to cram himself and

41

an accomplice into a narrow hidey-hole for nearly a full day. His ally had dropped off to sleep and started snoring, and Leo had strongly considered smothering him. Somehow they'd remained undiscovered without needing to resort to murder.

Which brought him back to the recent attempt upon his life — and Lady Hawkhurst's. While they were probably safe for the moment, he couldn't help but ruminate on who they could have been and where they could have come from. He and Lady Rosamund had left the Stanley estates mere hours before the ambush, and he'd had an uneasy feeling the whole morning. Had they been followed?

Leo had read the reports of increasing bandit attacks in border country, which was hardly surprising, and he'd been anticipating trouble within the next few days. But not so soon, not when they were still so far from their destination. He felt less confident than ever about Her Majesty's decision to send him alone with Lady Hawkhurst. If it weren't for that cursed fever, he could have assembled a proper vanguard, mitigated at least some of the risk. But no one else could be spared, and they could not delay.

Lady Hawkhurst herself, however, had surprised him. That she had her own sword was not unusual for a noblewoman, and he had assumed that if she had bothered to pack one, it meant she had been trained in its use. Still, he knew from experience that technical skill didn't always translate into practical butchery. But she hadn't hesitated.

He could well believe it wasn't the first time she'd been in a fight for her life.

And where had that knife come from? It was weighted for throwing, quite different from the one she kept on her belt to eat with. She clearly knew how to use it. And while hiding weapons on one's person was an entirely sensible thing to do in a hostile environment, he was a little uneasy about how else she might choose to employ them.

But she'd saved his life.

He was probably safe.

✕

When Captain Collins had finally dropped off to sleep, Caroline returned to Rosamund. 'So he didn't lecture you after all, hmm?'

Rosamund scowled. 'No, he didn't. Are you happy?'

'Honestly, I'm as surprised as you are. Maybe he has other things on his mind?'

'Like the men who tried to kill us?' Rosamund muttered. 'They worry me too, but I don't know what to do about it.'

'You could talk to him?' Caroline suggested.

Rosamund shook her head. 'No.'

'Really? He saved your life! You still don't trust him?'

Rosamund shrugged, watching the fire. 'I think that might be unwise.'

'Not even a feeling-him-out-for-information chat where you both misinterpret what the other is saying and then get into a heated argument?' Caroline said hopefully.

Rosamund didn't bother to answer.

Caroline pursed her lips. Well, if the pair of them weren't going to engage in a fight by their own choice, she'd have to get creative.

Chapter 4

WHEN LEO WOKE to a hand closing on his shoulder, instinct kicked in before conscious thought. He grabbed at his assailant as he pushed himself upright, twisting and shoving until he had the culprit pinned to the ground.

The intruder yelped—the pitch much too high for a grown man—and the figure on the stone floor of the farmhouse resolved into Lady Rosamund Hawkhurst.

Leo's blood ran cold.

It wasn't an attack.

She had woken him up for his turn at watch, and he had assaulted her.

Lady Rosamund stopped trying to struggle and instead drew a deep breath. Leo blanched, and keenly aware of the family sleeping upstairs, he clapped a hand over her mouth.

'No, no, shhh,' he whispered desperately, 'don't scream—it's all right, you just startled me.'

Rosamund stared at him, eyes wide with panic.

He leaned back, trying to take some of his weight off her. 'I'm so sorry, Your Ladyship.' He waited for a moment, watching her eyes until the terror had subsided somewhat. 'I'm getting up now.'

He took his hand off her mouth.

✕

'Leo Collins, are you joking?' Leo blinked as an exasperated Caroline appeared next to Rosamund, who had frozen in place still gaping up at him. 'You had your Hot Enemy pinned under you in the middle of the night and you *apologise?*'

Leo stared at her for a long moment. 'My who?'

'Your Hot Enemy!' Caroline exclaimed, waving an arm at Lady Rosamund. 'You're doing this all wrong! What is the matter with you both?'

Leo was flummoxed. 'I ... what should I have done?'

Caroline shrugged. 'Leaned in close and teased her about her fighting skills? Maybe made a slightly inappropriate comment about the fact that you're on top of her?' She looked over at him, clearly about to say more, but fell silent when he met her eyes.

Leo's voice, when he spoke again, was quiet. 'What kind of man am I?'

Caroline tipped her head to the side, confused. 'You're Rosamund's Hot Enemy? Obviously?' She started to walk around them. Leo tried not to look at the expression on Rosamund's face, uncomfortably aware that he was still pinning his so-called Hot Enemy to the floor, but Caroline didn't seem to care.

'You hate her, you don't trust her, but something about her compels you.' Caroline gazed off into nothingness, aided by the fact that the room her characters were in was a bit short on details. 'Something makes you want to be near her, makes you want her even though you shouldn't. You're conflicted, torn between duty and a feeling which might be lust ... or might be love?' She paused. 'Ooh, that's quite good actually, I should put it in the blurb.'

Leo realised that his mouth was hanging open. He shut it with a click.

'I mean, you think she's pretty, don't you?' Caroline went on, oblivious.

Leo considered how to phrase his next question tactfully. He decided that tact was useless with Caroline. 'So I should have . . . over-powered her in the middle of the night and then mocked her while she was helpless?'

Caroline stopped short, blinked, and took the seat that material-ised next to her, apparently thinking this over. 'Um . . . well . . .'

Leo bit down on the inside of his cheek to stop himself from shouting. 'I don't think that would help the mission,' he said finally.

Caroline frowned, but nodded. 'I suppose not. Never mind.'

She disappeared.

✕

There was a sudden easing of pressure as Leo pushed him-self off Rosamund entirely and backed away. She scrambled upright, her knife out in front of her, though she could not recall pulling it from its sheath. They stared at each other for a few moments, both breathing heavily, before Leo slowly raised his hands, palms out.

No threat, the gesture said.

Well. She would be the judge of that.

At length, when her breathing had slowed a little, she spoke. 'What just happened, Captain Collins?'

He had the grace to look ashamed, at least. 'I was star-tled, Your Ladyship. I'm sorry.'

Rosamund considered her options. On the one hand, Captain Collins tackling her to the floor in the middle of the night was clearly unacceptable. On the other hand, if she made him angry, he might do it again in earnest, and he now knew that he was quick enough to keep her hands away from her knives. The fact that she was currently armed was only because he'd been foolish enough to let her up.

She wanted to scream. She wanted this guard-turned-death-threat *gone*. Her body ached, both from the fighting and from the long days of travel. Her throat hurt, her lungs hurt, and her ears were ringing. For a moment she swayed, dizzy, sick, overwhelmed—desperate to be at home and *safe*.

But reality reasserted itself. She needed this man on her side for the most dangerous part of the journey. *I need him to trust me.* Rosamund took a careful breath and lowered the knife. 'It's all right, Captain. I am unharmed. Surprised, yes. More awake than I would wish to be, yes, but fundamentally unharmed. Are you injured?'

His eyes widened with relief. 'No, Your Ladyship.'

'Then be at ease, please.' She mustered her friendliest smile, but there wasn't much heart in it. 'Though if there is a way to wake you up in future without engaging in an impromptu wrestling match, I would be glad to know it.'

He was hard to see in the darkness, but she sensed him relaxing a little.

'Perhaps a stick?' he suggested, and she forced out a laugh.

'I'll bear that in mind.' Rosamund sat down in her bedroll, deliberately casual, and put the knife to one side. 'Good watch to you, Captain.'

'Goodnight, my lady,' he said absently, and she closed her eyes and pretended to relax.

✕

'I can't believe the pair of you; honestly, I give you the perfect setup, and I get nothing! Not a flirty remark or meaningful staring or even him noticing the way your chest was heaving . . .' Caroline huffed. 'What was the point of that?'

'What did you expect?' Rosamund growled, turning away from Caroline only to see Captain Collins sitting statue-like by the motionless fire. 'I thought I was going to die! I thought he'd decided that the bandits should have finished me off, and that my children were going to be left alone, and—' Rosamund swallowed hard, her breathing ragged.

Caroline despaired. Why were neither of them acting like proper protagonists? It was very annoying.

'I thought I was going to die,' Rosamund whispered again.

Caroline gave up. 'Well, go to sleep then. We'll talk about it in the morning.'

'I am *trying*,' Rosamund ground out through her teeth. 'But, shockingly enough, I don't sleep easily next to demonstrably dangerous men I barely know! We were supposed to be at an inn, in different rooms. Instead, we're on the floor of this farmhouse, and he just pinned me to the ground!'

'It was an accident!' Caroline protested. 'And he let you up! Far too quickly, in my opinion!'

'The fact that he can do it at all is the problem, Caroline!' Rosamund sat up in her bedroll, glaring. 'It is not restful to be reminded that I can be easily overpowered by someone who will be ten paces away while I sleep!' Rosamund's fingers strayed to her throat, and she swallowed again.

Caroline decided that, for everyone's safety, exhaustion should overcome her heroine swiftly.

×

Rosamund was tense and irritable the next day. She and Captain Collins didn't exchange more than a dozen words, and she recited the Litany for the Dead in silence at midday, mouthing the words while staring straight ahead. She had never been so glad to see a town as she was that evening. And when they entered the inn after handing over the horses, she found herself in luck: there were separate accommodations available for men and women and, best of all, someone to draw her a bath.

Captain Collins was not afforded that particular luxury, since it would dissolve the glue.

×

Caroline was wondering when "janitorial support for careless, incompetent executives" had been added to her job description when her phone pinged. This was inconvenient, crouched as she was under the expensive ergonomic — and completely drenched — desk of George Radley, CFO. Half-buried in a tangle of soaking wet electrical cables and very glad she knew where the fuse box was, she pulled all the plugs out of their sockets before snaking her hand to her pocket.

It was a message from Henry.

> **Henry**
> Just reached the part at the inn. Wouldn't they have a private room?

> **Caroline**
> Not if they're trying to avoid attention. I thought about having them travel as a fake married couple, but I decided it was too early for that, so I went for a more historical option.

> **Henry**
> Wonders will never cease.

Even cramped into an uncomfortably small space surrounded by wet electronics, Caroline couldn't help but smile.

×

Leo was also glad to see the inn. He had spent the entire day expecting an attack that never came, but he judged that the bustling, brightly lit town was unlikely to harbour many brigands. He was particularly glad not to be sharing sleeping quarters with Lady Hawkhurst again. The inn was safe enough, so he was relieved of his responsibility for her until the morning. She could take care of herself tonight.

She was certainly dangerous enough. He'd been struck by the absolute flatness of her expression when she'd told him, 'I did what I had to do.' She also appeared to have a tendency to hide sharp objects on her person.

For some reason, he found that reassuring rather than concerning.

Best not to think about it.

×

Caroline smiled triumphantly at her laptop screen. It would have been better if Leo had been having all these uncomfortable thoughts while sleeping in the same room (or better yet, the same *bed*) as Rosamund, but she'd take what she could get. Leo, at least, was shaping up to be a proper romantic hero, though a little less *enemy-ish* than she'd have preferred.

Her plausible explanation to Henry notwithstanding, Caroline had tried to get Leo and Rosamund to share a private room, but Rosamund had been adamant that she would do no such thing. And her expression had been so hunted when she'd said, 'Caroline, *please* stop pushing this,' that Caroline had conceded the point.

For now.

It was clear that her heroine was very *focused*, which she supposed was admirable, but that just meant she needed to wear Rosamund down over time. Caroline turned back to the woman in question, who was now relaxing in the bath, an expression of absolute bliss on her face. The bruises around Rosamund's throat were stark against her skin, and Caroline wondered if Leo would spot them under the collar of her doublet.

She resolved to make sure he spotted them.

In the meantime, the scene went silent and still, and Rosamund groaned as Caroline plopped herself down in a chair next to the copper tub. 'Will you be soaping your body when Leo barges in to tell you something vital? Or perhaps washing your hair?'

Rosamund closed her eyes. 'I already washed my hair in the basin, and I doubt Captain Collins is so lost to good sense and decorum as to burst unannounced into the women's quarters. Unless there are assassins.' Her eyes snapped open. 'There aren't assassins, are there?'

Caroline shook her head. 'Obviously I wouldn't be able to tell you if there were, but since you won't remember any of this when I leave anyway, no. No assassins. An actual night of sleep. For once.'

×

Captain Collins and Lady Rosamund tackled the next two days of travel with renewed determination, not least because they were well into Bevorian border territory by now and accommodations were few and far between. But if the first part of the journey had been trying, the second was not much improvement. The summer heat had grown uncomfortable, and the biting insects were out in force. The horses were miserable, and so were their riders. Their route took them through several areas that showed signs of recent fighting: too many carrion birds by half, the odd flashes of white on the ground that could only be human bones. They passed uncountable fields ripe for harvest with just a handful of women and children working in them, their pace frantic as they looked at the darkening sky.

That night the weather took a stormy turn, which might have been a blessing after the lengthy drought, especially for the farmers — but the onset of hail threatened both the travellers and the ungathered crops. The lady and her escort were forced to seek shelter once more from obliging, if puzzled, peasantry; this time, however, Leo spent the night in the barn.

✕

'Are you sure you wouldn't prefer to spend the night in the house?' Caroline wheedled.

Leo shook his head. 'No, thank you.'

Caroline considered arguing, then shrugged. She could handle a slow burn. They'd be forced into proximity soon enough. Maybe he would miss her while they slept.

✕

The next day brought unrelieved rain coupled with unseasonably chilly temperatures. This did nothing to improve morale, particularly when Rosamund overheard the farmer and her son having a murmured conversation away from the younger children about the possibility of flooding. Rosamund shivered. She and the captain should reach the Grenalla River, which marked the usual border with Abrenia, by the end of the day.

The relentless downpour after the drought had turned the river wild. The water was brown with silt, and Leo noted stray branches from uprooted trees racing along in the current.

Lady Rosamund wiped dripping strands of hair out of her eyes and tugged her hood lower over her brow.

'Captain Collins,' she said, her voice strained, 'I can see your promised accommodation for the night up that hill on the Abrenian side of the river. I am cold, it is pouring with rain, and I am exhausted. Please do not tell me you want us to take a day-long detour because you don't like the look of the bridge that you yourself led us to.'

Leo resisted the urge to snap at her.

The narrow, rickety rope bridge, the height of three men above the rushing river, required scrambling up and down a steep, scree-covered hill to access it, making it all but useless for soldiers. It had been long abandoned by its Bevorian owner, who lived on an estate far from the borders and probably didn't remember it existed. Leo had crossed it on a mission to Abrenia two years prior, but time had not been kind, and the river was wide. He was keenly aware of the risk to Lady Hawkhurst.

And the document she carried in her saddlebag, of course.

That said, when he glanced back at his travelling companion, he had to admit that she looked terrible. Her freckles stood out starkly on her pale face, there were dark smudges under her eyes, and her normally bright red hair had been plastered to her head by the heavy rain. Not to mention the despondent look on her face. Perhaps he had pushed her too hard the last few days.

He came to a decision. 'Fine,' he said shortly. 'We cross here. I'll go first.'

Leo's horse didn't like the bridge. Scout stamped and snorted as the captain coaxed him onto the first few boards. Leo couldn't blame him, but after a tense few minutes of creaking and groaning, horse and rider made it to the other side safely.

'See?' Lady Rosamund shouted, already sounding more cheerful.

Leo ground his teeth, forcing the words down. Now was not the time for an argument. The lady dismounted to lead Willow over the bridge, and he began to relax as she stepped carefully over the slippery planks. She and her mount were almost across when something cracked.

Willow squealed, charging forward and shouldering her owner aside.

The rotten wood gave way with a violent screech, and Rosamund tumbled into the water.

The river closed over her head, surrounding her with rushing ribbons of green and brown. Rosamund hit the bottom quickly and pushed off to strike out for the surface, her clothes dragging, her lungs burning.

She broke through the water and gasped, sucking in a great gulp of air. Regaining her bearings, she saw the river had drawn her a short way downstream. She despaired at the height and steepness of the Abrenian bank, but struck out for it anyway. If she could just get out of the current . . . she grabbed for the plants at the water's edge, ripping several out and slipping off several more, pulled along by the water once again before—there!

Rosamund clamped a hand on a tree root and hauled her upper body onto relatively dry land. She had a climb ahead of her to get back to the level of the bridge, but she was out of danger. For now. She paused, panting, for the space of a handful of breaths.

Then she heard, 'Catch!' and something hit her on the back of the head.

'Ow!'

The captain's face, white with worry, peered at her over the top of the bank, and now she espied the rope he had thrown down. 'Take the end!' She was about to grab for it when a nasty thought occurred to her: the declaration was safely stowed in Willow's saddlebag. All Captain Collins had to do to be rid of his troublesome charge was let go when she was halfway up, and unlike in the farmhouse, there would be no one around to witness it.

She knew Leo didn't trust her. Maybe Eudosia had never trusted her either. *Maybe she really does think I killed Hugo. Maybe this has all been an elaborate scheme to get me out of the way!*

Rosamund's head throbbed. She rested it against the tree root, trying to think. On the one hand, it was unwise to put herself at the captain's mercy. On the other, she was probably too exhausted and chilled to make it up the bank on her own. The rope that had caused stars to wink in her vision was dangling off to her left, waving from side to side as the end was pushed downstream by the current. Rosamund dived for it, grabbing on with both hands, and began to pull herself up the treacherous slope.

Halfway up her foot slid out from under her, and her left hand skidded off the rope. Her right shoulder slammed into a stout rock protruding from the bank, and she screamed at the sudden pain but held on. Over the rushing water she heard the captain shouting at her, and she grimaced at the thought of the talking-to she knew she was going to get when she managed to make it to the top.

For a moment Rosamund dangled, gasping, feet scrabbling for purchase. She had grit in her teeth, her wet hair had unravelled and hung full in her face, mud caked her boots and trousers, and sparks of agony shot down her arm.

But then the rope started to slide upwards, and Rosamund with it. She swung her left hand back to the rope, helping herself along with her feet as much as she could until finally, blessedly, she crested the top.

Leo gripped her by the forearm and let go of the rope. They both flopped to the ground – he to a sitting position, Rosamund flat on her back. She groaned gently, feeling the rain splash onto her upturned face.

A giggle burst out of her, unbidden.

'My lady?'

The laughter got more and more uncontrollable, until it was more like crying. She sucked in a few deep breaths, falling silent as the shaking started.

'Your Ladyship!' He sounded angry, but she couldn't control herself enough to speak. After almost a week of danger and misadventure, her body had rebelled against her.

'Up.' His voice seemed to be coming from a great distance away, but it brooked no argument. 'Now.'

She struggled to her feet, shivering. Her knees buckled, and she nearly fell. But then a cloak settled over her shoulders, and an arm snaked around her waist.

'The shepherd's hut is there,' he said, pointing up a small hill in front of them with his free hand. 'You said yourself that you could see it from the other side of the river. Move.'

Chapter 5

GOOSEBUMPS PERSISTED along Rosamund's arms and legs even after she entered the chilly, damp hut, but there was a small pile of cured logs tucked next to the hearth, and Leo soon had a fire burning in the grate.

Her escort dumped the saddlebags next to her. 'Get some dry clothes on,' he said curtly before going outside to settle the horses under the meagre shelter. She bit back a cry when her shoulder protested as she shrugged out of her riding doublet, and that was as far as she got. When Leo came back to find her still in her wet undershirt, he strode over to stand directly in front of her and scowled.

'Why aren't you changed yet?' he bit out.

'Because all of my clothes are wet!'

'What? Why?'

Rosamund drew a long breath, teeth chattering. 'The rope you used was in the saddlebag with my clothes. The rain is heavy, and the bag was left open, so everything in there is now wet. Not the documents!' she added hastily, as Leo blanched. 'They were in another bag, and well wrapped against water in any case. But . . .' She gestured helplessly at a length of soggy green velvet which was her usual formal daywear. 'The rest of my clothes are no better than my current set.'

His lips tightened. Rosamund tensed for a shouting match.

But instead, Leo knelt down to rummage in his own bags. A few moments later he thrust a white linen shirt, a pair of dark trousers, and a clean drying cloth into her hands. 'Here.'

She took them wordlessly, and he turned his back, shaking out another clean shirt for himself.

×

'You're not even tempted to look?' Caroline enquired sweetly.

Leo swallowed. 'Please don't ask me that.'

×

The compulsion to look and see if Lady Rosamund was all right was stronger than it really should have been. But he was responsible for this woman, which meant watching out for her wellbeing. And he had been. Although given the ring of bruises on her neck, the stiffness in her posture, the raw red colour of her palms and fingers from the rope . . . maybe he hadn't watched carefully enough.

Still, he'd noticed her reciting the Litany for the Dead under her breath at midday every day since they'd left the capital. He'd noticed the soft look she got on her face when her thoughts were wandering. He'd noticed that she had dimples on the rare occasions that she smiled.

He'd noticed a lot of things.

He really wished he hadn't.

Leo shook himself and pulled out some bread and cheese to slice for dinner, slowly counting in his head. When he reached fifty-five, Lady Rosamund coughed politely, and he turned around. Her teeth were no longer chattering, and she was squeezing water out of her hair with the drying cloth. His clothes were hopelessly big on her, but at least they weren't soaked . . . and the opening at the front of his shirt extended much further down her chest than it did his.

His thoughts in that direction were cut short when he saw what hung around her neck. He had previously caught flashes of a slim silver chain at her collar — even when the bruising from the bandit attack would have made it uncomfortable to wear — but it had always been tucked under her clothes. A ring hung from the necklace, just above her heart. A ring too big for any of Rosamund's fingers, but the right size for a man.

Leo turned away.

Their lodgings were small, but they boasted a well (the river water being of variable quality), an ancient cooking pot and kettle in the fireplace, and a long, narrow box full of hay, which presumably passed for a bed.

✕

'Oh, dear,' said Caroline. 'There's only one bed!'

Leo did not reply.

✕

The bed was not particularly near the fire, which did make sense given the risk of its going up in flames in the middle of the night, but was not ideal for one who had recently been immersed in cold water. Lady Rosamund consequently declared her intention to sleep by the fire and leave the bed to him.

'As you wish, my lady.'

✕

'Shouldn't you offer her the bed? As a gentleman?' Caroline smiled encouragingly.

'She's right to stay warm. By the fire is the best place for her.' Leo's brow knotted. 'And I'm a commoner, not a gentleman.'

'But —'

'Leave her alone, Caroline.'

×

Once they had eaten, Rosamund busied herself with hanging her clothes in front of the fire. Arranging heavy wet velvet with only one good arm was a tedious business, but she managed. It was a small mercy that her bedroll was still dry, and she shook it out near the hearth, trying to judge how close she could get without being in danger of errant sparks.

She cringed as she ran her good hand through her hair, snagging it on multiple tangles. Her hair fell to her waist when loose, which, combined with its thickness, meant it was still so drenched that it dripped onto the floor. Sighing, Rosamund attempted to divide the sodden mess into sections to comb it.

×

'You could ask Leo to help you wash it?' Caroline suggested.

'No, thank you. I'll just ... comb it out and braid it.'

But Rosamund sounded less sure of herself than usual, and after watching her glacial progress for a minute or so, Caroline understood why.

Rosamund froze while Caroline addressed Leo. 'Rosamund is having trouble.'

Leo, in the middle of repacking his saddlebag, looked over. 'With her hair?'

Caroline tutted. 'With her shoulder.'

Leo wished he hadn't noticed that.

✕

One minute and eight seconds turned out to be as long as Leo could stand watching Lady Rosamund struggle.

'My lady?' he ventured. Rosamund started.

'Yes, Captain?' Her voice was bright, but with a strained, brittle quality that wasn't entirely due to her bruised throat.

It was for the mission, he told himself firmly. If she caught a chill, then she was going to be unbearable at best and dead at worst. He needed her alive. And capable of diplomacy.

'Would you like some help with your hair?' He studied her reaction. Her breathing quickened—was that nervousness? He offered a mild smile. 'I'm going to need some assistance with my leg. It seems a fair trade.'

There was a pause. He thought she was going to decline, but then . . .

'Shall we start with you, then?'

He shook his head. 'I'm fine for the moment. Ladies first.'

She stared up at him, face uncertain, but then she handed him the comb.

Leo's mother and sister both had very long, thick hair, and though it had been a while, he soon remembered the knack of combing it out without causing agony. The fire was warm on his side, and Lady Rosamund had stopped shivering. Small victories.

She sat quite still, staring at the wall in front of her. Her whole body was tense, and she hunched her shoulders as if trying to make herself smaller. Leo tried not to touch her

more than necessary. Or to think about the other implications of a woman wearing his shirt. Instead, he thought
about her hair, which there was much more of than he
had expected, having heretofore only seen it bound up or
bedraggled.

It was, he had to admit, pretty hair, curlier than his
sister's. Juniper's hair had always been as straight as their
father's, though a different colour, while Leo had Aldous
Collins's fair hair and dark green eyes. Juniper had liked
to make fun of him for trying to emulate his father's neat
blond tail, plaited and tied with black ribbon. But that, a
tidy beard, and the smell of mint were the only things he
really remembered of Lieutenant Collins, who had died
some twenty years ago, when Leo was ten years old.

That was still a more comfortable thing to think about
than being alone with an attractive woman who was wearing
his shirt and letting him touch her hair.

✕

'Attractive, is she?' Caroline sounded smug again.

✕

He needed to think about something else.

Tangles. Tangles were like knots. How many kinds of
knots did he know how to tie and untie? Overhand, clove
hitch, bowline . . . these were just dozens of tiny knots. He
was good at unravelling knots.

After a few minutes, Rosamund started to relax.

✕

'Are you perhaps realising that it's nice to be cared for, Rosamund?'
Caroline offered.

Rosamund, unable to move without tearing her hair out of the comb currently frozen halfway down her back, narrowed her eyes. 'I beg your pardon?'

'It's nice to have people taking care of you, even when it's your Hot Enemy, hmm?'

'I have people who care about me, thank you very much,' Rosamund snapped.

'That's not the same as people who can look after you.'

'I—' Rosamund stopped short, wet her lips, then began again. 'I have my children. I have a house full of servants. I have a life outside this contrived journey you've sent me on!'

'Well, yes, but it's not the same, is it?'

Rosamund opened her mouth furiously, then checked herself and clamped it shut. Caroline was suddenly worried that her character was going to cry. But instead, Rosamund continued, a little shakily: 'No. It's not the same. But that's not important right now. Just like it wasn't important to send me on this mission with an adequate number of guards. Please, just let the man fix my hair in peace.'

'But—'

'Leave me alone, Caroline.'

×

It took some time for Captain Collins to braid Rosamund's hair, and, truthfully, it was pleasant to have someone else do it. How many days had it been since she'd had a maid to tend her? Her shoulder still ached, but she hoped a night of rest would put it right, and by the time Leo had finished combing, she had shaken off her feeling of melancholy. Regardless of what had brought it on, she mustn't show weakness. They had a job to do, and he didn't need her being a burden. The mission was dangerous enough as it was.

When he tied off the end of her hair with a bow and apologised that her braid was so messy, she managed to laugh. 'You've never seen my hair when Charlotte has decided it needs a restyle.' They smiled at each other for a moment. Then Rosamund remembered where they were and what they were doing. 'Shall I take a look at your leg, Captain?'

'Thank you, my lady.'

She tutted as he removed the bandages, revealing the fresh blood. She wiped it away and dabbed a fresh layer of the sticky, pearlescent caladrius glue onto his leg, grimacing when she used her right arm by accident.

'I'm sorry about your shoulder, my lady.'

Rosamund shrugged, only to wince again. 'These things happen.'

'I'm sorry anyway.'

She looked up at his face, braced for insincerity, but his green eyes were warm and serious, and she found herself soothed by his concern.

'I'm fine,' she said at last. 'But thank you.'

And even though she was sharing a room with him again, sleep came more easily that night, and Rosamund dropped off to the memory of a candlelit ballroom, a deep red curtain, and a chance encounter.

✕

Nineteen-year-old Rosamund Page pushed the heavy velvet aside, cursing wide-skirted ballgowns as she tried to flatten herself against the wall behind the draped fabric, safely out of sight.

There was a solid obstacle in the way.

'Oof,' said the obstacle, and Rosamund jumped, the curtain falling from her hands. There was not a lot of space behind it, and most of it was occupied by a dark-haired man in his early twenties who looked both aggrieved and somewhat panicked.

'Are you all right?' Rosamund whispered in Bevorian, conscious of voices approaching.

He grimaced. 'Madam, I am hiding behind a curtain in a ballroom. What do you think?'

At least she'd guessed the right language in which to address him. Abrenian men didn't tend to wear so much lace at their cuffs, so it had seemed a reasonable surmise. That said, he didn't look like the sort who would voluntarily don eveningwear in the first place. 'It seems safe to assume that your night isn't going well,' replied Rosamund, 'but perhaps you just really wanted some peace and quiet?'

The man gave her a tiny, fleeting smile, then bowed slightly. Which was fortunate; they were standing so close together that a full bow would have turned into a headbutt. 'I confess: I really, desperately wanted to be alone. Hugo Hawkhurst, misanthrope, at your service.'

'Rosamund Page. Sorry to interrupt your solitude, but . . .' She paused, then continued carefully, 'I also needed some peace and quiet.'

'Do you make frequent recourse to ballroom curtains for this purpose, Miss Page?'

It was Rosamund's turn to grimace. 'Usually not. But sometimes sacrifices must be made.'

A hint of curiosity broke through the stiffness of his expression. 'From whom are you hiding?'

Rosamund hesitated. Hugo frowned, and the silence that fell was made rather more awkward than normal by how close they were standing. 'Well,' he said at length, 'even if you wish to keep your secrets, I will further confess that I am back here to avoid making more intimate acquaintance of one Lady Cecilia, who . . . er . . .'

Rosamund had met Lady Cecilia before. 'Who was perhaps keen on making your slightly *too* intimate acquaintance?'

'She was more friendly than I had anticipated.'

Rosamund's lips twitched as she fought down a smile, trying to look suitably sympathetic. Hugo sighed. 'This is the part where you tell me that she's your cousin, isn't it?'

She giggled, then remembered that they were trying to be quiet and shook her head. 'I claim no kinship with Lady Cecilia, and she would not welcome the inference. But since you have been so honest, I am hiding from one Weston Mabry: apparently the second son of a baron, but also the sort of man who shakes hands like it's a competition and doesn't bother to apologise if he treads on your toes while dancing.'

> **HBWalker:** Shaking hands as a form of greeting? Really?
>
> ----
>
> > **CSLindley:** My fantasy world is not representative of any particular historical period, thank you very much!

Rosamund gave Hugo a lopsided smile. 'This is where you tell me he's *your* cousin?'

'Mercifully, no,' Hugo said dryly, 'but he is my neighbour, and his father is our liege lord.'

'Are bad dancing and competitive hand-shaking geographical traits?' She held out her hand. It didn't have to go very far. He discreetly wiped his palm on his coat before taking hers. Hugo, at least, could shake hands perfectly well, and she told him so.

'I'm gratified to hear it, since I'm a very bad dancer,' he replied. 'But I would at least be certain to apologise if I stepped on your feet. Which I'd do my best to avoid, but . . . well . . .'

'You can't be that bad at dancing.'

Hugo shrugged. 'Haven't really had much practice.'

'Too busy hunting, shooting, and/or fishing, Mr. Hawkhurst?'

'I prefer reading, honestly.'

> **HBWalker:** Novels are a very Regency thing.
>
> **CSLindley:** The printing press was invented in 1439, if I want novels in my novel, I am having them!

Hmm. 'Favourite book?'

'In what genre, Miss Page?'

'Poetry.'

'*The Epic of Fernisal.* Yours?'

Rosamund was startled into a grin. 'The same, actually.'

Hugo offered a tentative smile in return. 'Ah, but perhaps you are just saying that to entrap me with your feminine wiles. Though, if you are, at least you're being more subtle and thus more successful than Lady Cecilia.'

They were silent a moment. Hugo's face read like someone who hadn't quite meant to say that aloud. Rosamund's cheeks warmed. 'Well then,' she said, more lightly than she felt, 'perhaps you should ask me my favourite book in some other genre, and then we will be even.'

'Romance,' said Hugo, and now his face was pink as well. '*Eye of the Moon.*'

Hugo blinked. 'One of mine as well. Did you enjoy the sequel?'

Rosamund wrinkled her nose. 'Entertaining, but not a patch on the original.' The conversation continued along similar lines for some time until Rosamund remembered where she was and what she was supposed to be doing. 'Mr. Hawkhurst.'

'Miss Page?'

'We are at a ball.'

He nodded with mock-seriousness. 'I commend your powers of observation.'

Rosamund grimaced. 'We are supposed to be meeting people. Specifically, we are supposed to be behaving like good little girls and boys and—'

'—finding a suitable marriage partner from the correct country? Yes, but it's so *boring*, not to mention loud. Besides, my Abrenian has rather gone by the wayside since I finished my education, and my accent was always atrocious.'

'Many of the Abrenian ladies here were educated in both languages,' said Rosamund. 'So as you see, we are generally fluent enough in Bevorian not to embarrass ourselves.'

Hugo blinked. 'I wondered if I recognised you from school.'

'I don't think I recognise you, but I'm not the best at faces.' Rosamund shifted her weight a little, leaning back against the wall. 'If you're neighbours with Weston Mabry, we might be sitting near each other at dinner.'

'Really?'

She nodded. 'I saw the plan for the place cards.'

'How?'

'Never you mind.'

He grinned.

'That said,' Rosamund continued, 'if I am sitting next to him, I may end up resorting to murder, which would not be conducive to a pleasant evening. So . . .' Her eyes lit up. 'I think a little creative rearrangement might be in order.'

'Wait—' Hugo began, but she'd already twitched the curtain aside and slipped out, heading past the dance floor to the doors of the Great Hall.

Once there, Rosamund made quick work of finding the place cards, which merely confirmed her worst fears. She returned to the curtain and checked to see that no one was watching, then pulled Hugo out, slipping her arm into his. 'Mr. Hawkhurst,' she said softly, now steering him past the dance floor, 'if you're willing to take a quick walk with me, I think you'll find it to our mutual benefit.'

'Pray explain, Miss Page.'

'Well,' she whispered as they continued their circuit of the palace ballroom, 'I have just been into the Great Hall, and I have good news and bad news.'

Hugo braced himself.

'The good news: we are sitting near each other. The bad news: I'm sitting next to Weston Mabry, and you are sitting next to Lady Cecilia.'

'Do you have a proposed solution to this horrendous problem?'

She winked at him. 'Come with me.' And with that, she slipped through the half-open door to the Great Hall, pulling him along with her.

The room was currently empty and much darker than the ballroom. The fireplaces threw off some light, but as Rosamund led Hugo down the side of the table nearest the east wall, deep shadow lingered in every niche they passed. They reached their places, and Rosamund dispatched Hugo to move Weston Mabry's card down the table while she took Lady Cecilia's in the other direction. Spotting a card for a "Cecily", whom she thought she remembered from school, Rosamund swapped it with Cecilia's and returned to Hugo, flush with success.

'We don't want to move them too far,' she whispered, 'in case we get the serving staff in trouble. But I swapped Cecilia with a Cecily.'

'Great minds,' he whispered back. 'I swapped Weston with a Madeley. But we need to get out of here before someone spots us.'

> **HBWalker:** Why didn't Rosamund just . . . move them herself?
>
> **CSLindley:** Because that's no fun!

They made their way back down the table and had nearly reached the ballroom when a door on the west side of the hall opened with a creak. Rosamund squeaked as Hugo dragged her into one of the unlit niches, manoeuvering her behind a pillar to get her out of sight.

Rosamund was quite aware that her pale skin, red hair, and bright red gown would be extremely conspicuous, even in the dim light. Hugo seemed to have realised it too. He pressed her into the corner of the niche, attempting to flatten her unwieldy skirts and cover her body with his own. His green court dress and brown hair blended seamlessly into the dark, and she breathed out, trying to make herself smaller.

His mouth was right by her ear. 'Sorry,' he whispered, and she shivered, her pulse suddenly hammering in her ears. Not just because they'd nearly been caught. The ridiculousness of the whole situation struck her then, and she stifled a giggle.

'Miss Page?' Hugo sounded uncertain.

She smiled, though she wasn't sure if he could see it. 'I was just thinking that this is a very particular way to make friends at a ball. And that Lady Cecilia must never know.'

'If someone finds us in this, ah . . . compromising position,' he said quietly, 'we'll probably have to get married for decency's sake.'

She laughed gently. 'I am very sorry for you, sir, if that is the case.'

'Why for me?' They both froze at a noise from the south end of the hall. But then they heard a door creak, and silence fell again.

'I regret to inform you that the Page family is not highly thought of in Abrenia. We're really just peasants in fancy dress.'

> **HBWalker:** And yet her sister marries the heir to the throne?

>> **CSLindley:** Yes, and the only reason it's not an absolute scandal when Roland falls in love with Catherine is that Rosamund's marriage has given them such a leg up on the social ladder.

'I'm really only here to make up the numbers.' She shrugged. 'I'll probably end up married to whoever's left over from Bevoria. I hear a lot of the matches have been decided upon behind closed doors already. Which makes sense, I suppose. A situation in which aristocrats can marry off their children to other aristocrats in an act of selfless diplomacy won't stop them from seeking other more tangible benefits from the arrangement.' She sighed. 'I should be out there dancing and flirting and trying to figure out who my best option is, but . . .'

'You're stuck in a dark corner with me?'

'You're not so bad, even if I can't marry you.'

Hugo pulled his head back to look at her. 'Why not?'

'You . . .' She blinked up at him. 'You were hiding behind a curtain. I assumed you had been matched with Lady Cecilia and were hoping that if you disappeared, she might catch someone else's eye before you had to announce it.'

'A reasonable assumption, but no. I have no prior arrangement.'

'You're telling me,' Rosamund said slowly, 'that you have spent the last hour talking about books and rearranging place cards with me . . . and you haven't even got a wife in mind?'

'Yes.'

'You—' *idiot* was on the tip of her tongue, but instead she tried, '—don't want to choose your own wife instead of being left with one of the brides nobody wants?'

He looked back at her, then, something sympathetic in his expression. 'I'm told,' he said gently, 'by an impeccable source, that Miss Rosamund Page is among the "brides nobody wants". Which leads me to believe that everyone here is a fool, since she is quite the most charming woman I've ever met.'

Oh.

There was another noise behind them, but neither of them paid much attention. 'You know . . .' Rosamund said, edging towards him a little, 'you had a point earlier.'

'I did?'

'Yes. When you said that if we were found in a . . . compromising position . . .' She was radiating warmth now; he could probably feel her blushing from here. 'Then it would probably be required that we marry.'

There was a long silence. 'That being the case, Miss Page,' he said at last, 'may . . . er . . . may I kiss you?'

'I think I'd like that.'

They pressed their lips together, and it was tentative, and warm, and sweet.

When they broke apart, Rosamund frowned slightly, and Hugo winced. 'Are you . . . all right, Miss Page?'

'Well, first,' she said slowly, 'if there's going to be kissing going on, you should probably call me Rosamund. And second,' she said as she put her arms around his neck — and the smile she gave him was wicked — 'while I'm not what you'd call *experienced* at this kissing business, I think we can do better.'

And then his hands were in her hair, and her body was pressed up against his, and it turned out that they could, in fact, do better.

Of course, that was the moment one of the servants came into the niche to light the lamp.

Neither of them noticed.

✕

But as Rosamund drifted into deeper slumber, the memory turned on its head. Now she was holding her husband's body, trying to stop Charlotte from seeing, desperate to find the red curtain so that she could hide Hugo from view . . .

She woke up screaming.

Chapter 6

LEO HAD DROPPED OFF to sleep quickly, but he awoke a few hours later to the sound of whimpering. Though it was full dark outside, the banked fire gave off enough light that he could see Lady Rosamund stirring, her bedroll in knots about her.

'No — don't — I — ' Rosamund descended back into incoherent mumbling as her movements became more violent. Leo was no stranger to nightmares; usually he'd leave the dreamer in peace. Besides, she carried a lot of knives. Waking her up could be the last mistake he ever made.

But if she was thrashing about that close to the fire . . .

He got up. Just to make himself something hot to drink. The fact that this required him to stand between Lady Rosamund and the hearth was irrelevant. Her words became more distinct, Abrenian and Bevorian phrases jumbling together, with one name running through all of them.

'*Hugo!*'

Leo had just set down his tea when Lady Rosamund sat bolt upright in her bedroll, screaming. She scrambled back until she hit the stone wall of the hut and stopped there, gasping for breath. Leo's heart twisted as he watched her work out where she was. Her face crumpled. She curled her knees to her chest and began to cry. Very, very quietly.

Maybe she didn't like him very much. Maybe she didn't trust him. If he was honest, maybe she was right not to.

But watching her weep silently in the corner—only now, in the dead of night, after so much else had tried and failed to break her—he found he could not bear it. Whatever she might think of him, he wasn't heartless enough to let her cry herself back to sleep while he sat and watched. Picking up the tea, he crossed the room to kneel in front of her. 'My lady?'

She flinched, but her eyes met his, her face tear-stained and red. She took a deep breath, drew herself up, and wiped her face without speaking.

'Would you like some tea?'

Lady Rosamund pressed her lips together, her face still tight with pain, but nodded. 'Thank you.' He passed it over, and she wrapped her fingers around the mug, inhaling the steam. Leo fetched a blanket and his own drink and came back to sit down beside her, careful not to touch her. There were still the knives, after all.

Halfway through her cup, she wiped her face again before looking up at him. 'I'm sorry for waking you, Captain Collins. Especially after yesterday.'

Leo shrugged. 'Don't worry, my lady.' He hesitated, then offered, 'Would you like the bed? I was worried you'd roll into the fireplace.'

She set her tea down. 'I'm fine where I am.'

He waited to see if anything else was forthcoming. Often people who'd had a scare were more talkative, and now (though he wasn't pleased at the thought) would be the best time to get truthful answers from her. After all, there was more than one reason that Queen Eudosia had sent him with Lady Rosamund. But the seconds passed, and she showed no sign of speaking again. Finally, he ventured, 'Would you like to talk about it?'

She shook her head.

'Is there anything else you need?'

Rosamund opened her mouth to speak. There was no sound for a moment, and then she heaved a horrible, strangled sob before starting to cry again.

Afterwards, Leo would rationalise his actions by saying that he needed her to trust him, and so comforting her was the natural thing to do. In truth, he had just moved. A moment later his arms were around her, and she was sobbing violently into what was probably his last clean shirt. He reached up to stroke her hair and mumbled meaningless phrases into the top of her head like she was a frightened child. 'Shhh,' he whispered. 'It's all right.' After a long moment she began to relax—and then clung to him more tightly.

Leo considered his options.

He stayed where he was. Eventually, the crying eased. The self-recrimination followed.

'I should have listened to you, Captain Collins. You were right. The bridge wasn't safe, and I nearly got myself killed. I'm sorry.' Rosamund curled in on herself again, and Leo tightened his grip, hoping very much that she wasn't going to take this unasked-for physical contact amiss when she came back to herself.

'It's all right, my lady. It's not your fault. None of this is.'

Rosamund flinched. Too late, he remembered her shoulder. He relaxed his hands, and she reached for one of the freshly dried handkerchiefs hung by the fire to blow her nose. 'Ah, a man who doesn't listen to gossip. A rare commodity indeed.'

Now here was something. How far could he go with this line of enquiry? She had turned away from him, but he sensed her husband's death pressed heavily enough upon her in this moment to prompt a confidence, for all that she was trying to put a brave face on things. That was often true of the guilty. But then again, it was often true of the disbelieved, too.

'I've heard the rumours,' he said. 'But I'd rather hear it from you.'

The tears returned, and his damp shirt stuck to his skin as she cuddled into him again, all pretence of dignity forgotten. 'There's a rumour that I arranged his death, that it was an assassination.' She sniffed, and he would have called it derisive if it hadn't sounded so pitiful. 'Ridiculous. I loved my husband.' She looked up into his eyes, tentative. 'But I wonder sometimes if the gossips were right about an assassination. An Abrenian force big enough to kill his entire guard *just happened* to get past every single member of his—'

Caroline scowled, peering out the window at the darkness, and drummed her fingers on the chipped particleboard of her desktop. She had gone to bed straight after dinner, exhausted from her week at work, only to wake up a few hours later from a terrible dream she vaguely recalled involving Henry, George, and running away from a giant man-eating zebra. Unable to go back to sleep, she'd decided to mitigate unwieldy emotions the best way she knew how. And Leo and Rosamund had been most obliging, for once, but then—she sighed, looking at the clock. Maybe Henry was still awake. It wasn't *that* late.

Caroline
What's the word for the people you'd call up to fight
from your estate?

Henry
Do you mean the household guard (I think we
decided Hugo had about ten of those) or do you
mean the levy, the selection of able-bodied men from
the town called up for war?

Caroline
the latter, thanks

Caroline
sleep well :)

✕

'—levy and reach his command post?' Rosamund clamped
her mouth shut for a moment, her lips white, before she
went on. 'When Baron Mabry sent each of his knights
to a different Abrenian village to set up a perimeter, the
Hawkhurst levy was the smallest force. So why were they
sent to the most isolated position? Hugo would *never* have
been so careless with deployments.' She coughed and
dabbed at her nose again. 'Weston Mabry is a snake, but
he's not stupid. He wouldn't risk his forces with an inadequate picket. Would he? Sometimes I've wondered . . .'
She trailed off, burying her face in Leo's shirt once more.
He was grateful for this; it meant she couldn't see his
expression.

How much has she guessed? How much did she know?

'I miss Hugo so much that it's a physical ache.' The
pain in her voice jarred him back to the present. 'But
instead of sympathy, I get suspicion.' Her voice rose in agitation. 'And now there's a rumour at court that I'm a traitor
who killed my own husband.'

'Idle gossip is not evidence, my lady. You gained nothing by his death.'

She snorted. 'That hasn't stopped people talking.'

Leo shrugged. 'The truth rarely does.'

They sat for a while longer. The fire had begun to dim, but neither of them moved to stoke it.

'We should go back to sleep,' Rosamund said eventually.

'Yes, my lady.'

But they didn't stir. Even the silence was comfortable — in the same way, he realised, it had been with her from the start. And now he was also convinced that Rosamund wasn't behind the death of Sir Hugo Hawkhurst. How much of that conclusion was based on cold logic versus wishful thinking, he didn't wish to speculate.

At last Rosamund roused herself. Leo hurried to stand up as soon as she moved, embarrassed at his thoughts. 'I'll see you in the morning, Captain,' she mumbled, returning to her bedroll, and he grunted an acknowledgment as he followed suit.

When Leo woke with the sun, he let the lady sleep while he dressed and prepared breakfast. They couldn't afford a long delay, but giving her an extra half an hour before she had to deal with the world didn't seem so unreasonable.

✕

Caroline sat back, impressed. Maybe it would be a slower burn than she'd originally anticipated, but she could work with this.

If only Rosamund would *notice* how attentive and considerate Leo was being. Her heroine's preoccupation with the task at hand — well, when she wasn't weeping all over her aggravatingly respectful Hot Enemy — was most annoying.

Caroline shrugged, closed her laptop, and went to bed.

✕

Leo's watchfulness over the horses, their surroundings, the road conditions, and the weather as they hurried towards Quayforth no longer struck Rosamund as remarkable — but she was a little unnerved to find that he was watching her, too. He never said anything, but occasionally when she was riding ahead of him, she'd feel the hairs on the back of her neck stand on end, and she had to resist the urge to turn and look.

Still, the captain's vigilance had its uses; they had not progressed five miles into Abrenia before he spotted a border patrol. They scrambled off the road and out of sight, leading the horses and trying not to make too much noise. Rosamund focused on her breathing as the soldiers sauntered along the road towards them. These men clearly didn't expect to meet anything other than sheep on this lonely stretch of country road, and with any luck, they wouldn't.

The soldiers drew level. Rosamund put a hand on Willow's nose to keep her still, trying to ignore the prickling sensation on the back of her own neck. Of course Captain Collins was watching her; if they were discovered now, they would have to rely on her diplomatic skills to protect him, rather than the other way round. That was all.

After what felt like an age, the party passed them by, but the captain waited a full five minutes before deciding it was safe to move again. They met no more patrols that day and spent the night in a ramshackle barn, talking little. Rosamund noted that the silence they had so easily shared at the start of their journey had a different quality now. Traversing hostile territory was not sufficient to account for the tension in the air, but neither of them mentioned the nightmare or the conversation by the fire.

No matter. They were almost there. They just had to reach the capital and present the declaration. Then Rosamund could take a moment to breathe before making her way home to prepare for the peace talks . . . which would probably coincide with Hugo's Feast of Remembrance.

She shoved the thought down. *No.* No getting distracted now, not when they were so close. She could do this.

She had to.

The next day, as the road they were on grew gradually more well maintained, Captain Collins interrupted the silence to make a request: 'My lady, would you be so kind as to do the talking when we encounter Abrenians?'

'Certainly, Captain,' she responded mechanically, but then raised an eyebrow. 'I assume the queen wouldn't have sent you if you didn't speak Abrenian, but if you'd prefer . . .'

'I — ' He closed his mouth. For a moment, the only sounds were the clip-clop of the horses' hooves and birdsong. 'If your throat is better . . . If you would, my lady. I'd prefer not to have to speak.'

Rosamund refrained from asking how that was any different from usual. Instead, she smiled demurely and edged her mount on ahead of him. 'Stay with me, Captain Collins. I'll do the talking.'

They made it to a town that night, one far enough from the border that two relatively well-dressed travellers raised no comment. Rosamund started to smell the sea on the afternoon of the third day, and when the city walls came into view between the trees, she couldn't help but laugh with relief. That said, their arrival at the city gates provoked consternation.

The guards were not impressed at the arrival of a woman who bore a striking resemblance to their beloved sovereign, and there was a ripple of disbelief from the crowd when Rosamund announced that she was Queen Catherine's sister. Even producing the Declaration of Truce, sealed with Queen Eudosia's official insignia, did not much placate the city guard, who confiscated the pair's swords before permitting them entry. The captain was obviously uneasy about this, but Rosamund gave him a reassuring smile as they were escorted down the main thoroughfare. She could feel people watching her, and she sensed their confusion: What was Queen Catherine doing riding up Latimer's Way? Why was she accompanied by the city guard instead of her personal guard? Was it their imagination, or did Her Majesty look older than usual?

The horses were sweating by the time they had climbed the winding, cobbled road that led up to the palace. The men standing watch at the palace received them with careful courtesy. No fewer than three messengers were dispatched to announce their arrival, leaving Rosamund and Leo to affect polite nonchalance.

When a maid and a manservant appeared, Rosamund was led off in the opposite direction to Captain Collins, and she tried not to dwell on how strange it was to be out of his company. She followed the girl through halls of bustling staff—who bowed and curtseyed deeply while attempting not to stare too obviously—but encountered surprisingly few members of the Abrenian nobility. Perhaps her attendant had been instructed to prioritise discretion.

At last, when the maid opened the door to the stateroom and asked what the lady required, Rosamund barely resisted the urge to say, "five minutes alone." Instead, she washed, changed into her Hawkhurst green court gown, and schooled herself to patience while the maid dressed her hair. That complete, she gathered up the declaration papers and pulled the stateroom door open—to find Captain Collins already waiting outside.

His appearance came as a surprise, in more ways than one. He had shaved, polished his boots, and wore the blue and gold of Queen Eudosia's palace guard: altogether a very different picture from the road-weary companion to whom Rosamund had grown accustomed.

It suits him, she thought—then gave herself a mental shake. This really wasn't the time. Even if the colour made his eyes look very green.

'My lady,' he said, his Abrenian only slightly stiff.

She gave him an Abrenian curtsey instead of a Bevorian bow, aware of just how much the change in context necessitated the change in manners. She had a part to play. So play it she would. 'Shall we, Captain?'

'After you, Your Ladyship.'

They walked side by side down to the audience chamber. The heavy oak doors swung open, revealing honey-gold stone walls and crimson tapestries. Rosamund pulled her shoulders back and stepped inside, and Leo matched her pace.

An array of floral scents hung heavily in the air as they passed through the assembled crowds, Rosamund holding the documents before her like a shield. Almost all of the blooms were white, the colour of peace: white poppies nodded in vases around the doorways, and pale roses twined around candelabra. The only variation was provided by the bright blue lilies that flanked the golden eagle lectern that stood, wings outstretched, on the dais. The mitigating effect of the flowers on Abrenia's standard was limited, but the sight of so much floristry seemed to calm Leo, just fractionally, and Rosamund felt her own body relax a little in turn.

When they reached the front of the crowd, Leo stepped off to the side at the direction of a page. Rosamund, eyes locked on the grave figure of King Roland—a man she had not seen in some five years—strode forward at his signal to approach and took her place behind the lectern facing the assembly. Scribes at either side unfurled the scroll with a crackle of parchment. She took a deep breath.

'From Her Gracious Majesty Queen Eudosia, Sovereign over Bevoria and all its associated Realms and Territories, Ruler by the Light of the Wisdoms, to King Roland, son of Adelric the Third, Sovereign over Abrenia and the Isles of Dunlar, Ruler by the Light of the Wisdoms—Greetings.' Rosamund's voice rang out in the vault of the chamber, and she fixed her eyes on a point above the jewel-box colours of the audience. She didn't dare to make eye contact with any of the Abrenian nobles in attendance—many of whom she had known or else known of since childhood. 'It is no pleasure of ours that the citizenry of both of our nations is currently spent on warfare, for while it is wisdom to be prepared for war, it reflects most gravely on a sovereign if they are unable to make peace. Therefore, in the Light of the Wisdoms, and according to the statutes of our own nation, Bevoria presents these terms: first, that immediate truce be declared between the sovereign states of Bevoria and Abrenia.'

A collective breath was taken up by the room—whether more a gasp or a sigh, Rosamund couldn't tell. She ignored it, returning to the words on the scroll. 'Second, that peace talks be convened as soon as may be accomplished, and at a location appropriate for both parties. Third, that the ongoing dispute over river rights be resolved by . . .' Rosamund continued to read the details of Eudosia's proposal but risked a glance around the room. While Roland was only visible in her peripheral vision and seemed not to have stirred, the attitudes of perhaps a third of the nobles in the room started to soften as she made her way down the scroll. Most of them, she thought, would be those in the border territories.

She noted with slight consternation that Leo was not looking at her at all. He appeared to be taking in the entire room instead, his eyes sweeping back and forth. But when a scribe on the dais shifted position to assist her, the captain's head snapped around, his expression dangerous. Their eyes met for a moment, and even as Rosamund's pulse thundered in her ears, she saw him relax minutely before resuming his survey of the audience. As Rosamund neared the end of the scroll, fully half of the audience seemed at least somewhat mollified, though the expressions of the others ranged from deep scepticism to outright hostility. Her attention snagged on a particularly hostile face—and then on a familiar pearlescent shimmer on the bandage at his throat. *Caladrius salve? On an Abrenian?*

But this was no time to dwell on the implications. She dragged her eyes back to the scroll, concluding, 'Sent with our most loyal Lady Rosamund of Hawkhurst, whose estates we offer to host talks of peace, this day the twenty-second of Summer in the Year of the Fox.' Rosamund stepped away from the lectern, faced the throne, and curtseyed deeply, waiting with one knee on the ground while King Roland made his way to the centre of the dais.

'There is no wisdom in warfare with a neighbour who offers friendship,' he began, and Rosamund's heart leapt. She didn't dare raise her head, but the discontented muttering seemed quieter than it had when she'd first entered the audience chamber. 'Abrenia welcomes the opportunity for peace,' Roland continued, and Rosamund concentrated on staying upright. Her legs were protesting after a week of hard riding, but she couldn't move until he was finished. She wobbled, just a little.

Leo's eyes darted towards her, and he flinched, but she shook her head minutely and he inclined his head in understanding and remained where he was. Roland was still talking. '—interests of harmony between our countries and abundance in our storehouses, it is therefore our pleasure that a truce be declared and peace talks be convened. And so, in honour of this declaration, a celebration is in order.'

Relief and fatigue swept over Rosamund. Her legs were shaking in earnest as His Majesty, her brother-in-law, announced a masquerade ball in four days' time. Finally, he looked down at her. 'Rise, Lady Rosamund. Be welcome in our halls.'

She stood, still trembling, and Roland, whom she'd met all of three times in her entire life, smiled at her like she was his sister in truth. 'Hello, Rosamund,' he said gently. 'Cat will be pleased to see you.'

CSLindley: See? I TOLD you I could do politics!

✕

Henry Walker rolled his eyes with more fondness than he would ever admit to and closed his laptop. To be fair, he had no one to admit anything to, at least not in his immediate vicinity. He knew the names of two of his housemates (both Maria and Paul had lived in the five-bedroom house share in Birmingham for almost as long as he had), but they were both out at work, and he could not recall the names of the people who had recently moved in. This was not helped by the fact that one of his new housemates was one half of a couple, and he could not for the life of him figure out who had actually signed the contract and who was just living there for free.

As long as they followed the cleaning rota and didn't steal his plates, he'd decided not to bother protesting.

Henry stood up from his desk and replaced the chair underneath before backing through the narrow space between the single bed and the crammed-to-the-rafters bookshelf. When he'd first moved in, he'd taken the smallest bedroom out of necessity; freelance editing was a feast-or-famine business, and since he'd only just started, it had been famine almost all the way. Caroline had changed that, but he'd stayed anyway. The Midlands weren't the most expensive place to live, but there was no sense wasting money. Caroline, he knew, lived in a house share in Canterbury, and frequently complained about both the expense and her noisy night-owl housemates.

If Henry got antsy in his small space, he followed Caroline's example and ventured elsewhere to work. The smile in her voice when he'd told her that he was calling from next to a duck pond had been entirely worth it, though he'd sat on his hands to avoid texting her pictures of the ducklings. That would have been a step too far.

It wasn't that Caroline was his favourite author to work with. It was just that she was interesting, and funny, and very punctual with her payments. It definitely wasn't anything more than that. It was definitely not unprofessional for him to reach for his phone instead of using the comment function on the document.

Henry
A masquerade? From scratch? In four days?

Caroline
You're no fun :P

Henry
I'll have you know I'm a renowned party animal :P

There was a brief suggestion that Caroline was typing a reply, then nothing. Henry, now anxious about whether or not using a tongue-sticking-out emoji when conversing with your client constituted sexual harassment, decided not to think about it.

Chapter 7

'Oh, we knew that the declaration was on its way,' Catherine said to Rosamund as the sisters sat down to tea. 'We had a phoenix materialise in the courtyard a week ago. I couldn't work out why Eudosia hadn't just sent a pigeon; if it were me, I would have erred on the side of caution during a time of war rather than risk my most expensive pet being shot at by jumpy guards. But the engraving on the bird's leg ring was clear enough: an offer of truce was on its way. Who and when, she didn't have space for. But I'm glad to see you.'

'You . . . she . . .' Rosamund scrambled for a reply, but anger was rising in her throat. As if it wasn't enough to be pulled around like a puppet on a string, the fact that everyone else seemed to know far more about what was going on than she did had started to rankle. *And what about that Abrenian noble with the caladrius salve on his wounds?* What else didn't she know?

And how much of it could get her — or her sister — killed?

Clearly tact would have to remain the order of the day. 'Well,' Rosamund said, more lightly than she felt, 'that does explain how you're going to be able to throw together an entire masquerade ball in three days flat.'

> **HBWalker:** Fine. Handwave away.

Caroline scowled as she read the comment on her latest chapter. He knew as well as she did that a ball was an *expected trope*. Why was he being so dismissive?

She decided not to bother arguing.

✕

Catherine looked at her with something like pity in her expression, and Rosamund bit down on the inside of her cheek. Her sister being sympathetic might be a little too much to bear at the moment. They had met for tea in the queen's private rooms, lavishly appointed in burgundy and gold. It was their first chance since Rosamund's arrival for a quiet visit together, just the two of them. As soon as they were alone, Cat had flung her arms around Rosamund and squeezed until they were both breathless. 'I'm so sorry,' Cat whispered.

That Hugo had died? That they were technically on opposite sides of a war? That she hadn't been able to come to the funeral? Rosamund pulled back and shook her head, anxious to reassure her little sister. 'I'm fine, Cat. Really.'

Catherine looked sceptical, but her baby daughter chose that moment to wake up from her nap, and the sisters backed away from the precipice of uncomfortable feelings. Conversation, when it resumed, was strained at first, though Rosamund did give her sister the edited high-lights of the trip. Falling in the river made the cut.

'That sounds terrifying!' Cat exclaimed. 'Thank the Wisdoms the captain was there to fish you out.' She waited expectantly for her sister to continue, but Rosamund only nodded briskly, having decided not to mention the part where she'd wept in Captain Collins's arms in the middle of the night.

Cat gave her a suspicious look that Rosamund knew only too well, even after their years apart: it said, *You're holding something back again, aren't you.* But, after an uncomfortably long pause, Cat sighed and said, 'Did you have any trouble once you were over the border?' and Rosamund was able to continue.

However, Catherine also saw fit to invite Captain Collins to tea the following day. Rosamund knew better than to argue.

Leo sat still and straight on the edge of the upholstered chair and concentrated on not spilling his tea. He tried to relax his shoulders at least, hoping to avoid looking as uncomfortable as he felt. The sisters were polite enough to speak Bevorian for his benefit, but he could tell that he was intruding.

That said, Leo took careful note of Queen Catherine's murmured asides in Abrenian, most of which were either flattering-but-embarrassing comments about him — "At least she gave you someone pretty to look at while you were on the road!" had him fighting down a blush — or highly unflattering (but accurate) assessments of the Bevorian aristocrats the recently-crowned Queen of Abrenia had previously come across: 'Has Stanley managed to run off his third wife yet? No? Shocking. What about those awful twins who used to pull my hair at school?'

Leo managed not to make a fool of himself by staying silent unless asked a direct question and thought he was getting away with "Yes, Your Majesty" and "No, Your Majesty" quite handily — until Queen Catherine smiled at him and asked if he'd like to hold the baby. Her four-year-old son (who, after some prodding, had greeted him more-or-less formally in Bevorian) had been ushered away to his lessons after the first half hour, and Leo had just been starting to relax when the infant girl was sprung on him. He suspected it was a test.

Mindful of the need to at least attempt to be charming, and trying not to think about the number of people in the building who would kill him slowly and painfully if he upset the baby, he took the little princess in his arms, faced her towards her mother, and rocked gently from one foot to the other.

×

'What do *you* know about babies?' Caroline asked, incredulous.

Leo shrugged. 'I have two nieces and a nephew.'

Caroline made a note.

×

Catherine owned herself quite curious about her sister's escort, and much to Rosamund's dismay, she just would not stop passing comment. 'Are you sure you aren't thinking of a morganatic marriage?' Cat murmured to her sister in Abrenian as Leo shushed the baby.

'Don't be silly. The paperwork alone would kill the poor man,' Rosamund muttered back. She glanced over at Leo, who surely spoke at least some Abrenian, but when he caught her looking, he just gave her a polite smile before turning his attention back to the princess.

> **HBWalker:** Wait, did you actually make up a language?
>
> **CSLindley:** Who do I look like, Tolkien?

✕

Henry had typed:

> **HBWalker:** No, you're much prettier.

before he'd stopped to think. He deleted it, but mindful that if Caroline was in the shared document, she might have seen the typing, he wrote:

> **HBWalker:** No, your approach to worldbuilding is more Lewis than Tolkien. Oh look, Santa Claus!

There was no response.

✕

The next day, Leo declined the invitation to tea. 'I thought you would prefer to catch up with your sister without an acquaintance in tow,' he said, and Lady Rosamund didn't argue. She merely smiled, curtseyed in that curious Abrenian way, and left him alone with his thoughts.

He was relieved she did not press him for his other reasons to remain in his quarters, including the fact that hearing the Queen of Abrenia rate him as a marriage partner under her breath had been unsettling, to say the least. Pretending his Abrenian wasn't excellent was hard enough, and the lady's remark that her sister was being ridiculous hadn't really helped either. And he still wasn't sure what "morganatic" meant.

Still, the expression on Lady Rosamund's face when she'd turned to see if he was listening had been . . . fond? Maybe?

He was just seeing what he wanted to see. Rosamund

was a widow, and one still grieving her husband. There was the night by the fire they didn't mention, but there was also her daily recitation of Hugo's litany. Even the day of the bandit attack she had whispered it under her breath as they limped towards civilisation, and Leo hadn't had the heart to hush her. She may have been extending the period of its recitation far past its usual duration—one of the litany's secondary purposes being to discourage remarriage for that first month after a death—but after that . . .

After that, perhaps it was a comfort to one in distress.

He was being foolish. He needed to think about something else. Not the unexpected twist in his gut when she played with her niece and nephew, not the dimples in her grin when she teased her sister, not how her entire demeanour changed when she was safe with her family . . .

He pulled off his surcoat and slumped into a chair. Thinking about something else was not going very well.

✕

'Caroline, could you just—'

'Caroline, would you mind—'

'Ah, Miss Lindley, if you've got a moment—'

Caroline could *not* "just".

Caroline *did* "mind".

And she absolutely did *not* "have a moment".

None of this seemed to matter to any of the people in question, and since they were all senior to her (sometimes on the merest of technicalities), she spent her day running between offices to solve elementary problems, trying to extricate herself in time for her own meetings, and occasionally hiding in the toilets on the second floor until the people bothering her had left for lunch.

At a quarter past five, desperate for a few minutes to herself before she had to deal with George again ('I need this program working before you go home for the day, Carla!'), she hid herself away in the server room. The drone of the hardware and the lack of actual seats made it an unpopular place to hang out, but Caroline found the white noise soothing. Sinking to the floor, she closed her eyes and wished herself somewhere else.

✕

'Rosamund! We need to talk dresses.'

Rosamund groaned, still asleep. 'Caroline . . .' She stopped. She was no longer in her bed. Instead, she stood in a vaguely outlined mirrored ballroom wearing a red gown. Her curly red hair fell loose over her shoulders, held back by a tiara that she didn't remember owning. Caroline invading her dreams was a new one, but at least her body was getting some sleep, so Rosamund decided not to argue with the fashion show.

That said . . . 'Caroline, I only brought one ball-appropriate dress.'

'And you wearing it will make excellent cover art!'

Rosamund blinked, and her outfit changed. The new dress was a deep pink, one-shoulder number with sparkles on the bodice. Those must be cut-up phoenix feathers. As if she had that kind of money to burn on fripperies. 'Shouldn't you finish writing the book first?'

'It's important to think ahead! Now—'

'If the words "acres of leg" and/or "bosom" are about to cross your lips, then I should warn you—'

'Don't be silly! You don't even have acres of bosom!'

This, at least, was undeniable. Especially in the next dress. Which was blue. And short. And tight.

'Yes, I am aware,' Rosamund hissed, rescuing one of the spindly straps as it slipped down her shoulder. 'I just wasn't sure if your cover artist was!'

×

'Christabel! I can't get this login to work!'

The highly polished, pointy-toed shoes of George Radley, whose face and laptop Caroline never wished to see again, tapped the floor directly in front of her. Someone must have ratted her out; he'd never have looked for her among the servers otherwise.

She shoved her pen and notebook under the closest rack before following George to his office. For a wonder, he had actually managed to install the program correctly without her, but despite his having retained the physical letters containing the login details, Caroline got nothing but looping error messages no matter what she tried. She even rechecked the laptop's security settings to see if she'd missed something the last time. For some reason they seemed to have reset to their previous parameters, which was disturbing but shouldn't have affected anything she was doing.

By six o'clock, George was out of patience. 'I'm in a hurry—'

'You need to wait at least another five minutes for the program to finish reinstalling,' Caroline snapped, 'at which point I will test to make sure it's working properly this time before I leave for the weekend.' She tried to moderate her tone. 'And then I'll see you on Monday.'

'What if it doesn't work?'

Caroline ground her teeth. 'Maybe you could call the helpline?'

It did not, in fact, work, so she had to call the helpline. The time of the last bus drew dangerously near, and Caroline was staring at the clock in despair when the call centre finally connected her to her seventh technician. 'You've reached the Kirtle Node Interbank Financial Exchange Technical Support Department, you're speaking to Maya, can I take your company name please?'

Caroline explained who she was and the problem she was having, again, hoping against hope that this was the one day the bus decided to be late.

'Do you have your login credentials to hand?'

No one had bothered to ask that before. Caroline scrambled for the letters and recited the appropriate details into the phone.

'That doesn't match what we have on file, ma'am.'

'Wait, what?' Ninety seconds and a change of a single character later, the program worked perfectly. Caroline slammed the laptop shut and bolted out of the building without a single word to George.

She sprinted through the rain, her bag slamming against her back as she tried not to slip on the wet pavement, and arrived at the bus stop just as the number 43 did. Panting, soggy, and thoroughly fed up, Caroline set her bag in her lap, shoved her headphones into her ears, and indulged in a little vicarious dress-shopping.

×

Rosamund was not impressed by any of the options in the *Beautiful Things* folder on Caroline's phone. 'Can't you just pick something pretty but relatively practical? No weird cutouts, no thigh-high slits—just a nice formal dress that covers all my stretch marks and allows me to stash a large number of small weapons. Please?'

'Well, all right.' At least Rosamund knew the word "please", unlike other people of Caroline's acquaintance. She noted the bruising on Rosamund's neck, which was shaping up to be quite spectacularly purple and blue. Perhaps a little more coverage was called for. 'I think I have just the thing! Sleep well.'

As Rosamund disappeared and Caroline came back to herself, she saved an image to her *Murder Dresses* folder, then considered getting a second opinion. Not from Henry, though. She'd had enough high-handed dismissiveness for one day.

×

'Captain Collins, I need your help.'

Leo, like Rosamund, had been safely asleep. Or so he had thought. He swiped a hand over his face, blinking at his author with the half-fogged comprehension of a man unexpectedly awake in the middle of the night. She was not in the mood to wait.

'Listen, Leo, I have some masquerade dress options for Rosamund, and I can't decide between them.'

Suddenly Leo's head was full of Lady Rosamund. No, *multiple* Lady Rosamunds: in red, in purple, in white, her hair tumbling down her back, her shoulders bare, her lips red as blood. And then, just when he thought the worst of the shock was over, a Rosamund in a low-cut blue dress, her legs bare to mid-thigh.

He hadn't supposed his author would stoop to this level of anachronistic intrusion, but apparently he had been wrong. Closing his eyes did nothing since he was already asleep. And even Rosamund's imaginary form had a ring of bruising around her neck from the bandit attack. The sight of it did nothing to improve his mood.

Caroline was still waiting.

'I—'

'Yes?'

'You—'

'Yeeeeessss?' Caroline's smile was sharp enough to draw blood.

'She looks nice?' Saying "stop taunting me" seemed an unwise tack to take, even if that was exactly what was happening, but the words were rising in his throat anyway. He tried to back away and found the dream had left him with nowhere to go.

Caroline scowled. 'She looks nice?'

'Yes!' Leo tried to keep the panic out of his voice, but he couldn't make himself wake up, and the Rosamund in the blue dress was *grinning* at him in a way that he didn't think the real Rosamund ever would. 'Surely you should ask her what she prefers?' *And leave me alone?*

Caroline looked thoughtful, and the multiple Rosamunds coalesced into one. Leo would have been relieved, but it was the one in the blue dress.

'You fancy her.' Caroline sounded triumphant.

Leo fought for calm—and against the urge to blush. 'I really don't want to dream about her wearing'—the apparition was laughing at him now—'that.' The ball was already going to be awkward without his having to fight off mental images of Rosamund in varying states of undress. She was distracting enough fully clothed.

'Interesting,' Caroline said, and disappeared.

Leo slipped back into a mercifully dreamless sleep.

×

By the time Caroline had made it home and eaten dinner, it was already nine o'clock. All she wanted to do was fall into bed and sleep until Sunday morning. But no, she had told Henry that she was going to send him the next part of the manuscript by the end of the day, and she had never reneged on a deadline before. Not a writing deadline, anyway. This was the one part of her life over which she had absolute control, and she wasn't about to break her streak now, even if her notebook and favourite pen were still hidden under a server rack at Crossguard Solutions.

But she was also still soggy from her run through the rain. A shower, a change of clothes, and a hot chocolate were in order. The forms observed, she sat down at her desk, opened her laptop and willed herself to keep going.

Just . . . one more scene.

×

Rosamund had not planned for any pressing social engagements on the morning of the masquerade, so she hadn't even made it out of bed when there was a knock at her door and a maidservant announced that Queen Catherine requested her presence. 'At once, if you please, my lady!'

Such was Rosamund's haste to make herself vaguely presentable for the trip through the palace that she threw on her clothes and shoes and bolted out the door without a single weapon on her person. This left her feeling uncomfortably underdressed, but she shook it off. The palace was the safest place she had been in over a week, and she was going to see one of the most heavily guarded people in it. Besides, she wasn't about to set herself up as a target for idle gossip by arming herself while the maid looked on.

As it turned out, Cat just wanted someone to talk to while she was having her hair dressed. 'Tell me about Edmund and Charlotte! How is Ed finding school? Is Lottie still obsessed with horses?' Rosamund would have been more annoyed, but after a week of misadventure on the road and the last few days of ceaseless politics, it was a relief to do nothing and let someone else lead the conversation for a while. The hairdresser was particularly welcome as Rosamund's shoulder still twinged a little when she lifted her arm over her head. Still, it was healing.

Once Rosamund's hair had been arranged to her sister's exacting standards — 'How lovely you look, Rosy! Won't the captain be pleased?' — Catherine dismissed the servants to fetch luncheon. Rosamund was considering taking a nap in the exceptionally plush chair where she had settled herself, both in hopes of avoiding further pointed remarks from her sister and to refresh herself before the masquerade — when the window shutters crashed inwards and a short, bearded man in a mask rolled into the room.

The sisters leapt to their feet, and Catherine snatched up her sleeping child. The baby started to scream. 'Cat, *go!*' Rosamund dashed towards the low table in the middle of the room, trying to put herself between the assassin and her niece as Catherine clutched her baby to her chest and ran for the door.

Rosamund reached up her sleeve for a knife—and it wasn't there. She cursed in frustration, her eyes still on the masked figure. The table held little in the way of potential weapons, but Rosamund grabbed the cheese knife and then the cheeseboard and hurled them both at the intruder in turn. The door creaked behind her as Cat made her escape, and Rosamund dived across the room to her sister's bed, shoving the rich red hangings aside.

'Please please please—' *There!* Catherine's sword, underneath the frame. She drew it and faced the assassin squarely just as he recovered himself from a cheeseboard to the temple.

'Don't move,' she growled.

Then the door creaked behind her again, and the bearded man threw his knife.

Rosamund ducked and tried to deflect it with the sword blade. She missed, and there was a *thunk* as the knife embedded itself in the wood of the doorframe.

The assassin abruptly turned tail and scrambled back out the window, and the two members of the Queen's Guard who had narrowly dodged his weapon sprinted across the room in pursuit. Rosamund briefly considered hurling the cheeseboard after him again in hopes of accelerating his descent but instead decided to verify that her sister and niece were safe. Cat was nowhere in sight, but Rosamund could hear her down the hall shouting commands to apprehend the invader. She slumped against the wall and started breathing again—

But then her eyes snagged on the assassin's knife.

She could hear more voices approaching, Catherine's exclamations over her sister's bravery loud among them. But Rosamund couldn't move, couldn't speak. The deep blue hilt, the lily etched on the pommel . . . she'd seen that knife before. In Hugo's hand.

She grabbed it by the hilt, yanked it from the frame, and stowed it in her dress, hoping the guards shouting out the window to soldiers on the ground hadn't noticed anything. There was no good reason for Hugo's knife to be there, and a lot of bad ones.

Besides, she might need it.

×

Caroline finally made it to bed near midnight only to be woken in the small hours when inebriated students knocked over the bins outside her shared house. Unable to go back to sleep, she ground her teeth at their giggling and shouting and reached resentfully for her phone. How much worse could things get? Had Henry seen her latest work yet?

He had.

Henry

Caroline, I understand that you want some mystery, and it's an exciting scene. But is now really the best time to be introducing more complications like an assassination attempt on Rosamund's sister? The husband possibly being alive? It doesn't make any sense for the existing possible villains to try and kill her sister right now. Or for Rosamund to be set up to take the fall, which I assume is what you were going for? You need to rework this.

It was the final nail in the coffin of her awful day. Caroline fought back tears as she stared down at the words on the screen. How *dare* he? She had stayed up late to finish this chapter! She'd written several thousand words this week around her full-time job, and he was just coming along and disparaging all of it?

She dropped the phone into the drawer of her bedside table and buried her face in her pillow. If that was how he felt about her work, maybe she wouldn't bother sending him any more of it. She could do this on her own.

×

The next morning — Saturday — broke grey and wet, rendering her little white desk in her white-ish room paler and more nondescript than ever. Equally morose, Caroline hung up on her mother — 'Yes, everything is fine, I'm just tired, that's all, I'll talk to you on Thursday' — and sat down to write expecting a lecture from Rosamund on putting babies in harm's way.

But when she imagined herself into Rosamund's quarters at the palace, her heroine just looked at her with big, sad eyes and said, 'Caroline, I'm not seeing things, am I? That knife was my husband's.'

'Gosh!' said Caroline, who had discovered this fact at exactly the same moment as Rosamund and was still scrambling to figure out the plot implications. The blank page and blinking cursor on her laptop screen loomed in front of her, and she didn't even have her notebook to aid her. She decided to get back to the important things. 'Nonetheless, King Roland has insisted that the masquerade will go ahead, though your sister will not be in attendance.'

'Good! One less person to worry about keeping alive!' Rosamund paused. 'Caroline, are you ... all right?'

'Why wouldn't I be all right?' Caroline snapped.

Rosamund blinked. 'You look ... tired. That's all.'

'Well, I'm fine.' Caroline opened the file containing her notes for the masquerade scene. Rosamund faded from consciousness as Caroline concentrated on details of décor and costuming.

She *was* fine. This scene was all planned out; she just needed to write it up. And things were about to get good.

Chapter 8

LEO RAPPED LOUDLY on Lady Rosamund's door. He had almost run past her room on his way to the queen's quarters before realising a guard had been posted outside and, therefore, Rosamund must be inside. It was a good thing the men recognised him from his appearance at the declaration ceremony, or he might have found himself lying on the floor bleeding, rather than knocking. They looked edgy enough as it was, and no wonder; there had been screaming and then shouting and heavy footsteps everywhere, and by the time Leo had reached the royal wing, the whole castle was on high alert. *An assassination attempt on the queen? While Rosamund was there? Who would—*

Light steps from inside the room filtered through the door before it opened a crack. A blue eye looked him up and down before Rosamund threw the door wide and beckoned him in without a word. Her face was drawn with worry, but she took a seat and gestured for him to do the same.

'I heard—screaming . . .' Leo began. That was all it took to start the words pouring out of her.

'Someone just tried to kill my sister!' She jumped up again and began to pace in front of his chair, still talking. 'He could have done it, too, had he not been shockingly incompetent; he came crashing right through the window, even though we were several stories up. I can't believe nobody saw him climbing!'

Of course she got herself tangled up in the middle of another assassination attempt. Leo rose from his seat but stopped there, uncertain what else he could do to calm her down. 'They might have gone up last night, my lady, before climbing down from the roof?' he offered. Though, why hadn't they attacked under the cover of darkness then? Unless . . . but she didn't seem to be listening.

'Leo—' She stepped closer. He tried not to notice just how close. 'Something is very wrong here.'

The urge to hold her, to tell her everything, was suddenly very strong. The way she was looking at him, with her face upturned so earnestly, desperate for someone to comfort her and keep her safe. He could just reach out and . . .

But the moment passed before he could justify seizing it. Rosamund stepped away towards the small window. 'King Roland insists that the ball must go ahead, and I don't know why. The assassin hasn't been found; isn't everyone's safety more important right now?'

Leo considered this. 'A single attacker is unlikely to mount an assault against a large, well-guarded assembly. You said he was less than competent?'

Rosamund nodded. 'To put it mildly. I would never have bet my life on the offensive capacity of a cheeseboard, but there you have it.'

He raised an eyebrow, but she was too distracted to elucidate, so he continued. 'Then perhaps the assassination attempt was never intended to succeed, and the goal they had in mind was to disrupt the celebration of the truce.'

'Maybe.' Her brow furrowed in thought. 'Cat and the children have been removed to another location, so I suppose the threat here has waned. I just wish I could have gone with them—' Her eyes widened. 'Unless I was the intended target?'

Leo tried, and failed, to keep the scowl off his face at the thought.

'But that can't be right.' Rosamund shook her head. 'The assassin—he seemed surprised I was there. He was surprised that I tried to defend my sister. What else would I have done? And why didn't he just run me through and get on with it? I don't . . .' She sank down into her chair again, her head in her hands.

Leo resisted the urge to place a hand on her shoulder. He tried to resist the rage boiling up in his stomach at the thought of someone mortally wounding her. He didn't have much success with the latter.

'Something about this just doesn't add up.' Rosamund looked up at him, and he tried to assume a relaxed, confident stance that none of his feelings could currently support. 'But I'll have to think about it later.' She winced. 'I need to finish getting ready for tonight.'

'Shall I escort you down to the ballroom this evening, my lady?' he said before he could stop himself.

The look she gave him then was a little surprised, but there was a gentle warmth in it that made him want to reconsider everything he'd ever done.

'Thank you, Captain Collins. That would be kind.'

×

Rosamund shut the door behind the captain, pointedly ignoring Caroline's knowing smile.

'What now?' asked the author.

'I guess it's time to figure out *exactly* how many knives I can hide in that dress.'

Several, as it turned out. Rosamund's ballgown was long-sleeved and white, with a voluminous skirt into which she had sewn several large pockets and a couple of disguised slits on the bodice besides, which gave her at least half a dozen opportunities to hide sharp objects.

×

Caroline sat back, a satisfied smile on her face. She'd been so busy for the past two weeks that her writing had been forced to take a back seat. The preceding fortnight had been a nightmarish procession of angry phone calls from Crossguard's clients topped off with a sickness bug among the staff that meant Caroline had worked a truly horrendous amount of (likely unpaid) overtime. But she had held the thought of writing this scene before her like a carrot on a stick. It was Wednesday night, her phone was off, and she had no obligations until the morning. 'You look beautiful, Rosamund.'

Rosamund smiled back. 'Thank you! Although,' she added, 'it would be more of a compliment if we didn't have exactly the same face.'

Caroline chose not to respond to that.

Rosamund frowned slightly, looking down at the layers of white. 'I did wonder about the colour, though.'

'Well . . .' Caroline shrugged, a little awkward. 'White is a mourning colour, too.'

Rosamund's mouth, painted with red stain for the occasion, fell open. At length, she said, 'Thank you, Caroline. I appreciate it.'

Caroline sniffed, feeling a little guilty. 'You're welcome.'

No need to mention what else white was traditional for.

×

Rosamund's lace mask, hastily acquired in Quayforth by one of Cat's most discerning servants, matched the trim at the top of the dress. She donned it now, tying it over her carefully arranged hair — half pinned back, the rest of the auburn curls tumbling down her shoulders. It had been some time since it had been styled this way for any public occasion. When she had been younger, and the times happier. Rosamund permitted herself a small smile, then tucked the memory of dancing with Hugo away again before it could prompt tears.

She had just secured one final knife in her bodice when there came a knock at the door. 'Come in!'

A black-clad figure in a lace fox mask entered the room.

Rosamund's smile returned, and then refused to leave. 'Good evening, Captain.'

Caroline sighed. 'So you're not going to be surprised that the mysterious stranger you feel like you've known for years is actually Leo?'

Rosamund rolled her eyes, but her expression was still warm. 'He asked to escort me to the ball, remember?'

Another thing Caroline had not planned to happen until she had written it. On the other hand, she also hadn't anticipated how pleased Rosamund would be about it, so maybe it wasn't a total loss. Caroline was further heartened by the way Leo was looking at Rosamund just now — and his expression right before he had tied on his mask and entered the room had been a deliciously complicated mix of hope and anxiety.

It was all coming together. 'Oh, I'm *so excited*!' Caroline cried.

Her heroine winced. 'Can we get this over with, please?'

'Yes, of course, run along.' Caroline did her best to assume nonchalance. It didn't work. 'I'll see myself out.'

The captain returned her smile, and even behind the mask his expression was somehow . . . soft.

Rosamund blinked and reminded herself sternly that she had more important things to worry about, like not making a fool of herself as Queen Eudosia's official envoy at a celebration of peace talks. How long had it been since she'd danced? 'Are you ready?' she asked.

She was comforted to see the wryness of her tone reflected in his face as they both contemplated an evening of enforced jollity. Leo nodded, but his manner was decidedly ill-at-ease, and she sympathised: it wouldn't be pleasant to spend an evening as a commoner among foreign nobles, especially when he would have to stand around all night on an injured leg.

Rosamund recalled her own initial forays into the Bevorian court on Hugo's arm and had an idea. Reaching up, she tucked Leo's arm into hers, quite the opposite of the usual arrangement. 'Stay with me, for the introductions at least,' she said softly, 'and I'll keep you out of trouble.'

And then, before she could think too hard about the implications of taking this man under her protection, she led him from the room.

Try as he might to ignore it, Leo's heartbeat hammered in his ears as he escorted the lady to the ballroom. Upon their arrival, they were directed by an officiant to the dais, where the king sat alone. Lady Rosamund's white dress and red hair shone like a beacon as they made their way through the sea of colour; Leo, for his part, did his best to fade into the background.

'Lady Hawkhurst. Captain Collins. We thank you for the honour of your attendance this evening, particularly given recent events.' King Roland's resonant voice was not hard to distinguish even from behind his full-face helmet styled in imitation of an eagle's head. His dark feathered cloak contrasted sharply with his gilded—

×

Caroline scowled. Chainmail? Mail? Maille? Hauberk? Her phone was in her hand to text Henry before she checked herself and opened her Internet browser instead. She could do this on her own. She didn't need him.

Maybe it would have been quicker and less confusing to ask Henry than to fall down the rabbit hole of people arguing on Internet forums, but that was not the point.

×

—mail shirt, which gave him a striking appearance even as the helmet obscured his identity. Leo noted the king's very real armour with grim satisfaction: it was an outfit that could be worn by any number of decoys in case the assassins returned.

Leo and Lady Rosamund murmured their respects to His Majesty, and the king dismissed them as another noblewoman curtseyed before the dais. As he reluctantly disengaged himself from Lady Rosamund's arm so that she would be free to join in the dancing (he was almost grateful his leg precluded the need to explain that he didn't know how), Leo wished that he, too, could have hired a masquerade outfit that included a helmet. He had done his best—it wasn't the first time he'd had to acquire a change of clothes on very short notice—but the only thing they'd had left in his size was this all-black ensemble with entirely too many frills for his taste.

The man who approached Lady Rosamund some minutes later didn't have that problem. His costume was that of an ancient warrior and included a nearly full-face helmet. Added to this, his silvered cuirass and long red cloak rendered him impeccably dashing, whereas Leo looked more like a peacock in mourning.

×

'Envious, are we?' Caroline enquired. 'Wishing you were the one to hold Lady Rosamund's attention?'

'This room is full of masks, and the assassin was never caught. Please stop distracting me.'

×

The man in the red cloak bowed to Rosamund in the Bevorian style. Rosamund bowed back, her expression curious. 'A mysterious stranger wishes to dance with you,' the man said, his grin just visible under his helmet. Leo was not prepared for the stab of jealousy when the lady's face lit up.

'Robin!' she cried.

'Rosy!' Robin Waverley held out a hand, and Leo watched as he led Lady Rosamund out onto the dance floor, slipping gracefully through the thronging couples. Rosamund nodded politely to those she passed, still beaming, and she and her partner took their places as the next dance began.

Leo turned to survey the room. He needed to concentrate.

It was surprisingly difficult.

×

'She does look happy, doesn't she?' Caroline said, her face a little wistful.

Leo would have said nothing, but when she didn't leave, he realised she wouldn't until he answered. 'Yes.'

'Do you think I should stage an interruption?'

Leo wrestled with his conscience. 'She had a terrible shock today,' he said finally. 'I think she deserves a few minutes' peace.'

'But —'

'Caroline.' He turned to stare his author full in the face. Her eyes widened. He didn't care. 'Leave. Her. Alone.'

✕

The music began, and Rosamund and Robin fell into the familiar patterns of the dance. The surrounding couples, some of them in wigs that were bound to get uncomfortably hot by the end of the evening, were emboldened enough by their masks to stare shamelessly at the Bevorian envoy. But Rosamund didn't care. Her footwork had come back, and Robin was at her side. Bright capes and wide skirts billowed around them as the music picked up its pace, and Rosamund lost herself in the whirl of colour before the music slowed and each couple came back together.

'When did you get here?' Rosamund demanded, still smiling at the unexpected joy of seeing her friend.

Robin shrugged. 'Around the same time you did, give or take. Queen Eudosia thought it best to send more than one envoy to ensure the message got through, though she did a good job keeping us secret even from each other. I knew I wasn't the first, but I didn't know *you* were tasked with the mission, Rosy.' He eyed her. It was hard to tell behind the helmet, but his look seemed one of concern mixed with . . . surprised regard? 'She expressed confidence that the first envoy—you, as it turns out—was in good hands and would arrive safely. But she hasn't retained the throne by failing to plan for contingencies.'

Rosamund was less sure than Robin that Queen Eudosia had intended her to arrive at all—if her monarch had commissioned other envoys, didn't that make Rosamund more expendable than ever?—but she let it be. She was here, and so was Robin, and the peace talks were going ahead. She'd delivered the declaration, she would get through this ball, she would go home to Edmund and Charlotte, and no one was going to stop her. 'We did have an interesting time getting here,' she said, and left it at that.

The tempo picked up again, and Robin and Rosamund swirled in and out of the other couples as if they'd been doing it for years. Which, of course, they had. Their very expensive Calterian boarding school had insisted upon it.

'How so?'

'Captain Collins had to pull me out of the Grenalla, among other delights.'

'Really! What compelled you to put him through that?' The fond sympathy in Robin's voice belied his words, but he glanced over at the captain, and Rosamund followed his gaze. Her travelling companion still stood at the edge of the floor where she had left him. His posture was as upright as ever, but after a week of travel with him, she could see the stiff discomfort beneath it.

Perhaps she should have checked on his leg before— *hold on.*

Robin had looked right at him. Did he know Captain Collins? She hadn't introduced them yet, and Robin had arrived at the masquerade well after she and the captain had gone their separate ways.

'Have you met?' Rosamund said as Robin spun her through the next set of steps.

He nodded readily enough.

'When?'

'Oh, er . . . the spring before last, I think. Yes, when the queen asked me to visit Baron Mabry. Captain Collins is, or rather was, a member of his levy.'

Rosamund froze, and Robin almost tripped over her.

✕

'What's wrong?' Caroline demanded.

Rosamund didn't respond, her half-concealed face a rictus of abject horror.

✕

'Robin, I'm so sorry, I—excuse me!' Rosamund stumbled backwards.

Robin let go of her. 'Rosy? Are you well?'

Rosamund fought to smile at him, attempting reassurance, but her face refused to comply. She gave up and hurried to the dais, nearly tripping up the marble steps as she fell into a curtsey at the king's feet.

'Your Majesty—I fear you are in grave danger!'

✕

'Rosamund, what—' Caroline attempted to halt the scene, casting about for some way to redirect her protagonist. But Rosamund was heedless, entirely set on her course, and Caroline could only try and keep up as the words kept coming.

✕

King Roland's voice came out low and distorted through his helm. 'Lady Rosamund,' he said. 'Please explain.'

Rosamund took a deep breath. 'Roland,' she said, heart in her mouth, 'what do you know about Baron Weston Mabry of Bevoria?'

✕

'Wait!' Caroline said, truly agitated now. 'You can't just ask him that in the middle of a ball!'

'I can and I will,' Rosamund snapped, 'if by doing so I save his life!'

✕

The king nodded once, sharply, before beckoning her over to one side. He lifted the visor of his helmet, his dark eyes piercing hers. 'What's wrong, Rosamund?'

She shrugged, suddenly unsure. 'I don't—I don't know yet. But please, answer the question. I think it's important.'

Her brother-in-law gave a terse, bitter laugh. 'Oh yes, it's important all right.' He lowered his voice further. 'The short version? I have reason to believe Baron Mabry is deliberately stoking the war between Abrenia and Bevoria. It was a dispute over river rights on the border of his estate that started this most recent conflict.'

Rosamund's eyes went wide.

'And . . .' Here the king looked away. 'Our latest information suggests . . . that he may have been responsible for Sir Hugo's death.'

The music, her breath, her heart—everything—stopped.

The king took her hand. 'I'm so sorry, Rosamund. We're not completely sure, and ordinarily I wouldn't have brought it to you until I was—but the circumstantial evidence is strong.'

Black spots danced in front of her eyes. She swayed on the spot, desperately trying not to be sick. Only the thought that people were still in danger recalled her; she had no time for weakness. Rosamund took a shallow breath. 'Your Majesty, I just found out that my escort, Captain Collins, used to work for the baron, and he . . .' More things that didn't quite fit slotted into place. 'He may still.'

Roland's gaze swivelled to Captain Collins, and Rosamund had another, even more horrifying thought: if the captain was working for the baron, then he already knew the location and timing of the peace talks. *He may have already sent word to Mabry by messenger bird.*

What if the baron was closing in on Hawkhurst at this very moment?

'I have to get home, now,' Rosamund whispered, more to herself than anything. Roland searched her face, and when she met his eyes, she saw the deep compassion of which her sister spoke so fondly. He nodded and motioned her dismissal.

'Go.'

Rosamund turned on her heel and ran.

Chapter 9

'Rosamund, what are you doing? You're supposed to be dancing in an adorable but charged way with Robin and then in an angry and somewhat sexually frustrated way with Leo. I queued up my "Waltzing with Your Hot Enemy" playlist and everything!'

Rosamund, back in her room, yanked up her mask to glare at her author. 'I'm going home.'

'Yes, you said, but *why*?'

'Because I think I understand now.'

Caroline pulled her notebook over, desperate to make sense of this sudden intrusion of plot into her flirty scene. 'Well I don't! None of this is in the outline! Rosamund Hawkhurst, you get back into my masquerade *right now*!'

Rosamund tossed the mask into a bag. 'Caroline, here's what I know: Queen Eudosia sent me on a borderline-suicidal mission with a single—with a *lone guard* as an escort.'

'Yes, but—'

'We were attacked even before we had left Bevorian soil and barely made it out alive. And Eudosia's guard—well, even if he saved my life, he has *also* worked for Baron Mabry, who Roland believes—' Rosamund swallowed hard, then continued, '—killed my Hugo.' She yanked the laces at the back of her dress, her hands shaking. 'What if Eudosia and the baron *planned* all of this? What if the idea was to consolidate her power at court, make her look good by proposing peace, and then when killing me off in the borderlands and blaming Abrenia didn't work, oh no, Lady Rosamund is a traitor to *both* kin and country; she tried to murder the Queen of Abrenia! Off to the dungeons she goes, the truce is off, I suppose we'll just have to keep fighting! *And* there was that Abrenian noble with caladrius salve! What if Mabry is smuggling it? What if *that's* why he used so much of it?'

'I don't think—'

Rosamund shoved her arms into the sleeves of her black doublet. 'It all fits. Baron Mabry pressuring me to send Edmund to the front lines, a gentle suggestion that' — she mimicked the baron's nasal, whining voice — '"As long as the war continues, I must have a Hawkhurst knight!"' Rosamund bit her lip. 'My son is fifteen, Caroline. I'm not sending him off to war. But how easy it would be to arrange an accident for the Hawkhurst heir, how tragic, and Charlotte and I would hardly be long behind him. Which would leave Mabry with sole access to the caladrius and their salve, our most valuable resource!' Her hands trembled as she began to fasten her buttons. 'Of course, there are other ways he might try to remove me first in order to get to the children.'

Caroline scribbled rapidly in her notebook. 'Like your husband's knife turning up in an assassin's hand?'

'Yes. When Hugo was returned to us, that knife wasn't among his effects. At first I thought his attackers had stolen it because it was new and looked valuable, but Mabry escorted the body home himself; he would have had ample opportunity to take the knife even if he didn't arrange the murder.'

'And then when you heard that Leo used to work for Mabry . . .'

Rosamund pulled on her riding trousers. 'What did you expect me to think? That it is the *veriest coincidence* that Captain Leo Collins, formerly of Baron Mabry's levy, is here when an assassin tries to kill my sister and frame me using my dead husband's knife?' She ransacked the discarded dress on the floor in search of her knives, and swiftly replaced them on her person before tucking her necklace under her shirt. Hugo's wedding ring hung at her breastbone, a touchstone in a world gone mad. 'Is it not reasonable for me to suspect that

Leo Collins is a traitor to the realm who only saved my life so he could use me later?'

Caroline trailed Rosamund helplessly as her heroine threw the rumpled gown and various as-yet-unpacked oddments into her saddlebags before setting off down the back halls of the palace. The ball was still in full swing, and it was unlikely anyone would notice Rosamund creeping off towards the stables. Caroline, struggling to follow through reams of haphazard notes, broke in again just as Rosamund hauled Willow's saddle down from the wall. 'You don't seriously think that Leo was the assassin?'

Rosamund scowled. 'Of course not! I've spent practically every waking minute with him between Bevoria and here; I'd have recognised him. And Leo — Captain Collins — knew I was with my sister. He would have expected me to fight if she was in danger; I doubt he would have planned to murder her while I was in the room. But how else would the assassin have got the knife?' She reached for Scout's saddle.

Caroline, still trying to puzzle through Rosamund's panicked and not entirely coherent argumentation, started. 'Err, excuse me? Are you stealing Leo's horse?'

Rosamund sniffed and swiped at her eyes, then spotted one of the captain's saddlebags. She yanked it from the shelf, revealing a black cloak inside. Rosamund pulled the cloak on, shoving a mostly empty grain sack in its place. 'It'll be faster with two; one gets a break while I ride the other. Scout knows me, and if he's missing, it will detain Captain Collins a little if he tries to follow me.'

'Why can't you just — ask Leo about this? Let him explain himself?'

Rosamund shook her head. 'Too risky. Don't you understand, Caroline? I can't trust anyone right now. Not Leo, not Robin — not even Roland, really. If I hadn't taken that knife before the guards who stormed Cat's room saw it, he might have thrown me in a cell no matter what she told him. All I know is my children are in danger, and

I never should have left them. I'm going home. Now. I might already be too late.'

She yanked the hood of the cloak over her head, distress in every line of her face. 'If you want to stop me, you're going to have to kill me outright. Stop sending other people to do it for you.'

Caroline's mouth fell open; she could only watch as her protagonist mounted up and rode out alone. Her hand dropped to her side, still clutching the notebook, and she sighed. 'I had such a beautiful evening planned. Candlelight, dancing, maybe a few flirtatious threats. And what do I get? Grand Theft Equine.'

Caroline decided to let Rosamund get well away from Quayforth before trying to reason with her again, and it was a day later for her, and a few hours after sunrise for her heroine, when she broke back in. 'I still can't believe you told King Roland that Leo was a spy!' Caroline's usually neat hair wisped out of her bun; she shoved a stray strand behind her ear, scowling. She had slept badly, again; the bus was late, again; she'd torn the hem on her favourite trousers running up the staircase at work; and she was spending her lunch break arguing with the most stubborn character she had ever had the misfortune to create.

Rosamund had grown no more tractable in the interim. 'I can't believe I didn't realise this before! You even called him my Hot Enemy! Why didn't I see it?'

Caroline was already regretting her word choice. First, because Leo was stubbornly refusing to act like a proper Hot Enemy archetype, and second, because Rosamund was stubbornly refusing to act like the sort of woman who would fall for anyone who would put her loved ones in danger. 'That's not how that goes, Rosamund; you can't know things in the story until you actually work them out for yourself. Besides,' — she decided to try for honesty — 'this wasn't how the masquerade was supposed to go.'

Rosamund shortened Scout's reins and scowled down at her. 'What, was I supposed to be stupider?'

'Frankly, yes.'

'I'm not sorry.'

'Wouldn't have expected you to be.' Caroline attempted a wry smile, which her heroine did not seem to appreciate. She sighed and muttered, more to herself than Rosamund, 'It was a great dress, though.'

She wasn't really expecting a response, so she was surprised when Rosamund's mouth turned up a little at the corners and her heroine murmured, 'Yes, it was nice.' At least there was one thing they could agree on.

'I still think you should have talked to Leo.'

Rosamund huffed, and the hint of a smile vanished. 'You solved your problem with Henry by running away from him—'

'—I did not!—'

'—you can hardly blame me for doing the same. Especially since I doubt that Henry would do more than say mean words to you. Captain Collins is more than capable of killing me if I get in his way.'

Caroline accepted that she would not win this point. 'You could at least have waited for King Roland to provide you with an escort.'

'I think I'm better off on my own at the moment.'

That was a little close to the bone. Heroines making stupid decisions was par for the course, but it genuinely unsettled Caroline to see Rosamund in this state. Still. She could work with it.

She hoped.

'Honestly, Rosamund, I was hoping your Bad Decisions Arc would be more romantically related, but . . .' Caroline shrugged, casting an eye over the tattered remnants of her outline as the character in question outdistanced her over the rise of a hill. 'Here we are.'

✕

Caroline didn't write a word for the rest of the week. She wanted to pretend it was because of work, but it wasn't, even if she had spent Thursday morning wandering the car park looking for George's key card. He'd insisted he had it when he left the house and also that he could not possibly spare the time to find it himself. 'No, you're much too *busy and important!*' Caroline had hissed under her breath as she stalked up and down the rows of cars, eyes peeled for a piece of white and gold plastic.

But even the weekend brought no relief. She washed her clothes on Saturday, but the weather was so miserable she was forced to put up the clothes rack in the space between her bed and her desk. She'd been planning to go for coffee with one of her friends, but Jasmine cancelled on her for the third time in a row. Then, after she had spent a discouraging evening researching current cover art trends, one of her housemates (Greg, by the sounds of it) steamed in near midnight with three equally drunk friends, who proceeded to have an unnecessarily loud hour-long conversation about their favourite children's cartoons. When Caroline got out of bed to look for her earplugs and give them all a piece of her mind, she tripped on the clothes rack and stubbed her toe on the wardrobe. The crash that the metal rack made when it folded itself up and hit the desk at least encouraged them to keep the noise down, but she spent the next five minutes on the floor hugging her own foot and trying not to cry.

On Sunday, even a cup of strong tea and two custard creams after the morning service weren't enough to wake her up. When Betty (generally good-natured busybody and distributor of tea, biscuits, and sound advice) made some gently probing enquiries as to Caroline's general well-being, Caroline answered, but later couldn't remember the questions or what she had said. She turned down Betty's offer of lunch and walked the long way home from church to mull over her story instead. That was when she discovered that her phone battery had finally ceased holding charge and she'd need to take it to be replaced the next day. The perfect end to the weekend, really.

What was she going to do about her story now? Rosamund had jumped the plot rails, and Caroline needed something drastic to lure her back on track. But nothing, absolutely nothing, came to mind. The right thing to do — anything to do — refused to present itself. She'd cleaned the bathroom (and spilled bleach on her new top), she'd watered the plants (and dripped water on her not-new carpet), and she'd even gone so far as to dust her bookshelf (which, fortunately, contained nothing to spill or smash). But still her brain refused to present a solution to Rosamund's rebellion.

And then the weekend was gone.

Caroline arrived at work on Monday with barely a minute to spare — and in the blue-carpeted, white-walled reception of Crossguard Solutions, she found herself facing a furious CFO. He had apparently been trying to call her for the whole of the previous day.

'I can't believe you didn't pick up. I must have called a dozen times as well as emailed you—'

'—I don't actually check my work email on the weekend—' Caroline began, but it was no good. George was off and running.

'My quarterly report files are all over the place, and each and every one has had its name changed. I can't believe you'd be so careless!'

'But I didn't—'

'—displaying a complete disregard for the needs of the company—'

Caroline's temper rose, and she bit down on the inside of her cheek, trying to tune out the words while looking suitably attentive. She must have succeeded because she was jolted back into the room at the phrase "disciplinary action". 'Excuse me?' she squeaked.

George smirked, scenting blood. 'It's just not acceptable, Christine—'

Caroline was seriously considering common assault when help arrived in the unexpected form of three members of the board.

'We'll finish this later,' George muttered forcefully under his breath before hurrying off to glad-hand people more important than her. Caroline escaped upstairs to the Ladies and stared at herself in the mirror. Her face was pink with suppressed rage. She splashed cold water on it, thinking furiously.

She hadn't moved any of George's files, or changed their names. And she could prove it, if she could manage to access anything on the company server. Naturally, the person who could give her permission for that wasn't in the office. 'Of all the times to go on your *dream holiday*, Susan!' Caroline muttered, running more cold water over her wrists and trying to calm down.

Something very bad was going on, and even worse, she'd somehow become the scapegoat for it (though really, what else could she expect with George?)—but there wasn't a thing she could do until her colleague returned. She'd just have to wait. But she didn't want to wait; she wanted help. Just . . . someone to talk to. Anyone, really, as long as they could make intelligent suggestions about what she should do and tell her that she wasn't going mad.

Caroline let out a long, wavering breath, smoothed her hair, straightened her blouse, and strode back to her desk. It was going to be fine. She would gather her wits, track down some advice . . . and spend the morning emailing her CV to all Crossguard's competitors. George and the board members would be ensconced in a conference room by now, and since they always went out to a restaurant after long morning meetings, she was safe enough for the moment.

After a lunchtime trip into the city centre to get her phone working again, Caroline's first message was to her former colleague Nick.

Caroline
Just wondering if you've got a minute to chat?

And then she tried to find something productive to work on. She really did. But by three o'clock, her nerves were stretched to the point that even her terminally absent-minded line manager noticed. 'Caroline, you don't look well at all.'

Caroline shrugged feebly, hating her own show of weakness but too grateful for the save to demur. 'I think I might need to go home.' Annabel agreed with such alacrity that Caroline was forced to conclude that she looked as bad as she felt. Getting out of the building was a relief, though she didn't feel properly safe until she was home with all the doors locked behind her.

Nick texted her at half past five with the instruction to call any time. She took him at his word.

'Caroline, how are you?'

She took the plunge. 'Nick, I need to talk to you about George Radley.'

Instant suspicion. 'Oh?'

'He's acting very strangely. Even more than usual. And he screamed at me today because there's something wrong with his files.'

Nick drew a long breath. 'This goes no further than us, right?'

'Of course.'

Another pause. 'I think file names are the least of his problems. I think he's a security risk.'

It only went downhill from there. By the time she hung up, Caroline was utterly drained. Even given her newfound decisiveness, she concluded it would be better to tackle Henry in the morning. As Rosamund said, one crisis at a time.

Chapter 10

HENRY WALKER LOOKED FORWARD to all his chats with Caroline Lindley, but especially the video calls. Officially it was because she was far and away the most successful writer he'd ever edited. His usual clientele were non-fiction authors who self-published books about trains, planes, and/or automobiles. They appreciated his meticulous attention to minute details in a way that few people did, and it mostly paid the bills. Mostly.

When Caroline had first contacted him, it was ostensibly to help her with the same things, but given the genre gap, he had almost turned her down — until he saw she had one book already published and three more in the works. Most of his clients wrote one-offs, so as soon as he finished working with one, he had to scrounge about for another. He thought he'd done quite well gaining clients by word of mouth alone, but his bank account didn't always agree. Thus, Henry's name had appeared inside the cover of *A Tale of Two Cafés*, and every other novel Caroline had published since. It had been the beginning of a long-standing and financially profitable venture for both of them.

But — unofficially?

Unofficially, it was possible he enjoyed the good-natured battle of wills that constituted Caroline's editing process a little too much.

Truth be told, in his personal life Henry was quite shy, which his mother informed him came across as "brusque and uncommunicative, love". As an editor he had been able to turn this into a reputation for being persnickety and blunt. It wasn't an approach that suited everyone's tastes, but he found enough people who appreciated it to get by. Admittedly, he was happiest indulging his persnicketiness to its fullest extent on Caroline's manuscripts. After all, he had to make sure she got good value for her money.

In the privacy of his own head, Henry was willing to admit that the schoolboy crush he'd developed was a bit pathetic. But while he knew that Caroline openly called him a stickler behind his back (and sometimes to his face), he'd always thought they had a good working relationship, so it was a little surprising when he'd sent a text about her latest chapter (far too late on a Friday night, which was also a bit pathetic) and didn't get a response. At all.

She *always* responded, even if it was only to tell him she'd seen it. She'd been silent for weeks. Henry had no idea what the problem could be, but there definitely must be one . . . and he didn't feel comfortable asking what it was.

She had a job. It might be family stuff. It wasn't his place to intrude.

He had gone back to catching up on work for other clients, things he had previously put off so that he could fit in more of Caroline's last-minute edit requests. Somehow, mechanical engineering didn't have the same romance as it had before.

Then she texted, and his heart raced when her name appeared on the screen. *Definitely pathetic.* He marked an incomprehensible paragraph about Spitfire engines in Jack Price's latest manuscript with:

> **HBWalker:** Not sure what your main point is? Maybe use a bulleted list?

and sat back with a sigh. He'd text her back and set up a call.

Professionally. Soon.

Now.

'How are you?' Henry asked when the call connected.

Caroline looked down. 'I'm . . . fine.'

She didn't look fine. A nasty thought occurred to him. 'Are you taking a break from writing?'

She shook her head. 'Not exactly. I just . . .' She seemed to be searching for the right words. 'It's just . . .'

'It's just what, Carrie?'

She slammed her hands on the desk in front of her and wailed, 'It's just that I am a special snowflake with delicate and easily hurt feelings, all right?'

Oh.

'And sometimes you can be a bit . . .'

'Rude? High-handed?' The words came readily enough; Henry had heard them used to describe him on a few prior occasions. Sometimes by Caroline. The expression on her face told him he hadn't quite got it, though. 'Tactless?' he offered.

'Yes.' Her lip wobbled, but she smiled the smile of People Pretending They Are Okay When They Are Clearly Not Okay, shrugged, and said, 'Everything has been a bit . . . all over the place lately, that's all. I might need more encouragement and a bit less fixing, going forward. At least until I have a working draft. The story has rather got away from me.'

Ah. 'Do you know what's going to happen next?'

Her face was a picture of misery. 'No.'

This, at least, was more his area of expertise. 'Why don't you tell me what you've got so far, and I'll see if I can help. Nicely.'

Caroline then launched into a long rant about the conclusions to which her heroine had jumped and the impossibility of winding it back without changing something fundamental. This then segued into how Caroline had queued up her favourite waltz music to write the Dancing With Your Hot Enemy scene, and it was all for nothing.

Henry took a deep breath. He needed to be delicate. Sensitive. Not-tactless. He could do this.

He hoped.

'What does Rosamund want to do?'

She told him.

'Why don't you just write that?'

'Because I don't know what I'm doing. And I usually feel like I know what I'm doing. But I don't. And it's unsettling.'

'Maybe she's too much like you,' Henry suggested, and Caroline blushed much more deeply than the comment really warranted. *Huh.* Then again, Caroline's characters usually weren't blue-eyed redheads. Come to think of it, Captain Collins had fair hair and green eyes.

Best not to dwell on that too deeply. It probably didn't mean anything. Henry hurried on: 'Leaving halfway through the ball to go home because she thinks her kids need her is not stupid, it's admirable. Calling in a higher authority to arrest Leo instead of confronting him herself? That's just the grown-up decision to make. And from everything we've seen of her so far, you can't deny that she is a grown-up.'

Caroline sniffed, but at least she still seemed to be listening. 'She doesn't trust easily, but that's not surprising,' Henry went on. 'Maybe you just need to demonstrate who she can trust a bit more concretely.' He attempted a smile. 'Not that they would have concrete. Unless they're Roman-inspired.'

Caroline still didn't look convinced. And she didn't even smile at the joke. That was worrying.

'Look,' said Henry, 'even if she's not making the most rational decisions right now, she's still acting according to her own guiding principles. It works. She feels real.'

That got her attention, so he plunged on. 'I think Rosamund is the most compelling heroine you've ever sent me, and her supporting characters are all . . .' He paused for a moment before deciding to throw out a feeler: 'Familiar, yet distinctly themselves.'

Caroline went pink again — and wait, was he right, was Leo — *no, no, think about that later, cheer her up now. Say something nice.* 'You're always telling me to trust your process. Maybe you should take your own advice. You're doing fine, Carrie.'

He hadn't meant to call her Carrie. Again. It had . . . slipped out. But she just said, 'Thank you.' And her smile had dimples in it again.

'When you're ready, send me what you've got. I promise to be nice. I'll even run a find-and-replace: substitute "nitpicking" with "encouragement".'

That startled a giggle out of her, which was better than he had hoped for. Caroline nodded and thanked him again before signing off the call. If he had a modicum of self-control, he would not immediately search her existing draft to figure out exactly how much of Leo was based on him.

If he had a modicum of self-control.

×

Robin Waverley, second son of the Duke of Waverley and occasional spy, was not a man given to indecision or regret. But the look of horror on Rosamund's face when he told her that he met Captain Collins when Leo was a soldier in Baron Mabry's levy?

That was probably a sign that something was about to go wrong.

She had turned to glance at the man in question, who looked, as he always did when surrounded by aristocrats, stoically uncomfortable—and then she curtseyed in the middle of the dance and rushed off, causing a minor commotion as she wove through the other couples.

Robin decided that "mild concern for the lady's wellbeing" was the expression to adopt to avoid suspicion and started to make his way in Leo's general direction.

'What did you say to her?' Leo demanded as soon as Robin was in earshot.

Robin winced. 'I don't know! But I seem to have caused a minor issue.'

'What'—Collins narrowed his eyes—'Did. You. Say?'

'She asked me how I knew you, to which I replied that I met you last year on Baron Mabry's estates, back when you were part of his levy. Then she said "oh no" and ran off!'

'You told her—oh, no.'

'No, *she* said "oh no," weren't you listening?'

'Shut up, would you?' Leo glowered at Robin, then looked back at Rosamund, who was still on the dais with King Roland. 'I may be in a lot of trouble. We need to leave.'

They made their way towards the exit. Slowly. Trying not to draw any attention, just two friends chatting at a masquerade. By the time they reached the great doors, they could see Rosamund was leaning forward to listen intently to the king. Leo picked up his pace. 'The whole conversation, Waverley. Now.'

'Fine.' The recounting took them out of the ballroom and up the stairs. They had almost made it to Leo's rooms before the King's Guard caught up with them.

'Captain Leo Collins?'

'Yes?'

'Come with us.'

✕

Caroline was *not* happy with him, but Robin wasn't too worried. Well, not about Caroline. He was a bit concerned for Leo.

'I can't *believe* you were so careless,' Caroline raged. 'You've thrown off my *entire* outline! Now Rosamund is absolutely convinced that Leo is a traitor, and she's run off! Without you! How am I supposed to get her to feel uncomfortable feelings in your presence if you're not even there?'

Robin shrugged. 'She doesn't think of me like that, so your point is moot. And I thought you were trying to get her together with Leo, anyway?'

'It's a love triangle!' Caroline seethed. 'The whole *point* is that she's torn between two completely different choices!'

'The dashing childhood best friend or the grumpy younger man?' Robin ventured, waggling his eyebrows.

Caroline was affronted. 'He's thirty! He wasn't *meant* to be a younger man! I just ... hadn't intended her to be so old!'

'You do realise Rosy and I are the same age, don't you?' Robin quirked an eyebrow, trying to hide his smile. 'But don't fret, you're not *that* much younger than us, and isn't Leo only a couple of years older than you?'

'Yes, but Rosamund was meant to be twenty-four!' Caroline pinched the bridge of her nose, avoiding his gaze, and Robin frowned. He could have sworn he'd seen "Rosamund – red hair, blue eyes, fiery personality – 19" scribbled somewhere among the author's notes. She hadn't lifted him from the life of an honest if lazy nobleman and trained him as a spy for nothing. But that aside, he was sure there was another reason he and Rosamund wouldn't work as a couple. But thinking about it gave him a headache, so he decided to focus on the task at hand: rescuing Captain Collins.

×

Luckily for Leo, Robin had already formulated a plan.

It wasn't a very detailed plan, but a plan nonetheless. Good thing Her Majesty The Queen had been whisked away to a secret location that even her sister didn't know about – right here in the palace. He really was that good, he thought to himself.

'Cat? Cat? I know you're under lock and key in there but I really, really need to talk to you!' After nearly a minute, during which Robin hopped from foot to foot with agitation, a grey-haired lady's maid answered the hidden chamber door in the servants' quarters. She was entirely unmoved by his not-inconsiderable charms.

'Her Majesty Queen Catherine is asleep,' she snapped, 'because it is night, sir. Return in the morning. With an appointment.'

'But her big sister's boy-toy has been arrested for espionage, and if I know Rosy, she's probably doing a runner on bandit-infested roads at this very moment!' Robin shouted.

There was a wail from within the chambers, and two burly guards materialised from behind the maid. Robin had almost thought better of his plan when the queen herself appeared, shushing the crying baby in her arms. 'Stand down,' she said to the men, looking Robin up and down. Then she motioned him to enter. 'Disarm. This had better be good.'

Robin divested himself of his sword belt and his masquerade helmet before one guard patted him down and the other ushered him inside. He declined a chair, instead choosing to pace the border of the rug as he explained what had just transpired. Cat shushed the baby throughout his catalogue of disasters before sending one of her other maids to the stables.

The woman returned quickly. 'The stalls marked "Willow" and "Scout" are both empty, Your Majesty.'

'She stole his horse?' Robin barked a laugh. 'I am never, ever letting him live this down.'

'Assuming he survives the night. Thank you, Pippi,' Cat said shortly. 'Mildred, would you pass the paper, please, then go and arrange two fast horses?' The grey-haired woman complied, and the queen wrote a short note, handing it to Robin with the words, 'Take this to Master Florenz in the dungeon.'

He bowed over her hand and kissed it, and she held his grip a moment longer until he met her eyes. 'Don't. Get. Caught.'

He inclined his head towards her again and departed. Then he noticed that the note hadn't been folded or rolled, so he read it.

> *Dear Florenz,*
> *This prize idiot is tasked with removing my sister's travelling companion from the dungeons. Half a day's head start before raising an alarm will be ample. I will explain all to His Majesty in the morning.*
> *Catherine*

And wasn't that Rosy's little sister in a nutshell. Robin grinned in anticipation. Time for a daring escape.

HBWalker: Are we going to get details of the daring escape?

CSLindley: Maybe in the next draft.

HBWalker: Looking forward to it :)

Rosamund was forced to stop and make camp the next afternoon, if only because killing the horses wouldn't get her to Hawkhurst any faster. She coaxed Scout and Willow off the road and into a copse of birch trees, which, she hoped, would provide a decent screen from prying eyes. By the time the animals had recovered, it was dusk. She had travelled far enough from the city for bandits to be a real concern once more, so she undid her bedroll and tried to rest. Her stomach pinched; she hadn't had anything to eat since before the masquerade, but anxiety had completely crowded out appetite, and the little sleep she did manage was plagued by memories and nightmares in equal measure.

'I don't like it, Rosy.'

Rosamund watched Hugo pace the command tent. She gestured for him to sit down next to her, wrapped an arm about his side, and put her head on his shoulder. 'What's the issue?'

'The deployments don't make sense. Baron Mabry' – they shared an eye roll – 'says the priority is holding Oakbridge, but he sent us all the way out here.' Hugo pointed to the map with his free hand. 'I understand the need for a defensive perimeter, but there's no need to be this far from the town . . .'

'I'm sorry I can't stay longer.' Rosamund leaned back from their embrace, fighting tears.

Hugo pulled her in again. 'I love you, Rosy.'

She could barely speak. 'I love you too.'

He clutched her to his chest, and she inhaled, breathing him in. When he finally released her, she steeled herself to walk away – but at the edge of the camp, men shouting and hurrying about her, she turned and looked back.

Outlined in gold by the late afternoon sun, he looked like an oil painting.

The women wouldn't let her see Hugo's body until it was laid out.

'No, my lady. Please. Remember him as he was in life.'

Even after they'd cleaned and covered his body, the sight of him lying there, unmoving, had shattered her into pieces.

'Though we perish to darkness and decay, we will rise to Light . . .'
The priest continued to intone the litany, but Rosamund could no
longer hear it. Her world had narrowed to the children clinging to
her, and the wooden box draped in Hawkhurst green.

'I simply must have a Hawkhurst knight to lead the levy at the front.'
Weston Mabry's whine grated on her ears.

Rosamund forced herself to stay calm. 'I have no knight to
send you, my lord.'

'Then I will have to send orders directly to the Hawkhurst levy
at the front myself. Perhaps some of my own men will suffice to lead
them in the interim.'

Charlotte had cried for her father for half the night, and
Rosamund was too tired to resist. 'Whatever you think best, my lord.'

He hadn't finished. 'Perhaps Edmund will be free to assume
the duty soon, despite his tender years.'

No.

This time, when she awoke from the nightmare, there was
no one to comfort her.

Chapter 11

BY THE TIME SHE ARRIVED in Oakbridge, Rosamund was nearly spent. Her muscles ached from days of riding, her head swam from lack of sleep, and she was parched and famished after abandoning Quayforth too quickly to acquire sufficient provisions. And unfortunately for her homeward ambitions, the Mabry estate lay directly across the bridge, and the Bevorian force occupying the town consisted almost exclusively of the baron's soldiers. Rosamund halted the horses at the outskirts, pulled her hood up, and bit her lip, considering how she might avoid drawing attention.

She would need to leave Scout outside the town. A lone woman on horseback was not that unusual, but a lone woman with a warhorse as her spare mount would certainly attract unwanted notice. Thankfully, it would only take a few hours to cross Mabry lands and reach her estate; Willow could carry her the rest of the way.

She pulled off Scout's tack and dumped it under a tree, loosing him on what seemed to be some common land. He immediately put his head down to graze, and she smiled wearily. Trust a horse to know what was important.

Her passage through the town was blessedly uneventful, but the bridge was another story. News of the truce might have reached Oakbridge, but as she neared the line of travellers leading onto the crossing, she could see the guards questioning everyone and their grandmother before allowing them to pass. Many people were turned away, likely because they couldn't grease the soldiers' palms.

'Of course it couldn't be simple,' she muttered resentfully. But maybe there was another way to make it home. Rosamund remounted Willow and rode a short way upstream. The river was generally far too broad here to swim, but maybe she'd get lucky and find a spot that could be forded. She refused to think about what had happened the last time she attempted to cross the Grenalla under less-than-ideal circumstances. Or the fact that this time, she was on her own.

The problem, of course, was that the bridge had been located where it was precisely because that was the easiest crossing point for several miles. Rosamund clutched the reins and scanned the water, feeling more desperate by the minute. She did not have the kind of time that a side trip would require.

✕

'Could you shoot an arrow with a rope attached across the river?' Caroline suggested.

Rosamund shrugged. 'Normally I would ask where the bow would come from, but right now I just don't care.'

Caroline pursed her lips as she considered the width of the river depicted on the map she'd been forced to draw on the back of some Christmas wrapping paper. 'My editor would never let it slide anyway, he's a total stickler. Maybe you should rest a while? There's obviously nothing you can do right now, and you've barely eaten or slept in days.' Rosamund blinked at her, suspicious, but Caroline held her gaze. 'You can't cross right now, Rosamund, and you know it. Take the time to regroup a little. Please.'

Her heroine's nose twitched with irritation, but she nodded. 'Fine. I'll go stable Willow and see if I can get some sleep in a real bed for a few hours. Maybe tonight I can sneak over the bridge.'

✕

Leo and Robin passed the third mile marker from Quayforth before they slowed their horses to a walk. The jailbreak had gone off without a hitch, and while Leo had been as silent as usual while they made their escape, Robin assumed that was just his natural reticence. But after they'd passed the fourth mile marker without Leo so much as looking at him, Robin said, 'Everything all right, Collins?'

A stream of invective poured forth in Abrenian, Bevorian, and what Robin tentatively identified as Ellanish as Captain Leo Collins gave vent to his feelings. Of which there were many. Quite a lot of them revolved around Rosamund and how she had got him arrested. Some of the censure was also spread onto Robin, particularly his inability to "keep his fool mouth shut" and "maintain operational security". Other points touched on included the conditions in Abrenian dungeons and Leo's complete inability to ever undertake a clandestine mission near Quayforth again.

Robin waited patiently while the tide washed over him, keeping an eye on his surroundings and paying his friend no mind. Here and there he'd pick out a phrase like "utterly irresponsible" or "jumping to conclusions" or "Wisdom-deficient aristocrats" and then tune back out again. When Leo at last ran out of words—which took a surprisingly long time, considering he normally used them like they were rationed—Robin merely nodded and said, 'Yes, Collins, that all sounds very difficult. But tell me how you *really* feel.'

There was a dangerous rustling sound before a wrinkled apple shot at Robin's head. He ducked and waited to see if any further missiles were incoming. But then Leo's head drooped. 'This could have gone better,' he muttered.

'True,' Robin allowed, 'but look on the bright side. You're alive and well, you're no longer in Quayforth, and you never have to attend one of their balls ever again.' He shrugged. 'Shame. It would have been hilarious watching you try and dance with Rosy.'

'I've put her in danger.'

Robin shook his head. 'Technically she put herself in danger. You were merely an accessory. Besides, I thought she was a Wisdom-deficient aristocrat who jumped to conclusions, surely you're better off without her?'

It wasn't easy to see Leo's face in the dark, but the set of his shoulders was hunched and miserable. 'What if she doesn't make it home? What if her children are orphans and it's *our fault?*'

Robin turned his face away, stared out at the moonlit road ahead, and thanked the Wisdoms for a clear night. 'Rosamund is not dead. And we didn't kill Hugo.'

Leo scoffed. 'He didn't last long as a Blue Lily, did he?'

That much, at least, was undeniable. Robin himself had recruited Hugo Hawkhurst to the society a mere fortnight before his death. Whatever had happened after Robin left Mabry's border territory last summer, something had tipped off the baron, and the consequences for Hugo had been fatal.

'We have to find her, Robin. We have to get her home.'

'Even if she's an untrusting harpy who got you thrown in prison?' Robin said sweetly.

Leo swallowed, looking a little shamefaced. 'I . . . We have to get her home.'

And with that, he urged his horse into a trot, and they were off again. They made very good time; Leo's ill-concealed panic meant they took turns that first night leading each other's horses while the other slept, and they subsequently avoided drawing attention at inns and settlements by encamping off the road. In three days they had reached Oakbridge, where they made straight for the Golden Elm Inn: an establishment with no interest in asking questions (nor hearing answers).

Leo had been scanning the inn yard, vaguely hoping to spot Rosamund, when he realised that Robin had been speaking. '—You want to find Rosy, but the first priority is getting you out of the country. I can look for her on this side of the river, but we need to get you back on Bevorian soil, and she might already be over there anyway.'

Leo grunted acknowledgement. 'I still know a lot of Mabry's men. I'll need a cover story for why I'm in Abrenia, but I can get across the bridge. I can bring you with me —'

Robin shook his head. 'I don't want us travelling together. We still don't know where—*oh*,' he finished, in quite a different tone. He darted back into the stable, yanking Leo after him.

'Are you —' Leo stopped, equal parts annoyance and confusion, as Robin made frantic shushing motions and gestured for him to peer around the door frame. Leo did so, following his companion's eyeline.

It was probably a bad sign that his heart stuttered when he spotted Lady Rosamund Hawkhurst leading Willow to the watering trough. It was probably a worse sign that the feeling associated with her was one of disappointed hope, rather than anger.

But the worst sign of all was the one Robin was making with his hands. *Go on. Bring her here!*

Leo shook his head vehemently before mouthing, *Do it yourself!*

Rosamund was halfway across the stable yard when strong arms grabbed her from behind. A hand clapped over her mouth before she could do anything more than squeak, and she was dragged into the narrow, dead-end alley between the stable and the neighbouring wheelwright. She tried to breathe, tried to reach for a weapon, but the arms around her tightened like a trap, lifting her feet off the ground, immobilising her.

'Rosy.'

She knew that voice.

'Easy, Rosy. It's just us.'

Us? The arms holding her let go, and she stumbled away, drawing Hugo's knife from her wrist sheath and whirling round to see Robin, palms up, half-apologetic, half-wary.

And there, blocking her exit, was Captain Leo Collins.

Am I hallucinating? Rosamund backed up against the stone wall, closed her eyes, and took a deep breath before opening them again.

Still there.

Still *them*.

Her head spun. Were they here to kill her? To hold her hostage? *Is Robin a traitor too?* What was going on? She swallowed. She couldn't win if they wanted a fight. Not in such close quarters, not with her reflexes shot after the last few days of death threats and hard riding. Talking might be her best—her only—strategy. And maybe a little bravado.

She steadied herself, allowing the blade of the knife to catch the afternoon light. 'I have barely slept in three days, so I am just going to let you explain. In short sentences, please: what do you want?'

It was Robin who answered, his familiar voice eminently reasonable. 'The same things you do: to inform Queen Eudosia of what you've learned about the baron, and to make the peace talks happen.' He smiled at her—warm and reassuring, close to her as a brother—and she thought her heart might break. 'For queen and country, Rosy.' So saying, he slowly pulled a knife of his own from an inner pocket and held it out to her, hilt first.

She took it with her free hand, confused. Dark blue hilt, a lily engraved on the gilded metal of the pommel: it was the twin of Hugo's knife. Hugo had received his when he was on the front lines. She had assumed it had been from Queen Eudosia, perhaps a token she gave to knights or noblemen.

But then Captain Collins produced an identical knife from a wrist sheath—a wrist sheath just like hers. There was a roaring in her ears.

'I know this is going to come as a bit of a shock, Rosy,' said Robin apologetically, 'but there are things about me, and Leo—and Hugo—that you need to know.'

> **HBWalker:** A secret society? I have to admit, I was convinced that Robin was going to sell them both out to Mabry and skip off to live a fine life alone in Country C or something.
>
> ---
>
> **CSLindley:** Good to know I can still surprise you!

✕

'Wait, aren't you supposed to be the traitor?' Caroline snapped.

Robin graced her with a smile that had slightly too many teeth in it. 'Betray my country, my colleague, and my best friend all in one swoop? For what possible reason?'

'For love, obviously!' Caroline shouted.

'If that's what you wanted, you really should have foreshadowed it better, Carrie. And made me an entirely different character, frankly.'

Caroline bared her teeth. 'I do not take writing advice from figments of my imagination! And don't call me Carrie!'

'You don't mind when Henry does it.'

'That was one — fine, *two* times! Leave me alone, Robin!'

✕

Rosamund's legs threatened to give way beneath her, but her mind raced as the pieces she had missed belatedly fell into place. 'You're a spy. You're *both* spies. Just like — just like my Hugo.' This last came out in a very small voice indeed. She stared from Robin to Leo, then back again. 'And you!' she added, focusing more intently on her oldest friend. 'All that capering about, pretending you don't care about politics — well! You had me fooled, at least.'

Robin nodded, a little shamefaced.

'Which means you . . .' Rosamund turned to Leo. 'You weren't working for Mabry. You were spying on him.'

Leo nodded as well.

Rosamund let her legs go at last and slid to the ground. 'I've been a fool.'

✕

Caroline bit her lip, and the scene around her heroine froze. This was the part where Rosamund was supposed to take charge! Rally the troops! Be decisive! Do all the things that made her so difficult to work with! 'Rosamund — are you all right?'

'I've been so stupid.' Rosamund looked up tearfully at Caroline, who had knelt down in front of her. 'You tried to warn me, and I didn't listen.'

'I couldn't have told you,' Caroline said gently, 'because you can't know things —'

' — unless I work them out myself. Yes. You said.' Rosamund sniffed. When she spoke again, her voice was still very small. 'I don't know what to do.'

'I know the feeling,' said Caroline. She sat down next to her heroine. 'At some point, should you wish to hear it, I'll tell you about my "Mabry".'

Rosamund looked horrified. 'He's in your world too?'

'Every world has one,' Caroline said wryly. 'But don't worry about that. I may not have knives, but I have some options. And at least a few people I can trust.' She eyed the men standing a short distance from them significantly. Rosamund followed her gaze briefly before her head dropped again.

Caroline let the silence stretch out for a moment before her next overture. 'May I offer you some advice?'

'If you think I'll remember.'

Caroline sighed. 'You don't have to do this alone.'

Rosamund blinked, rubbed at her face, then looked over at the two men who had spent three days following her from Quayforth. 'I take your point. If they were here to kill me, they'd have done it already.'

Well, that was a start. 'Not quite my point,' Caroline said, 'but it'll suffice for now.'

✕

Robin looked over his shoulder, suddenly conscious of the attention two armed men cornering a noblewoman might garner if they lingered. 'This is no place for a conversation. Let's find somewhere a bit less conspicuous.'

The three of them made their way to a grassy spot near the river, Robin and Rosamund leading, Leo trailing behind. The slender silver birch trees at the bank would provide some shade from the afternoon sun but no cover for anyone trying to sneak up on them.

'I'm afraid that thanks to your shenanigans, Rosy, you aren't the only one who needs to leave the country in a hurry.' Robin looked back at Leo as they walked, and Rosamund felt a little twist in her heart at the genuine affection on his face. 'Such a challenge you set me, and no warning at all, as usual! There I was, all set to be my usual charming self: dancing, eating, practicing diplomacy—' Leo snorted. Robin ignored him. 'When Leopold over there gets himself arrested by the Abrenian authorities!'

'It was your fault, Waverley,' Leo retorted. Rosamund didn't even bother to hide her surprise at his— mostly—good-natured tone.

'Nonsense, Collins. If you hadn't insisted on silence as the best policy, Rosy would have already known that you worked for the baron last year, and it wouldn't have been a drama!'

They drew to a halt a short distance from town, and Rosamund gathered her focus enough to glare at her erstwhile attackers. Robin stopped mid-jab at Leo and had the grace to at least pretend to look embarrassed. 'I got you into a lot of trouble,' she said, looking at Leo. He didn't deny it. 'By jumping to what I don't think was an unreasonable conclusion.'

Leo slanted a sideways glance at Robin. Robin made a face at him.

'If you want me to help with whatever it is you're planning,' Rosamund continued, 'and I assume you do, because here we are wasting time talking when I could be on my way home to my children, then I need to know what you know.'

'That's what we've been trying to tell you!' protested Robin, but a "cut it out" gesture from Leo reined him in. 'Yes, you do,' he continued in a more conciliatory tone. 'But sit down, Rosy. You look worn to a thread.'

Rosamund sat, wary just as much as weary, and gave him a flat stare. Leo eased down onto the grass a few feet to her left. She noted that he was careful to stay well within her field of vision. Robin, in his element as storyteller, remained standing.

'About two years ago now, Queen Eudosia came to me with a problem,' he began. Rosamund listened with growing incredulity as Robin sketched his own heretofore unchronicled involvement behind the scenes of the war, and the exploits of half a dozen Bevorian men known as the Blue Lilies. Queen Eudosia had made extensive use of them as ambassadors and spies in an effort to counter the warmongering rife in her own court. The Blue Lilies had been unable to prevent a second war outright, but it was in large part thanks to their efforts that King Roland had always remained amenable to peace. Robin went on to summarise his trip to Baron Mabry's estates the spring before last, where he met Captain Collins and received his report on the baron's less-than-legal activities.

Eventually, reluctantly, Robin handed the tale over to Leo, who gave a much more succinct account of his dealings with the baron and his role as an officer in Mabry's levy. Sorting out which rumours of Mabry's conspiracy and probable smuggling activities held water occupied another few minutes: 'We never saw any caladrius salve at the front, my lady, and Wisdoms know we needed it. If you were sending extra, then he's been making a fortune.'

Rosamund shook her head, trying to clear it. Her exhaustion was wreaking havoc on her concentration, but it all made too much sense to ignore: Why Queen Eudosia would have chosen this single—this *one particular* member of her guard to accompany Rosamund to Abrenia. Why she would have attracted scrutiny by her mere association with the caladrius. And that time Leo had joined in when she recited Hugo's litany . . . he hadn't been honouring just any of his fallen comrades. He had known her husband.

And the back-and-forth between Leo and Robin was too natural to be contrived. They had clearly known each other for a while. It was possible, she supposed wearily, that they were *both* traitors, that this was all part of some elaborate scheme too complex for her to grasp—but she hadn't imagined those knives. She had to confess that the simpler explanation made the most sense.

Did she trust them completely? No. Not even Robin; if his words were true, he had hidden a great deal from her. As had . . . Hugo. But she pushed that thought aside. She couldn't think about it right now. The important thing was getting home, and if nothing else, it seemed that both Robin and Leo were keen to help her put an end to Baron Mabry's machinations.

HBWalker: Are you going to add more detail to this section?

CSLindley: Maybe when I've worked more of it out?

HBWalker: Best to keep going. You can always come back.

Chapter 12

'If I understand correctly, and you have been tasked with ensuring the safety of the peace talks—the ones happening in *my home*—then we all need to get to the same place,' Rosamund said. She looked between the two men, beseeching. 'Can you help me?'

'Luckily,' said Robin, 'Captain Collins still has an intact cover as a former member of Baron Mabry's levy. And in spite of his surly and uncommunicative demeanour, I assure you he did in fact make some friends among his colleagues.'

'He's not surly and unco—' Rosamund began, stopping as a smirk crossed Robin's face. She was too tired to try to interpret it, so she turned to Leo instead. 'You can sneak me across?'

The captain shook his head. 'Sneaking won't work. But we'll get you home to your children, my lady. I promise.'

Robin lifted his eyes to the heavens. 'So dramatic, Collins.'

Leo snorted. 'Takes one to know one.'

'*Gentlemen*,' said Rosamund, 'do you have a proposed solution?'

✕

'I think,' said Caroline, chipper again now that she'd regained some control over the plot, 'that it might be time for a good old-fashioned fake wedding! It'll give you a plausible reason to cross the bridge, an

excuse to hide your face, and —' She beamed. 'The trope possibilities
are *endless.*'

Rosamund stared at her for a moment, too weary and overwhelmed to argue. 'Fine.'

✕

'Before we can get to solutions, we do have another problem,' Robin said apologetically.

✕

Caroline blinked. She hadn't expected him to say that.

✕

'Um.' Robin looked genuinely embarrassed now, and
Rosamund got even more worried. Nothing *really* embarrassed Robin. He was utterly shameless.

'You're still alive, which,' Robin held up a hand to fore-
stall comment, 'is obviously a good thing. But we know that
Mabry is after your estates and the caladrius thereon. And
he has myriad means at his disposal. Good old-fashioned
brute force, naturally, but there's also the . . . legal route.'

Rosamund blinked. 'What?'

'Even if we get to Hawkhurst before he does, even if
the peace talks go ahead and Edmund is safe from being
called up to lead the levy in battle — there's still the Feast of
Remembrance.' Robin's face was sympathetic. 'Remember,
Edmund isn't technically of age to take over the estate until
he's twenty-one, and you are a citizen of a country we are
currently at war with. If the peace talks get disrupted for
any reason . . .' Robin trailed off, and Rosamund saw it.

Right now she was the caretaker of the Hawkhurst
estate. But at the Feast of Remembrance, it would be

officially handed over to its regent until Edmund came of age. This should also have been her, but as long as Bevoria remained at war with Abrenia, she was still the citizen of a hostile power. And, she realised with a start, the time of the feast was very near. The peace talks would be happening right on top of it.

'Mabry will claim I'm not legally allowed to manage the estate alone, *generously* offer to marry me, then kill us all at the first opportunity.'

'Well, I would suspect that he'll merely threaten to kill you before going to all that trouble,' Robin said cheerily, 'but you've got the general idea.'

Rosamund groaned and closed her eyes to consider the shape of the problem. Mabry planned to bribe, threaten, or blackmail her into marrying him. Then, if a tragic accident just so happened to befall her and her children, he would be entirely within his rights to claim the estate. If she didn't marry him, he'd try and kill her and her family anyway.

The sun neared the horizon; Robin swatted absently at the midges that had come out, while Leo got up and began to pace. At last Rosamund stood, turning to face him. He visibly braced himself. 'Captain Collins. You were working for Baron Mabry a year ago.'

'Yes.'

'Do you think he arranged Hugo's murder?'

'I do, my lady.'

Rosamund swallowed. 'Was it you who killed him?'

The captain stared at her, then slowly shook his head. 'No.'

Rosamund let her breath out in a great rush. 'Is there a reason you didn't tell me that Mabry was behind it?

After — after I told you I suspected him . . .' Tears suddenly pricked at her eyes; she fought them back fiercely.

Leo bit his lip. 'At first, it was because we weren't sure if you . . . had been involved.' Rosamund winced, and he looked down, abashed. 'After that, well . . . one crisis at a time, my lady. It didn't seem fair to burden you with yet another problem.'

'I see.' She looked away for a long moment.

Do I have the strength to do this?

It didn't matter. Edmund and Charlotte needed her. She'd find the strength.

Rosamund drew herself up into a formal posture and took both of Leo's hands in her own. He looked surprised but didn't resist. 'Capt — Leo. I realise that you probably don't like me much right now, and I don't blame you, and I realise that this is a little forward, but . . . will you marry me?'

✕

Caroline was forced to break in. 'Wait, what?'

Rosamund scrubbed at her eyes with her sleeve. 'I'm getting married.'

'No, you're getting fake married, it's right here in the outline! I mean, first you're supposed to agonise over the choice of who you get fake-married to, but eventually you pick Leo!' Caroline fought to keep the panic out of her voice.

Rosamund glowered in exasperation. 'I can see how a fake wedding might — *might* — help to solve the immediate problem of getting over the bridge. But actually marrying Leo' — she stared at the ground — 'assuming he'll have me, is better.'

Caroline wrung her hands. 'But your Hot Childhood B — Robin is right here! He's a Bevorian citizen too! You've known him since you were at boarding school together! Why aren't you asking *him* to marry you?'

Rosamund stared at her, swaying slightly. 'Robin doesn't know the bridge guards. Leo is my best chance of getting across and home, now.'

'Yes, but—'

'Robin is an aristocrat with sufficient political connections that he can probably get out of trouble without my help. Leo . . . can't, and it's my fault he's in this mess in the first place.'

'Yes, but—'

'Also—' Rosamund looked more than a little confused now. 'Robin is rich, personable, and attractive—'

'He is, isn't he—'

'—I was under the impression that he was already married, but every time I try to think about it, I get the vague impression of the name "Elinor" and a headache.'

Caroline put her head in her hands and groaned.

Elinor.

This was the problem with using previously conceived characters in a new book. You sometimes forgot important details about them. Like their wives, with whom they had a superbly adventurous courtship and an action-packed marriage, most likely in more ways than one. Caroline watched in despair as the last chance of a love triangle faded rapidly over the horizon—probably sailing off in the trading ship she'd just remembered Elinor owned—and tried not to sigh.

Maybe it was for the best. Robin had barely featured in the narrative, Rosamund and Robin had refused to be even the slightest bit attracted to each other, and Caroline was tired of fighting them on it. She was still concerned about Rosamund's mental state, however. 'You'd really marry someone you've known less than a month?'

Rosamund shrugged. 'It wouldn't be my first political marriage. Besides'—her smile had teeth in it, but no humour—'we both know you'd have found some way to make this fake wedding into a real one.'

Caroline made an uncomfortable noise.

Rosamund squared her shoulders. 'At least this way, I chose it.'

✕

'. . . Will you marry me?' Rosamund said, and Leo wondered if he had gone mad.

Him, married? He lived a rootless life, and had for some time. His father had died when he was young, so to support his mother and younger sister, he had joined the army when he turned sixteen, too poor for promotion and too clever to be popular.

Then he'd been pulled into intelligence work in his early twenties, rendering his life even more unsettled. Always on the move—a new cover, a new place, new people he shouldn't ever trust. He tried to visit home when he could, which was almost never. His sister Juniper wrote to him as often as possible, even now with three young children underfoot—but she didn't ask him about what he was doing. She just urged him to be careful and wise.

This seemed to be neither, and yet—and yet.

Before he could formulate an answer, Rosamund gripped his hands more tightly and rushed to explain her reasoning. 'You know the bridge guards from your time in the Mabry levy, yes? You'll know who can be bribed or blackmailed to look the other way.'

'Yes, my lady, but—'

'You're a Bevorian citizen; if we're married, you would be eligible to administer the Hawkhurst estate until my son comes of age.'

'Yes, my lady, but—'

'You wouldn't actually have to do anything,' she hurried on. 'I've been the sole administrator since Hugo's death, but on paper, you would be in charge.'

Ah. A marriage of political convenience. He wasn't going mad after all. For a moment he'd wondered if she might —

'In the marriage contract, we —' She paused her headlong recital with an uncomfortable look, then pressed forward. 'We can include a clause where you and any issue renounce a future claim on the Hawkhurst estate. You would be entitled to my personal assets, should I predecease you, but Hawkhurst belongs to Edmund and Charlotte. I won't have it taken away from them.'

Leo's brain snagged on "any issue." Momentarily distracted by a vivid mental picture of Rosamund cradling a baby — *their* baby — in her arms, he realised she was still talking. Rosamund bearing his children was not what he should be thinking about right now. Focus. He needed to focus. Maybe her sleep deprivation was catching.

'. . . Mabry can't force me to marry him, and most important for you, Catherine will have substantial grounds to plead your case with King Roland and explain that I made a horrible, terrible mistake.'

'In accusing him of spying, or in marrying him?' Robin enquired with a grin, and Rosamund glared. He held up his hands to ward off comment and fell silent again.

'Leo, you —' Rosamund stared at her feet, clearly upset. 'I got you locked up by the Abrenian authorities. You could have been executed for espionage! I won't abandon you to the whims of political expediency, though, granted, the only solution I have might expose you to attack from the baron. Getting married to King Roland's sister-in-law might not provide complete protection, but it's the best I can offer you. And—I need your help.' Her eyes lifted to meet his once more. Big, sad, blue eyes, bloodshot from too many hours on the road and Wisdoms knew what else. 'Will you marry me, Leo? Please?'

She was about to cry, and that was probably more than he could bear.

Robin was no help at all, his head bobbing back and forth between them like a spectator at a tennis match. But he wasn't proposing any better plans, was he? And this could work. It solved many of their immediate problems at a stroke, including giving him and Rosamund a plausible excuse for a bridge crossing. As for any future problems it would introduce . . . well. As he had told the lady. *One crisis at a time.*

'Yes,' said Leo. 'I will.'

> **HBWalker:** Well. This took a turn.
>
> **CSLindley:** You're telling ME?
>
> **CSLindley:** I might require a little help with this.
>
> **HBWalker:** Whatever you need.

✕

'Really, Leo?' Caroline paced around him, agitated. 'You're going to marry Rosamund just like that? You're not going to agonise over the decision? Not going to finally admit your feelings about her? You're just going to say yes?'

Leo pushed a hand into his hair, closing his eyes. 'This is a workable solution. And if it's not, divorce exists.'

Caroline looked taken aback. 'You think Rosamund would divorce you?'

He didn't want to think about it. 'I think that this will help both of us. It's . . . convenient.'

Caroline scoffed. 'You're really happy to enter into a marriage of convenience? Complete with obligatory public displays of affection? Sharing a bed? Really?'

Leo pushed away the images that Caroline's words produced and opened his eyes. 'It's the best plan we've got,' he said firmly, 'and so I'm agreeing to it.'

Caroline sighed. 'You really do like her, don't you.' It wasn't a question. 'You wouldn't do this for just anyone . . . but you'll do it for her.'

There was something in her voice that Leo didn't quite understand, but Caroline's problems were her own. He wasn't going to add to his by prying into her psyche.

✕

Thank you seemed inadequate, but it was all Rosamund could think to say. She raised Leo's hands and pressed her forehead to them, a supplicant before a lord. 'Thank you. Thank you.' Then she pulled herself upright again and turned to Robin, numbness spreading through her body. She welcomed it.

'Robin, I need a lawyer, a priest, and a second witness, and I need all of them before it gets dark. We'll be back at the Golden Elm getting ready.'

She expected a smart comment, or at least a negotiation on the timescale. Instead, he pulled her into a hug. 'Give me half an hour.'

Rosamund watched him saunter off along the riverbank towards town, sticking to the shadow of the trees. Then she turned back to Leo and pulled the necklace with

Hugo's wedding ring out from under her shirt. A lump rose in her throat.

She swallowed it angrily. It was a good plan. It would help keep the children safe, keep Leo safe, keep her safe. All she had to do was marry a near-stranger.

Well. She'd married Hugo under similar (though less dire) circumstances, and it had worked out all right.

And Hugo would have understood. Given his slightly odd sense of humour, he might even have approved. After all, the Bevorian court was going to be scandalised that she was marrying a commoner, even if he wouldn't inherit.

She had responsibilities. Those came first. Her feelings, such as they were, came a distant second. Hugo would have understood that too. Indeed, recent discoveries indicated he would have understood all too well.

✕

'You are allowed to have feelings, Rosamund,' said Caroline.

Rosamund closed her eyes, fighting to retain the detachment. 'Yes. They're just not helpful right now.'

✕

'So what's the problem?' Henry tried his best to sound sympathetic, but Caroline scowled at him anyway. She wore a pink, blue, and cream summer sundress, and her hair fell around her shoulders in tumbling curls. He'd never seen it like that before. Every other time they had talked over video, she'd had it pinned back.

He blinked and nearly shook his head before remembering that she could see him. He should focus on what she was saying.

'I can't get Rosamund to keep her mind on the plot at all. She's too preoccupied with keeping everyone safe!'

'But that *is* the plot.'

'I mean the romance plot! Leo has fallen head-over-heels in love with her for no reason I can determine, but she's just too preoccupied to notice!'

Fortunately, Caroline was also too preoccupied to see the look on Henry's face.

'How do I get her to see what's happening, Henry? I just . . . can't get them to talk about their feelings!'

Would laughing at the irony of the situation be inappropriate? Henry decided it would be. 'I don't think you can. But you can sell the audience on the relationship, such as it is, and once the, ah — *action* plot is resolved, you can give her the space to think about it.'

Caroline nodded, thoughtful. 'Yes, I think you're right. Thanks.' She looked at her watch and made a face. 'Ooh, I should get going. My cousin's getting married this afternoon, and I need to catch this train so my mother can pick me up from the station. See you soon!' She cut the connection, and Henry found himself staring at a blank screen.

It wouldn't work out between them. He didn't know how to talk about his feelings any better than Caroline's characters, and he wasn't even sure that she had feelings for him anyway.

He needed to stop thinking about it.

✕

Rosamund unhooked the chain around her neck. Hugo's wedding ring, a simple ellunium band, dropped into her palm.

She held it out to Leo. 'Will this fit you?'

Leo took it wordlessly and pushed it onto his finger. It fit well enough.

'Good.' With a little effort, she pulled her own wedding ring off her finger and held it out to him. 'This one is for you to give to me.'

He took it, tucking it away in a pocket before removing Hugo's ring from his finger and returning it to her, closing her hand over it. 'You don't have to do this, my lady.'

Rosamund shook her head, stars winking in her field of vision. She ignored them, trying to focus on Leo's face instead. 'You saved my life, twice, and I repaid you by ratting you out to my brother-in-law. This keeps you safe, or,' she amended, 'at least safer. It makes me safer too.' She drew a quavering breath. 'I went to Queen Eudosia to get her to stop Baron Mabry pestering me about the lack of a knight to lead the Hawkhurst levy. I can't let him take Edmund like he took Hugo. And I'm hoping there will be peace. I'm hoping no one else has to—' She broke off, blinking furiously, then resumed. 'But if we don't have peace, we shall have you.' She looked up at him, and even though her eyes were damp, her smile was wry. 'And you won't let Weston Mabry push you around. But if you'll excuse me—we need to return to the inn, and I need to dress for the wedding.'

Leo remained outside the room while Rosamund went in to change. He stood with his back to the door, checking the corridor in both directions before glancing out the window, alert for signs of trouble. Or Robin. It was sometimes hard to tell the difference.

The chatter of patrons in the room downstairs was soothing, and while Leo waited, he spun himself a plausible story for the bridge crossing. But that took no time at all, leaving him to the inescapable reality that Lady Rosamund was going to marry him.

Granted, she was mainly doing it to protect herself and her children, but she had asked *him* to marry her.

That wasn't nothing. And she had clearly loved her first husband, for all that their match had also been politically convenient. Leo had only met Sir Hugo Hawkhurst once, but he remembered Robin twitting the man about the good luck he'd had in his arranged marriage. Hugo had taken the joking in good humour, dryly commenting that if Robin had been more open to political marriage himself, maybe *he* would have been the one married to Rosamund. 'Clearly she just likes me better, Robin,' he'd said, with a bland smile that had not at all matched the amusement in his eyes. Robin's face had been a picture.

Leo rubbed his tired eyes, thinking. Rosamund had loved Hugo. Maybe she could love him, too. Maybe he could make her happy. Maybe it didn't have to be all duty and obligation.

In the quiet of a summer evening, as the sun started to dip behind the buildings of the town, Captain Leo Collins considered his upcoming alliance with Lady Rosamund Hawkhurst . . . and found it appealing.

Dangerous, yes.

But still appealing.

A few minutes later Rosamund, once again in the white dress she'd worn for the masquerade, opened the door of the room and invited him to sit. The only available space was the bed, and she sat down next to him, her shoulder touching his. 'Thank you.'

He didn't know how to respond, so he moved his arm a little way around her. Just to make them both more comfortable.

Robin returned within his allotted half-hour, grinning and bouncing on his toes like a giddy schoolboy. 'Everyone ready?'

Leo pulled his fiancée to her feet, trying not to notice how strange her left hand looked without its wedding ring. 'Let's go.'

Chapter 13

ROBIN HAD THANKED the Wisdoms when he arrived at Oakbridge's Church of the Light and discovered that the priest in charge was still Marian. She knew him, albeit under odd circumstances, and he was sure he could charm her into performing a wedding on extremely short notice. He ran a hand along one of the columns as he walked under the portico, recalling how slippery they'd been to climb when last he'd been there. It had been a nightmare getting from the top of the northeasterly column onto the roof of the building, and without a rope and Leo's help, he'd have been a broken heap on the pavement before the men chasing them had even arrived.

Inside the church, all was quiet. Mother Marian's expression when he pushed the double doors open (he'd always loved a dramatic entrance) had been surprised, pleased—and slightly suspicious. It turned wholly suspicious when he explained that two very dear friends of his wished to tie the knot, immediately if not sooner, and could she please facilitate this? Also, did she happen to have a spare veil lying around?

Marian stared into his face, muttered something under her breath, dispatched Gretel (who had been dusting the wooden pews) to fetch a lawyer, and ordered Robin to retrieve the happy couple before bustling into the vestry to replace the tablecloth on the altar with something more wedding-appropriate.

All he had left to do now was take a small detour on the way back to the inn. He needed to collect Scout, after all, and it was only another minute or two out of his way.

Leo and Rosamund didn't speak at all on the way to the church. Rosamund stared straight ahead, so lost in concentration that Robin didn't wish to interrupt. Leo, by contrast, was as vigilant as ever, though he watched his betrothed as much as his surroundings.

Robin hadn't really decided how he was going to explain away Rosamund and Leo's urgent need to be wed, but Mother Marian did not ask. She just shooed him away towards the pews and beckoned the intended couple closer. He watched as Leo's fluent Abrenian in response to the traditional opening questions made Rosamund start and suppressed an eye roll at the man's continued mania for compartmentalisation.

Robin would have stayed to eavesdrop further, but the growing cacophony outside had attracted even Rosamund's attention. At Marian's look he carolled, 'Don't worry, I'll go and see what the commotion is!' and climbed the stairs of the spire to take a peek. The chaos in the village square was clearly visible from the tower, and he smiled in satisfaction. His distraction was working beautifully.

Half the villagers had run to the north end of the town to herd the cattle, horses, and goats back into their pens at the market. He was sure the noise of the animals stampeding through the narrow streets could be heard for miles, and multiple scuffles had broken out as people fought over whose cow was whose. And, in response to this, every able-bodied Bevorian soldier in Oakbridge had either headed off towards the commotion or gone to reinforce the bridge.

Robin whistled merrily on his way back down the stairs to rejoin the lovebirds (he could see, no matter what either of them said, that there was a definite *spark* there). He calculated that the mess would be sorted within the hour, maybe two, and by then, the tired soldiers should have left a reduced force to guard the bridge, making crossing easier. In the meantime, the likelihood of any ill-intentioned pursuer disrupting the ceremony had been significantly reduced. Not a bad result for a few minutes' work.

'Just a little trouble in the marketplace; you know how livestock can be, nothing to worry about!' he called to the priest as he reentered the chapel. Mother Marian raised her eyes to the heavens but made no further comment.

✕

'Are you trying to stop me disrupting the ceremony?' Caroline hissed.

Robin shrugged. 'I am merely thinking ahead and enjoying the chaos. Both of which are entirely in character.'

✕

The wedding ceremony comprised two parts. First came the public declaration of vows, to which Robin and Gretel were party, and included the signing and witnessing of the marriage contract. Second was the private declaration of fidelity, which took place with the priest behind a screen.

To Rosamund's great relief, the pre-ceremony questions regarding fitness to marry were short and to the point, but she did get a shock when Leo responded in perfect Abrenian. She had previously wondered how much of his ignorance of her native language had been feigned, but it was . . . disconcerting to hear an accent from her home country come from the mouth of a Bevorian. One who wasn't Robin, anyway.

At some point she and Leo were going to have a chat about things it would be useful for her to know.

Geoffrey, the town lawyer, had declined to participate as the second witness, allegedly due to what had happened the last time Robin had stopped by. Instead, he had sent the requisite papers and his seal along with Gretel, charging her sternly to return it first thing next morning. She had preened a little as Robin offered his arm to escort her down the aisle.

> **HBWalker:** Are all your minor character names lifted straight from children's stories?
>
> **CSLindley:** I respectfully decline to answer that question.

The relative peace of the sanctuary was soothing to Rosamund's tattered nerves, notwithstanding the muffled sounds of dozens of confused, angry, and frightened animals outside, but nothing could entirely abate her sense of urgency. Still, her voice did not tremble, and her eyes did not stray from Leo's. If her hands were shaking a little, well . . . she thought that his might be too, so perhaps it didn't matter. Her hands had shaken last time.

It's not important.

Leo made his vow first.

'. . . to love, honour, and cherish you till death parts us. By the Light of the Wisdoms, in the presence of these witnesses, I make this vow.'

A wave of grief threatened to overwhelm Rosamund, but she swallowed it down, blinking furiously, and focused on the tapestry of the Wisdoms speaking the world into being over Leo's left shoulder.

Don't think about it. Don't think about it. You'll be home soon.

Afterwards, she could not recall saying her vows, but subsequent events suggested she had indeed made it through them. The contract swam before her eyes. Regardless, she could see that Geoffrey had assembled it with consummate skill and perfect courtesy. Robin would have settled for no less; she knew it was sound.

The priest swung the censer as Leo signed the pages, then handed Rosamund the phoenix quill.

'By the Light of the Wisdoms, I so vow,' she whispered, and signed her name.

Now it was time for the private declarations. Robin and Gretel stepped back from the altar, and Mother Marian indicated for Rosamund and Leo to take their places behind the painted screen in the chancel, where she would bind their hands together while intoning the ritual words. Then they'd emerge for the final declaration . . . and then Rosamund would be expected to kiss her new husband.

It wasn't *required*, true. But it would look a bit suspicious if she declined.

Rosamund's head throbbed: from the incense, from the exhaustion, from grief. But it didn't matter. Her children mattered. Protecting the man in front of her mattered. Getting home mattered.

Robin slipped outside as soon as Rosamund and Leo disappeared behind the embroidered screen. Gretel had looked at him curiously, but he'd just smiled in a winning fashion, made a vague sign with his hands like he'd forgotten something, and exited through a side door. He positioned himself comfortably in the gloom of an alley near the church, just out of sight.

The main doors to the church stood open, as was required during a public ceremony. Less than five minutes after Robin had settled into his hiding spot, he saw a bearded man in a brown cloak approaching those doors.

He might have been an innocent bystander. He might just have been very fond of weddings. But Robin was taking no chances. The man never heard him coming.

How the brown-cloaked stranger would feel when he woke up in a tiny alley with his feet bound was anyone's guess; Robin didn't particularly care.

A chime sounded, signalling the end of the private declarations, and Robin quietly let himself back into the church. He'd done a huge amount of work to pull all of this together. He deserved to see the results of his efforts.

The newly married couple reappeared, holding hands. 'I present to you Leopold and Rosamund Collins, husband and wife,' announced Mother Marian. The congregation clapped, all two of them. The priest turned to Leo, and Rosamund's stomach clenched, because this was the part where —

×

'Yes, yes it is,' said Caroline slowly. 'Rosamund — are you sure you're all right?'

'This was my idea,' Rosamund whispered, trying to keep her expression calm. 'It's fine.'

×

Leo looked at his wife—his *wife*—read the determination in her face, and hated it.

She had married him for his sake and her children's. She didn't want to kiss him. But she would, because it was her duty to do so.

×

'Yes, it is.' Caroline didn't sound as pleased about this as Leo had anticipated.

'She doesn't want me to kiss her, Caroline.'

Caroline sighed, slumping back into a pew, which—Leo squinted—was also a blue-upholstered seat inside a long metal carriage. 'I don't think she knows what she wants at this moment, but conventions of the medium mean that she'll probably enjoy it. She just isn't expecting to.'

'Not good enough.'

×

Leo ignored the priest and focused on holding Rosamund's gaze. Their hands were still intertwined. Slowly, as gently as he could, never dropping eye contact—he raised her hand to his lips and kissed it.

Rosamund, whose face had been pinched and pale, dropped her head and smiled in a way that made his heart pound in his ears.

He might, Leo admitted to himself, be a tiny bit smitten.

They made their way out of the church, and Rosamund pulled away from him; he immediately released his grip on her hand. Then Robin caught up and slung an arm around her, and she visibly relaxed. Leo suppressed a spike of envy.

Robin's voice was low, but Leo had long practice at listening in on other people's conversations. 'Honestly, Rosy,' Robin said fondly, 'all that effort getting you a lawyer—well, half a lawyer—and a priest and a veil, and you don't even indulge me with a proper kiss?' He squeezed her shoulders. 'You're going to have to be more convincing than that.'

'Leave her alone, Robin,' Leo said shortly—and Rosamund gave him a tired smile that made his stomach flip. 'She's fine. We're fine. It's done.'

'Well then,' Robin said cheerfully—but he let his arm around Rosamund drop. 'Let's get this party started!'

Marian declined their kind invitation to the Bridge and Rabbit tavern for the celebrations, but Gretel adjusted her iron-grey bun and declared herself in urgent need of a sherry. Robin offered her his arm once more when she came out of the church. Already swapping stories about their families and their shared penchant for bothering with other people's business, the pair started down the street.

Leo and Rosamund walked after them, side by side, but not touching. After the first moment of silence had passed and a second threatened to follow, Rosamund drew a breath. Better to get the awkward conversations out of the way now. 'I know it's not the done thing for newlyweds to discuss,' she began, hesitant, 'but if you absolutely can't bear to be married to me, you can just divorce me as soon as Edmund comes of age. I won't fight you.'

Leo didn't answer for a moment. 'Why wouldn't you just divorce me when Edmund comes of age?'

Rosamund blinked, confused. 'But I—I just made you a promise. I wouldn't—I—'

'So,' Leo continued. Rosamund tensed at his tone. 'You intended to keep your wedding vows but didn't expect me to keep mine?'

'I didn't mean it like that! I—' Rosamund bit the words off, looked away, and drew a hard breath. *No*, she told herself sternly. This was not the time to start a fight. She needed Leo to get her home; it was imperative that they didn't get into an argument right now. 'I'm sorry. I really appreciate you doing this for me, and . . .' She turned back to look once more up into his face. 'I don't want to be a burden to you.'

He frowned more deeply, opened his mouth—

'Who wants a drink to celebrate the happy couple?' Robin yelled, bursting through the tavern doors.

Rosamund swallowed her sigh.

Leo looked down at his wife. Her shoulders were slumped forward, her face a picture of exhaustion and grief. He was abruptly reminded that they were meant to be carefree newlyweds. 'My—erm. I mean, Mrs. Collins?'

'Um. Yes?'

For the mission, he thought. He took her hand. 'We need to cheer up a bit.'

Rosamund frowned, fleetingly, then stood up straight, her face clearing. 'Ah. I do apologise.'

He took a step towards her and took her other hand, leaning down closer to her face. She looked a little nervous, but she didn't move. 'Don't worry,' he said softly. 'As long as we're standing close together and not scowling, it looks convincing.' He raised an eyebrow. 'Are you all right?'

She nodded. 'Thank you.'

He wasn't quite sure what for. 'You're welcome?'

One side of her mouth quirked up. 'Thank you for marrying me,' she clarified. 'And' — she looked down again — 'thank you for . . . for the kiss, at the church. It won't happen again.'

The early evening light made it difficult to tell, but . . . was she blushing? Leo was still wondering exactly how to parse this last statement when Rosamund disentangled her hands from his own and placed them softly on his face.

'The priest is still watching us from the door of the church,' she said gently. 'And Robin is right.'

Leo stayed still. 'He is?'

'I need to be a bit more convincing,' she said, and kissed him on the mouth.

×

Caroline stared at the blinking cursor on her computer screen. 'Wait, what?'

She had just arrived back from her cousin Jenny's wedding reception, which had taken place in a warm, brightly lit pub. She was beginning to suspect that the trifle she'd had for pudding might have been alcoholic. That would explain the light-headedness.

It wasn't that she wasn't pleased about Rosamund kissing Leo. She just hadn't expected it.

×

Leo hadn't been unexpectedly kissed very many times in his life. The most notable occasion had been when he was sixteen; that particular evening had ended with Joanna Becker's older brothers throwing him into the millpond. If he'd had the wherewithal to recall that episode just now, he might have wondered if it was a bad omen, but the second Rosamund's lips touched his, his mind went blank.

Her kiss was firm and insistent, but she held his face lightly in her hands, her fingertips brushing the stubble on his cheeks and jaw. Some distant, calculating part of his mind told him that he could move away, that by this point it had been a long enough kiss that no one watching would find that strange.

He threaded his arms around her waist and pulled her in closer.

Rosamund put the light-headedness down to a sudden lack of air.

Obviously, she'd needed to kiss him, before she lost her nerve. The hand kiss in the church had been sweet, and respectful. She might even have fallen a little bit in love with him at that moment when he'd looked into her eyes and understood. But it was important to play the part, so "a little bit" was insufficient. Her children needed her. To get to them, she needed to be Mrs. Rosy Collins, smitten new wife of Captain Leo Collins. Lady Rosamund Hawkhurst's thoughts on the matter weren't relevant, even if they were technically the same person.

And Leo wasn't a bad kisser. Quite the contrary. It was strange kissing someone who wasn't Hugo (*don't think about it*, she told herself sternly), but it wasn't unpleasant. Judging from the way Leo responded, he didn't seem to hate the experience either. She was just starting to relax when a loud whistle made them break apart, blushing like a pair of guilty teenagers.

Robin had come back out to find them. He was standing in the doorway of the tavern, his brown hair backlit in a halo by the lamps inside, and the expression on his face could only be described as "smug".

'See what happens when I leave them alone for five minutes?' Robin shouted, and there was general laughter from inside the doors. He extended his hand. 'Come on, Rosy Collins, you need something to eat!'

'Keep your strength up for tonight!' cackled a woman walking past. Rosamund ducked her head, her face still pink. *Robin couldn't have asked for better acting*, she thought absently, and let herself be led inside.

Rosamund and Leo were presented with two flagons and a wooden trencher of bread, cheese, and berries to share before being shoved onto a curved bench that put them elbow to elbow. She started to pick at the food, mindful that she really did need to keep up her strength, if not for the reasons previously left unmentioned. She was definitely not thinking about those right now.

It was just the sleep deprivation. That was all.

Leo covered her hand with his, thumb stroking her palm. She shivered in spite of herself and tried to relax. 'I would guess,' he murmured as Rosamund attempted to navigate eating and drinking one-handed while wearing a veil, 'that we need to stay for at least three rounds of drinks before we can go.'

She tried not to groan. 'All right.'

'Maybe you should pretend to fall asleep,' Leo continued. 'The guards will be less likely to question you.'

'I am . . . quite tired,' Rosamund admitted.

'I didn't like to mention that I've seen healthier-looking corpses, but . . .'

She snorted. 'There's a vile accuracy if ever I heard one.' He laughed, looking for all the world like a lovestruck groom, and Rosamund closed her eyes against another pang of loss.

'Finish your food,' he said softly. 'That's an order. Then you can pretend to fall asleep on me, and we can get out of here.'

'An *order*, Captain?' She'd meant to sound stern. She definitely hadn't meant to smile.

He grinned back at her. 'If it makes you eat faster, consider it more of a suggestion.'

It was probably the haze of perpetual fatigue that was giving her the warm fuzzy feeling when he looked at her. But it was nice, nonetheless. It took her some time to eat her fill, but when she was finished, Rosamund sighed in a way that wasn't feigned at all and leaned against her new husband's shoulder, closing her eyes. It registered only distantly when Leo curled his arm around her to keep her from falling off the bench.

Some time later she felt warm breath tickle her ear as Leo "attempted" to wake her. 'Mrs. Collins?' This was followed by the sensation of air on her cheeks as a hand waved in front of her face. Then there was a loud discussion of how worn out she must be by the events of the day followed by a certain amount of speculation regarding whether she would be too worn out for the events of the night.

There was a swish of wool as Leo picked up his cloak, and her stomach lurched as she was hoisted into his arms. He carried her bridal style out of the tavern to where Scout was waiting and lifted her onto the horse's back.

✕

'You're so close together in the saddle that you're practically sitting in his lap,' said Caroline, who had been oddly silent during the entire performance.

'Fascinating,' Rosamund mumbled, too tired and worried to care.

✕

Leo kept half an ear on whatever it was Robin was doing to entertain the crowd. The snatches he could overhear suggested the man was deploying yet another one of his longwinded and frankly implausible stories to distract everyone. Leo caught the phrases "dastardly Bevorian uncle", "hidden inheritance", and "saving the farm from collapse" before tuning it out and merely watching as Robin's lanky arms gestured expansively, urging the crowd down the street towards another tavern. This created a long, slow-moving line of drunks that would serve to prevent any extra soldiers from reaching the bridge if things went poorly. He hoped.

Leo pulled his cloak a little further around Rosamund and himself as they approached the guard station. He tried to relax.

'Collins! It's been an age! How have you been?'

Leo made frantic shushing motions at Popplewell and Selley, two of Mabry's levy and apparently tonight's bridge guards. 'Blessed by the Wisdoms, Popplewell!' he stage-whispered back.

The guards laughed. 'Finally found someone to put up with you, then?' Selley chipped in, reasonably quietly.

Leo smiled down at the veiled face of his wife before replying. 'Yes, but don't worry, Selley, I'm sure there's a girl out there for you.'

'I have a cousin who's very short-sighted,' Popplewell put in helpfully. 'I'm sure she wouldn't mind your face!'

As the guards seemed to be gearing up for a good-natured slanging match, Leo tried to head them off. 'I just got married—'

'To an Abrenian?'

'We've got to take the one who'll have us.'

'And will she have you, then?' Selley's grin was sly. 'Or has she had you already?'

Leo's flare of temper wasn't entirely feigned. 'Less of your cheek, Selley.'

He held his breath. It was a bit of a dangerous move, to cut Selley off like that, but Popplewell was senior, and if he guessed right . . .

'Ah, leave him alone, Selley, he's in love.' Popplewell stepped aside. 'Cross quickly then, Collins, and your lady wife too, and good luck to the both of you. When you get across, tell Miller I'll need my replacement sooner rather than later.'

Leo nodded, gave a terse salute, and urged Scout forward.

Chapter 14

THE NIGHT WAS QUIET, but the clip-clop of hooves on wood and the splash of water against the bridge supports were unbearably loud to Rosamund's frazzled nerves. She concentrated on trying to appear relaxed, leaning back against Leo's chest and taking the slow, even breaths of a sleeper. None of her efforts stopped her pulse from thundering in her ears, and it raced all the more when she heard a guardsman shout a greeting. She bit the inside of her cheek and kept her eyes firmly closed — unable to participate in her own flight, entirely dependent on the goodwill of those around her.

Don't panic. Breathe.

The conversation and the crossing both seemed to take an eternity, but finally Scout's hooves struck solid ground again, then slowed to a stop. Rosamund held still as Leo relayed Popplewell's message to Miller. There was a low grunt in response, but he let them pass without further comment.

They set off through Gressan, Scout clip-clopping down silent streets until the sound of cobbles under hoof changed to muted thuds, and Rosamund concluded they had reached the edge of town. After a few more minutes, she risked a whisper. 'What's Robin doing?'

She felt as much as heard Leo's reply. 'When we left, he was passing around hard liquor to the guards. He'll catch up when he can, but it's more important that no one has reason to suspect anything.' He shifted in the saddle. 'I don't know what patrols are coming up. Until we cross onto your lands, you need to stay where you are.'

Rosamund let out a sigh, mumbled assent, and made herself comfortable in the crook of his arm.

It wasn't long before Leo discovered his wife had fallen asleep on him in truth. He tried not to move. Scout, for his part, was unbothered by the weight of two passengers but understandably confused when they reached a familiar fork in the road and turned right onto Hawkhurst land instead of left towards the Mabry house.

'No, Scout, this way.' Leo tried to pat the horse's neck without disturbing Lady Rosamund. She'd told him she had barely slept since she left Quayforth. Small wonder that she was out cold now.

×

'And what happens when she wakes up?' Caroline demanded, drawing up alongside him on a horse of unknown origin. Or was it a metal frame with two wheels?

Leo blinked and shook his head. 'I take her home. She hosts the peace talks and Hugo's Feast of Remembrance. She gets the baron off her back.'

'And then?'

'She can do what she wants,' Leo said firmly.

'But what do *you* want?' Caroline pressed.

'I'm safe. That's enough.'

'But she kissed you!'

Leo avoided her eyes. 'I told her we needed to be convincing. She was convincing. It didn't mean anything.'

'You're sure about that?'

Leo adjusted his wife's weight in his arms and said nothing. Caroline tutted, then disappeared from view once more, leaving him to his thoughts.

×

Rosamund woke up pleasantly warm, but with a tickly nose, an unpleasant taste at the back of her throat, and the ache in her legs that generally accompanied too many hours on horseback.

×

'Good morning, sunshine!' Caroline sounded much too cheerful.
'I'm on a horse, Caroline,' said Rosamund, her voice a little croaky.
'Correct.'
'I must have fallen asleep?'
'Also correct.'
Memory returned in a rush. 'I . . . got married.'
'Yes you did.'

×

The events of the last few days came flooding back, and Rosamund jerked awake. Leo tightened his grip, and there was a confused moment as they clung to each other while Scout danced nervously beneath them.

Once everything was back under control, they dismounted. Rosamund's knees buckled as she hit the ground. Leo sat down in front of her. 'Good morning, my lady.'

'Good morning.'

'I would ask if you slept, but' — his expression could only be described as a smirk — 'I heard you snoring.'

Rosamund decided to ignore this. 'Did you ride all night?'

He nodded, and she struggled to her feet, shivering a little in the pre-dawn cool. Leo frowned and pulled off his cloak to drape it around her shoulders. If she was honest, the gesture warmed her more than the heavy black wool.

A short while later they walked together beside the horse for the last stretch of the journey. Rosamund's legs complained every step of the way, but she couldn't find it in her to care. She was on her own land now, the landscape growing more familiar with every passing minute, and dawn had just begun to filter through the trees, touching the branches with orange and gold and pink.

But then another sensation invaded her consciousness. A stench in the air, different to the smell of sweaty horse and unwashed humans.

×

'What a delightful pair you make!' Caroline interjected, unable to resist.

×

'Leo, can you smell that?'

'What is it, my lady?'

Rosamund walked faster up the hill, a sense of foreboding growing in her chest, too distracted to answer. *Don't think about it*, she told herself sternly. *You're exhausted; it's probably nothing. Think about . . .* Unfortunately, the other pressing matter that required consideration was her new husband. Rosamund wasn't entirely at ease with those thoughts, either.

Well, no matter. She could be pleasant, at least.

'Thank you for bringing me home. I . . .' She stopped. 'Is that—smoke?'

They crested the hill. The scene below her was a jumbled confusion of noise and light. The smell of burning filled her nostrils.

Her home was on fire.

'The children!'

Leo secured Scout and grabbed his sword before pelting down towards the house after his wayward wife. Rosamund had raced up the other side of the valley, heedless of the burning debris in the dry ditch that surrounded the outer walls. The stone archway of the main gate stood open as people hurried in and out with buckets, and she sprinted through it, screaming for her children.

Leo charged around the corner of the gate in time to see her stop short next to a large stone chapel and clutch a dark-haired girl to her chest. Charlotte. The girl gesticulated in the direction of a bucket chain comprised of a handful of older men, a few housemaids — and a skinny, red-headed teenage boy. Edmund? Leo turned to look back at Rosamund; her expression was naked relief. *She's home, and her children are safe. For now.*

Of course, there was still the small matter of various parts of the estate being ablaze. Leo ran to join the bucket brigade.

✕

Five minutes before the end of the work day, Caroline sat at the desk in her shared office, whispering a silent prayer of thanks that no one could see her screen right now. After seventeen days spent arguing that she needed server access, she'd finally got the correct permissions.

Having been granted it, she was now wishing she hadn't. Hundreds of files on the company's supposedly secure server were inaccessible, their names and contents turned to gibberish. She could feel the blood pounding in her ears. *Ransomware.* And ten to one, it had come from George's computer. Which meant it was *all her fault*: she had assisted him in getting his hideous computer, with its four-colour glowing keyboard and entirely inadequate security settings, access.

But . . . that couldn't be right, could it? For a start, where was the ransom demand? She clicked through to another folder.

Oh. Her heartrate slowed, just a little. Nick had been right. This went beyond the last few weeks.

Way beyond.

Hands shaking, Caroline picked up the desk phone and called her line manager. 'Annabel? I need you to come down. Yes. Now.'

×

Leo had just noted another fire in the formal gardens to his left when a fresh outbreak of screaming snagged his attention. Rosamund, having joined Charlotte to herd a dozen large, pearly-white birds to safety, stood up straight and paused, indecisive, then turned on her heel and bolted for what looked like the stables. Leo sprinted after her, weaving his way through the bucket chain and skirting the vegetation on fire near the chapel.

Rosamund pulled out a knife—

×

Caroline started, too frazzled by the events of the day to concentrate properly. 'Wait, did she have that on her at the wedding?'

'Obviously!' Leo panted, and kept running.

×

—and cut the rope tying the draw bar for the stable in place. As he drew nearer, Leo spotted flames creeping closer to the building from a fourth fire.

Arson.

Not that he hadn't suspected that at once—but deliberately trapping the horses and, from the sound of it, the grooms as well was nothing short of a cold-blooded murder attempt. But Rosamund herself wasn't even meant to be present, so what was the target? The house? The peace talks? The Hawkhurst children? All of them?

Time enough for those thoughts later. Rosamund was straining to raise the bar, but she was a slight woman, and the pressure of the panicking grooms inside pushing on the doors meant she hadn't a hope of lifting it on her own. Leo reached her side right as she shouted, 'I need *help!*'—her words even then barely audible over the general mayhem.

He braced himself a little distance down from his wife and heaved; she turned to stare at him, hair loosed from her wedding bun and flying everywhere. They lifted together. The bar moved—slowly at first, and then all at once. Leo tried to pivot it away, but that meant it cleared Rosamund's door first, which immediately burst open. The speed and force of it knocked her back onto the summer-hardened ground, where she lay still.

Leo's heart stopped, and he almost dropped the bar. It took precious seconds to move the heavy piece of wood all the way clear of the doors, and crossing to where she lay was impeded by the grooms trying to lead the horses out and keep them out.

HBWalker: Are horses really that stupid?

CSLindley: YES.

By the time Leo got to his wife, praying she hadn't been trampled in the commotion, a fair-haired woman around his own age was kneeling beside her.

'Is she all right?' he demanded.

Rosamund groaned, opening her eyes blearily for a moment. He started breathing again.

'Hugo?' she mumbled.

Leo bit his lip until he tasted blood.

The fair-haired woman's mouth sagged half-open; she was clearly fighting panic. 'I think she's been knocked unconscious,' she said, a renewed medley of screaming horses and shouting men nearly drowning her out. 'My lady?'

Rosamund's eyes opened again. 'Sally?' She tried to turn over before yelping and falling back to her prone position.

Sally looked at him again, suspicious. 'Sir? Are you—'

'Captain Leo Collins, of the Queen's Guard,' he broke in quickly. 'I've been travelling with Her Ladyship.' *I also married her, but I'll let her explain that.*

'I'm Her Ladyship's maid. Sally,' the woman said, as if Rosamund hadn't just said that. 'We need to get her somewhere safe.' Sally rose and scanned her surroundings. 'I'll get—'

But Leo had already stooped to pick up his wife.

'This way please, Captain Collins. We'll take her to the Rose Room.'

They made their way to the southeastern corner of the house's inner ward; mercifully, none of the fires appeared to have touched the house proper. By the time he reached the stairs, blessing the fact that this part of the house seemed to be free of smoke, Rosamund was definitely conscious, though not quite coherent. 'Where's Edmund?' she mumbled, looking around. 'I saw him with the buckets, but it's past his bedtime, you know.'

'I'm sure he's fine, my lady,' Leo responded, shifting her weight a little as he climbed. Rosamund relaxed, curling in towards his chest and raising a hand to gesture at his shirt collar. 'You know, Captain Collins,' she said, and Leo tensed — what if Sally was still in earshot? 'You have the softest shirts I've ever worn.' She petted his chest. 'Soft like . . . feathers, or . . .' She trailed off, wrinkling her nose. 'You smell funny.'

He smiled as they reached the landing. 'I hate to mention it, my lady, but it's not just me.'

Rosamund *hmphed* at him, closing her eyes and relaxing further into his arms. 'There's lots of soap here, you know. You don't have to smell like smoke and horse if you don't want to. You can smell like . . .' She considered, eyes still closed. 'Flowers. All kinds of flowers, but we do run to lavender, because of the caladrius. Or mint. You can smell like mint if you want to. Mint tea is my favourite. Hugo says it tastes like licking a tree, but he has no discernment.' She gulped and opened her eyes to stare at him. 'Someone murdered him, you know.' She looked suddenly miserable.

Leo's heart constricted. 'I'm sorry, my lady.'

She sniffed. 'I miss him.'

What else could he say? 'I know.'

'And now I'm a burden.' She glanced around, bleary-eyed. 'A very literal burden.'

'No. You're not.'

He wanted to say more, but Sally had opened the door to a well-appointed solar and then carried on into a lavish, if violently pink, bedchamber. Leo followed, trying his best to be gentle as he set Rosamund on top of the covers.

'Thank you, Captain Collins,' said Sally, and Leo judged it the right moment to make himself scarce. But no sooner had he exited the solar when he was accosted by the brown-haired girl. Close up, she was unmistakably Rosamund's daughter.

His stepdaughter, now.

His responsibility.

Charlotte scowled at him. *Remarkably* like Rosamund. 'Where's my mother, and who are you?'

'Captain Leo Collins of the Queen's Guard. Lady Rosamund is with Sally, Miss Hawkhurst.'

Charlotte narrowed her eyes. 'How do you know who I am?'

'Family resemblance, miss.'

She, too, *hmphed* at him before skirting around him to the door.

Leo kept walking, intending to go back outside to offer assistance. He made it to the outer ward of the house and rejoined the brigade working to smother the remaining flames. The household had been busy; only the fires in the gardens and the dry ditch remained. Another half-hour of beating them down with branches and dousing with water put them out, and Leo collapsed to the ground with everyone else, spent. A short, stocky man in marginally nicer clothes than everyone else soon took charge, and before long Leo found himself at a table in the Great Hall, seated between the red-headed boy he strongly suspected was his new stepson and an older woman in a head wrap that had probably been beautiful before the soot got to it.

'Five fires!' Edmund said between bites. 'Five! It beggars belief. Where were the guards?'

'That's a very good question, my lord,' said the woman.

Leo, suspicions now confirmed, did not look at his new stepson. But a few minutes later, the boy turned to look at him. And he didn't look happy. 'It's rude not to introduce yourself, sir,' Edmund said.

Leo bowed acknowledgment, still seated. 'Captain Leo Collins of the Queen's Guard, sir. I've been travelling with your lady mother for the last few weeks.' *Has it only been that long?*

Edmund looked surprised. 'My mother?'

'Yes sir. Lady Rosamund hit her head on the ground trying to open the stable doors. She's in the Rose Room.'

'No one tells me *anything*!' Edmund leapt to his feet and ran off.

Leo kept eating his porridge, aware that people were now looking over in his direction. It was awkward. 'Did you really arrive with Lady Rosamund?' said his neighbour.

'Yes, ma'am.'

'I saw him carrying her,' a younger female voice piped up from further down the long wooden table.

'She was injured when freeing the grooms from the stables,' Leo offered, and several of them nodded. He finished his porridge as quickly as was decent, and then, as others stood up, took his leave. He climbed the spiral staircase of the tower for the second time that day and made his way back into the Rose Room's solar. The fires had not been an accident; they might even have been an inside job. He needed to keep Rosamund safe.

Leo dragged a wooden chair from the table to the corner near the fireplace, removed his — or, rather, Hugo's — wedding ring, and settled down to wait.

He shouldn't have sat down.

Rosamund woke up in her own bed. Her initial fear that she had died was rapidly quelled when she tried to get up. Being dead probably didn't hurt this much.

When she opened her door a few minutes later, a robe hastily thrown over her nightgown, she found Leo sound asleep by the fireplace. Had he been there for—Rosamund glanced out at the sky—the whole of the morning? It was noon. The pair of them had arrived to chaos around dawn, and she had apparently been asleep since . . . since . . .

She left that thought aside, smiled at the twist of fondness in her stomach at the sight of him curled up outside her door, and crept down the corridor towards the kitchen.

×

'You seem remarkably sanguine about someone changing your clothes while you slept,' said Caroline. Her smile turned sly. 'Could it be that the thought of your hot *husband* peeling off your torn, soot-stained wedding dress isn't so unpleasant after all?'

Rosamund frowned, ignoring the curl of sensation in her stomach at Caroline's words. 'He didn't change me. That was Sally.'

Caroline huffed. 'Yes, I know. Shame, really. I was hoping you would at least try to kiss him again as he carried you up the stairs . . .'

Rosamund blanched. Had she? Then memory unrolled. No, she hadn't kissed Leo. But she had petted him. Like a puppy.

She shoved down the feeling of mortification with a thought that was much, much better. After all the danger and intrigue and travel . . .

×

'I'm home.' She hadn't been sure where her children would be, but she walked into the kitchen, and there they were. Rosamund opened her arms as they ran to her, aware that she was sobbing and not caring in the slightest. For a long while after that, no one said anything at all.

Eventually they disentangled themselves, and Rosamund sat down to eat. When she had control of her faculties again, she addressed the table at large. 'What happened?'

It took some time for the story to come out, given how much Edmund and Charlotte kept interrupting one another, but Rosamund gathered that someone had slipped past the guard the previous night to set the fires. Charlotte, however, had been awake. When she heard the intruder and saw the light inside the house, she had hurled her chamber pot at him.

'Of course you did,' said Rosamund, grinning.

Half the household had been roused by the almighty racket, but by that point several fires were already burning, and it had taken a couple of hours to get them under control. Then, of course, there were the stables. That fire seemed to have started later than all the others — after the grooms had rushed to release the animals into the pasture in the event of the first fires' spreading — and Rosamund and Leo had arrived just as it had become evident. That the grooms were subsequently trapped inside the stables spoke to someone with intimate knowledge of the estate — perhaps even to an inside job.

But aside from an awful lot of coughing due to smoke inhalation, everyone seemed to have made it out intact. That was all Rosamund could ask for.

After she had sent Edmund and Charlotte to check on the caladrius (who knew how the temperamental birds would respond to *this* level of chaos), Rosamund sat alone at the table, thinking. She had arranged for Captain

Collins's belongings to be moved to the Rose Room (which was going to be an awkward conversation with the children, but — practicalities first, complicated emotions later) on her way downstairs to the kitchen. Now she took a moment to consider . . . other necessities.

✕

'The Rose Room is your room!' Caroline interjected. Had her heroine hit her head harder than she'd thought?

Rosamund shrugged. 'Obviously?' More accurately, it was the room she had exiled herself to when her screaming nightmares began waking her children and the household staff on a weekly basis, but the point stood.

Caroline sat down at the table next to her and said hesitantly, 'Rosamund, you know there isn't any rush — I mean, you don't —'

Rosamund chose to examine her piece of cheese more closely rather than look Caroline in the eye. 'Have contractual obligations? I think you'll find I do.'

✕

Removing the consummation clause from the marriage contract would have raised far too many questions. Rosamund wasn't even sure if the marriage would have legal standing in Bevoria without it. Technically there was ample time before anyone could officially call on either of them to confirm the marriage's validity, but . . . best just to get it over with. She could decide afterwards if sex with Leo was an experience that bore repetition, though she supposed he'd likely have an opinion on the matter too.

And there were the trifling inconveniences of the peace talks, the Feast of Remembrance, cleaning up after an arsonist, figuring out how to prevent future arsonists,

Baron Mabry, and who knew what else to deal with. They weren't exactly short of other ways to occupy their time.

Still, Leo was handsome, considerate, and thoughtful. They made a good team. She could probably trust him. She'd enjoyed kissing him. It would be fine.

×

'But I—you . . .' Caroline looked genuinely distressed.

Rosamund frowned at her. 'Is something wrong?'

After several false starts, Caroline finally stuttered out, 'I'm not writing that!'

Rosamund had some more cheese and wondered at this sudden prudishness from the woman who had gleefully been trying to engineer her into awkward situations with her now-husband since the day they met. But . . . who was Captain Collins to Caroline, anyway? Her surface thoughts had always been readily apparent, probably since all their conversations took place in Caroline's head, but now Rosamund was curious enough to reach deeper into her author's mind. The answer came to her, and she felt a glimmer of sympathy. 'Is this about writing intimate scenes where one of the characters has your Hot Editor's face?'

Caroline squeaked in protest. 'What? No! They're nothing alike!'

'Are you afraid Henry's going to notice?' Rosamund went on. She couldn't see it happening herself. Everything she had gleaned from Caroline's internal ranting about him suggested the Hot Editor was hot on details, but surely it would be more difficult than Caroline feared for him to recognise himself from a sparsely written description. Even if Rosamund herself was described as looking suspiciously like Caroline.

But Caroline only got more agitated. 'No, I . . .' She seemed on the verge of tears. Rosamund could only stare as Caroline stammered out, 'Excuse me!' and faded from her awareness.

Rosamund turned her attention back to the here and now. It was time to talk to the children about their new stepfather.

×

'Are you all right, Mother?' Edmund asked, returned with his sister from the caladrius pen, and Rosamund roused herself. She gave the question due consideration before shaking her head.

'Not really, sweetheart, but I'm home. That's what matters.'

'Who's that man you brought with you?' Charlotte demanded. Rosamund was a little surprised it had taken her this long to bring it up. Charlotte was usually the designated speaker. Edmund took after his father, and when in company, Hugo had been quiet to the point that people would wonder if he had taken a vow of silence. Something he and Leo had in common, it seemed.

Rosamund looked around, unwilling to have this conversation in public, but the kitchen was otherwise empty. She took a deep breath. 'He—'

'He's her husband.' Edmund's voice was absolutely level. Rosamund felt pride well up at his self-control even as her heart ached for him. She wasn't sure if Leo had told Edmund, or if Ed had just spotted his father's ring, but there was no sense in dancing around the subject if he already knew.

'You said you weren't going to get married again!' Charlotte cried, and Rosamund shook her head.

'No, darling. I said I didn't want to get married again. I also said I'd do everything I could to avoid it.' She put her cutlery down. 'I tried. I really did. But Baron Mabry wants this estate, and I am a foreigner' — Charlotte scoffed — 'and so Captain Collins, as a Bevorian citizen, agreed to marry me to keep us safe.'

'We don't even know him!' Charlotte protested.

Rosamund grimaced in acknowledgement but tried to keep her voice level. 'Was there some other Bevorian man you would have preferred?'

Her daughter screwed up her face indignantly. 'No!'

'Captain Collins has done us a very great favour,' Rosamund said firmly. 'He has *voluntarily* placed himself between Baron Mabry and the Hawkhurst estate, putting himself in additional danger. He has *also* renounced all claim to the land, which means if I die, he gets my money, but you can throw him out at your leisure.' Both her children's eyes widened at this. Rosamund was just wondering if it might have been too soon to use black humour with them when Charlotte giggled, and Ed ran his hand through his hair and grinned. Rosamund snorted too and softened her voice a little. 'He's not your father. You are not required to obey him, or even to speak to him. But he is a stranger here, without friends or connections, and I would very much appreciate any kindness you show him. As would he, I'm sure.'

'Aren't you his friend?' asked Edmund.

Rosamund blinked. 'I suppose I am.'

There was a short silence.

'I don't want him here,' Charlotte said mutinously, tossing her head.

'I know. But here we are regardless. So please, if you can't be kind, at least be mannerly. Have we an accord?' Rosamund held out her hand, and Charlotte took it grudgingly before pulling her mother into a hug. Rosamund closed her eyes and breathed in the scent of home.

When Charlotte exited the kitchen, muttering something about needing to see to the caladrius enclosures after the fire, Rosamund glanced over at her son. 'I'm here if you want to talk about it, Ed.'

'I know,' he said, and she decided to leave it at that.

It was time to check on Leo. As Edmund had so astutely pointed out, she was his only friend here. Rosamund smiled in spite of herself, finding the thought of being friends an unexpectedly comfortable one.

She could make this work. She could make his stay here, however many years it ended up being, pleasant enough that he wouldn't resent her for it. It was going to be fine.

Chapter 15

'It is *not* going to be fine! What am I going to do?' Caroline shouted at her screen. She dropped her head into her hands. *What a mess.*

She'd thought that writing would help her calm down after the crisis she'd just been through at work. The whole of her Tuesday had been spent in a state of high tension: when Annabel had arrived at her desk at the end of Monday, Caroline had filled her in on the situation only to have her supervisor narrow her eyes and say, 'Leave it with me,' then wander off without any further explanation. Caroline hadn't heard a word since. And now, just to put the icing on the cake, Rosamund had run away with the story again. Truly, a wonderful start to the week.

Caroline peered out through her fingers, muttering things she definitely wouldn't have committed to print. A *sham* wedding would have got Rosamund and Leo past the guards at the bridge and safely home. That the aforementioned sham wedding and its aftermath would naturally have entailed all manner of faked public displays of affection would have been a nice bonus. There might even have been a counterfeit consummation (which was actually an excellent book title, she should make a note), in which both parties involved could have ended up partially clothed and ever-so-close to admitting their feelings.

But Rosamund, aided and abetted by Robin, had thought further ahead than that. Caroline hadn't even needed to suggest a public kiss; she'd decided that all on her own. The problem was that Rosamund refused to take her own feelings into account, and Caroline could tell it was going to end badly. Her heroine wasn't going to be able to run on the strength of duty and love for her children much longer. At some point she was going to have to deal with her own emotional turmoil, or else it would deal with her, not to mention Leo.

The worst of it was that Rosamund was much too straightforward to countenance a sham marriage, and she liked Leo enough as a person not to want to shame him with an annulment or a divorce. Which meant . . .

Caroline groaned and allowed her forehead to hit the desk. It was highly embarrassing to admit, considering whose face Leo had — but she really needed Henry. He'd have some ideas on how to fix this.

But she just . . . couldn't. Not yet; not after the last thirty hours on top of the last thirty days on top of the last . . . well, it felt like thirty weeks, even if it hadn't been nearly that many. It was all just too much. Her books were supposed to be an *escape* from her life!

Perhaps she could skip this part for now and write an upcoming scene that didn't include the newlyweds. They were the main viewpoint characters, so it wouldn't be particularly easy, but she might need something referencing how Robin got to the estate from the bridge?

Caroline closed her eyes to better watch the scene unfold. Robin cracking wise with the bridge guards, plying them with alcohol, his blue eyes glinting, his brown hair reflecting red in the torchlight. Robin offering, oh so winsomely, to convey refreshment to their colleagues on the other side of the bridge . . .

✕

'I really *must* get an early start tomorrow,' Robin slurred. 'The quill — the quam — the *queen* is expecting me, you know.' It was past midnight, and his drinking companions, warmed by the glow of a large amount of strong liquor — *Wisdoms, this has been an expensive evening* — nodded with overt sympathy and waved him across towards Bevoria. But not before he'd given them two more bottles to share.

Willow clopped patiently across the bridge, and Robin slumped further into the saddle, every inch the louche aristocrat. 'Gentlemen!' he stage-whispered as he approached Mabry's second pair of watchmen, 'a toast!' He passed a bottle to the astonished guard by his right knee before raising another. 'To His Majesty Queen Euphoria, and to being back on Beverainian soil, where I heartily hope to stay!'

Mabry's men exchanged mildly confused glances, but Robin could see them calculating. He waited for them to draw the most obvious conclusions: an aristocrat on a horse throwing around absurdly expensive alcohol and drunkenly toasting the queen was unlikely to be a threat. And if the watch on the Abrenian side had let him across, surely he was a legitimate envoy. Besides, the bottle he had just handed them was worth two months' wages. Better to let him get far enough away that he forgot where he'd left it.

'Carry on, my lord.'

Robin nodded with somewhat wobbly solemnity. 'Quite so, chaps. Good watch to you.' And with that, he nudged Willow forward, keeping up the not-entirely-feigned façade of drunkenness until he was safely ensconced in a private room at a nearby inn.

×

'I don't know what to do with them, Robin,' said Caroline, and Robin raised an eyebrow as he tugged off his boots before collapsing back onto the bed.

'I'm really not seeing the problem here,' he said to the ceiling. 'If I'm reading your mind correctly, Rosamund married Leo, brought him back to her house, moved all his belongings into her room, and plans to consummate the marriage. Why are you so upset?'

Caroline whimpered.

Robin raised his head enough to grin at her. 'Wait. Is this about Henry the Hot Editor?'

'That's a separate issue.' And one that she wasn't ready to think about just yet. Because while Rosamund wasn't exactly like Caroline, and Leo wasn't exactly like Henry, a man who was such a stickler for details was not going to miss the similarities that *were* there. Caroline honestly wasn't sure if Henry was being deliberately slow about it or if he'd just decided not to bring it up out of embarrassment.

She wasn't sure which was worse. 'Look, Leo thinks that Rosamund married him out of duty and/or guilt —'

'Not entirely inaccurate.'

'Rosamund thinks that Leo married her out of duty, or possibly pity —'

'Less accurate, but I'll grant you that she thinks that.'

'And Leo isn't an aristocrat. He's not going to know that they need to consummate the marriage to make it valid!'

That got Robin to sit up again. 'Wait, why wouldn't he know that?'

Caroline sighed, twisting her hands into her hair and trying to frame the problem. 'In Leo's mind, poor people get married for love, and so obviously they have sex. Rich people get married for money or status, so they only have sex with their spouse so they can have a legitimate heir. After which, at least in Leo's experience of noble households, they go back to merrily' — she waved a hand, searching for the expression — 'copping off with their mistresses. Their wives sleep in an entirely different room, and sometimes an entirely different house! Rosamund already has an heir, and Leo . . .' She flailed both her hands, incoherent. 'Well, all he knows is that she likes him enough to save him from rotting in an Abrenian prison for the rest of his life and is fine being stuck with him for the next five-and-a-half years! He's just hoping that at some point she decides to fall in love with him.'

'But instead of giving herself time to fall in love, she'll just —'

'Spring it upon him at the earliest opportunity. Yes.'

Robin lay down again, smirking, and closed his eyes. 'That's going to be an awkward . . . conversation.'

'Was that a pun?' Caroline shouted, incensed.

'Caroline Lindley,' said Robin, not bothering to open his eyes, 'you are talking to a character you made up in your own head. If there are terrible euphemisms going on, you only have yourself to blame.'

Caroline decided to ignore this, on the grounds that: a) he was probably right, and b) she was concerned that she might be going mad. 'Rosamund is going to assume that Leo knows about the consummation requirement, and so she's not actually going to talk to him about it, and it's all going to go wrong!'

Robin frowned.

'I've spent hours trying to work around it,' Caroline continued, 'but I just can't see how! Every scenario that I try ends the same! They all start optimistically enough, but then it just gets bad!'

'Bad like you have to write an intimate scene that's basically between facsimiles of you and Henry?'

'Bad like I start the scene and she has a breakdown!' Caroline cried. 'Then Leo, whose life and livelihood depend on reading people correctly, notices that she's not doing very well and asks her what's wrong, and she loses her temper and shouts at him, and . . .' Caroline paused for breath. 'She's just not very good at dealing with sympathy! I don't want her to have sex just to fulfil a contract, and I especially don't want her to do that right now when she's still ignoring her own feelings! She loves Leo, I think, but she still loves Hugo too, and learning that he was murdered over something he never even told her about has torn open the grief of losing him all over again, and she's ignoring both of those things in favour of —'

'Securing her children's future?'

'Yes! I want her to be *happy*,' Caroline wailed. 'I don't want "seduce husband for legal reasons" to be an item to check off her to-do list!'

'It's not as if that's an uncommon trope—'

Caroline lost her temper. 'I don't *care*! Every character in this story'—here she paused to glare at Robin—'runs around setting boundaries like I gave them free will or something. Well this boundary is mine. I'm not writing that. No!'

'Then fix it.'

Caroline scowled furiously at him, and then stared, her mouth falling open.

Robin could fix it. That was the solution. He'd already set himself up as Rosy and Leo's wingman, regardless of their wishes or Caroline's. He was tactless enough to bring the subject up, but also sympathetic enough that he would explain when he realised that Leo was working from a faulty set of assumptions. And, Caroline reasoned, if Mabry had arranged the arson attempt, he'd surely have a follow-up plan. All she needed was a minor crisis that would require Robin and Leo to share a room. She could do that.

'Listen,' Caroline said sternly, 'you just need to have a chat with Leo so he understands what's going on in Rosamund's head *before* things get . . . spicy. They're grown adults, I trust them to work this out. All they need is time, and some actual communication, and to be apprised of all the relevant information.'

'Which is where I come in.'

'Yes. If I can keep them out of the same bed for a few days, could you please explain the realities of politically married life to Leo, so if Rosamund does get away from me again—'

'She will,' Robin said merrily.

'—he at least has some idea why she's being so weird?' Caroline ended this with a glower, but Robin took it all in his stride.

'Certainly. It would be my genuine pleasure.' He looked far too pleased for her liking, but she let it go.

'Thank you. I appreciate it,' she said stiffly.

'Will this mean I'm rooming with Leo again?'

'Yes, I should think so.'

'Last time he tried to smother me with a pillow.'

'Not my problem, Mr. Waverley. Try sleeping on your side this time.'

Robin wrinkled his nose. 'If this is the last uninterrupted sleep I'm going to get for the foreseeable future, I'm making the most of it.' He pulled the blankets up over his head, and Caroline left him to it.

Well. That solved *that* part of the problem. Not that Robin was going to remember this conversation beyond a vague impression that Leo might need an explanation of the birds and the bees, but still. She'd made the effort.

As for what she was going to do about Henry? She'd think about that when nothing else was on fire.

×

Robin awoke around noon with a mild hangover and a great desire for breakfast. He was just descending the stairs into the common room when a soldier wearing Mabry purple strode through the front door and marched over to the innkeeper. 'His Lordship the baron will be returning to Bevoria within the hour, along with a squad of soldiers. They will require food, water, and fresh horses and will depart at the second hour, so make yourselves ready. The baron will stand for no delays.'

That's not good. Robin made his way more slowly down the stairs.

Maybe Mabry wasn't headed directly for Hawkhurst, but Robin hadn't lived as long as he had by banking on maybes. He paid the innkeeper, tipped Willow's groom, and set off at a brisk trot through the cobbled streets. As soon as he was out of Gressan, Robin pushed Willow into a canter, and then a gallop. So much for breakfast, or lunch, or whatever meal he was missing right now; he wouldn't have time to stop if he wanted to have any hope of beating Mabry to Hawkhurst.

'Welcome home.'

Leo woke to afternoon sunlight pouring through the windows and Lady Hawkhurst prodding him with a stick from some distance away.

The stick still had leaves on it.

She caught him looking at it and set it down by his chair. 'You can't blame me for exercising a little caution, considering what happened the last time I woke you unexpectedly.'

Her eyes were firmly on the floor, but there was a definite smile in her voice. 'Behold your wife,' Mother Marian had said. *Maybe we can make this work.*

Leo realised that he hadn't responded. 'Of course not, my lady.' His wife glanced up, a complicated expression on her face. He did not like it very much.

'I have, so far today,' she said wearily, 'had more than one awkward conversation where I have been obliged to explain to various people who need to know that you are my husband. This includes conversations with my monumentally unimpressed fifteen-year-old son, my bewildered eleven-year-old daughter, and my baffled steward, whose age is unimportant. Can you at least try to leave off the "my ladys", even if "Rosamund" is beyond you?'

'I can try, m—' Leo caught himself. 'Yes.'

'I appreciate it.'

They were both silent for a moment. Rosamund looked him up and down. 'Martin is just down the corridor. I'll fetch him in a moment. He'll be able to provide anything you need.'

Leo frowned, thinking over the faces he'd seen while helping fight the fires. 'I think we met last night . . . I mean, this morning.'

'Seems likely. Not very tall, grey hair, big beard? He's my second-in-command. He already moved all your belongings into the Rose Room, which,' she gestured behind her, 'I assume you're already familiar with.'

The words "but that's your room" were on the tip of his tongue, but he nodded instead.

'I'm afraid I have far too much to do and nowhere near enough time to do it,' Rosamund continued apologetically, 'but anyone here will get you anything you require. You've slept through luncheon, but if you'd like to have supper with us later, we'll eat at the seventh hour in the small hall.'

Leo stood, bowing acknowledgement, and Rosamund strode off to return with Martin, who treated Leo to a truly spectacular "make trouble for us and I'll end you" glare when she wasn't looking. 'Be nice,' was her parting shot, though whether that was directed at Martin or him, Leo was unsure.

Martin, after his initial flash of hostility, was scrupulously deferential. He made no comment on the manner of his lady's arrival, her subsequent misadventures, where she was, or what she was doing. 'Will Your Lordship require anything else?' he asked when Leo was washed, clothed, and fed. Leo shook his head.

'No thank you, Martin, I'm sure I'm keeping you from much more important work.'

Martin's bow was ornate and faintly mocking. 'If you wish to dismiss me, I will take my leave.'

Leo bowed briefly in return. 'My thanks.' And then he was on his own again.

Being alone in a strange place was not an unusual experience for Leo, though he supposed these circumstances were somewhat outside the norm. Nonetheless, the same principles applied. *What is the tactical situation?* It was time to find out. 'I'm going home,' Rosamund had said. But the way she'd said it was clashing hard with the stone-walled fortress in which he found himself. How had the arsonists even found their way in? It must have been carefully planned sabotage or else very sloppy gatekeeping.

Making his way up the honey-coloured stone steps onto the outer walls, Leo spotted four towers, one large gate, and a bustle of activity in both the inner and outer wards. The outer walls were surrounded by a dry ditch where, he recalled, one of the fires had been set the night before. Leo had to assume it was a diversion, though he supposed that the crops growing nearby would have burned if the fire had lasted longer into the morning and the winds had picked up.

Inside the outer walls there had been three fires: one in the gardens that must have been the initial decoy; one by the chapel, which would almost certainly contain plenty of wooden accoutrements and cloth decorations; one behind the stables, which were built of timber and filled with hay and straw. Either of the latter two would have drawn ample attention away from the main house on its own.

That left, most worrying of all, the fifth fire. Set within the house itself, it would have required the arsonist to make their way through the inner ward. Leo traced the culprit's probable path, and when he reached the granary door and pushed it open, it groaned like a dying horse. That must have been what had alerted Charlotte. The conversation around him at breakfast had told him she'd seen the fire from the top of the first flight of stairs and hurled her chamber pot down at the arsonist, dousing the freshly started fire at the same time.

Why wasn't the granary door locked? *Did* the door lock? If it didn't, why not?

Leo shook his head, determined to overhaul the watch system that clearly wasn't working and to confirm exactly how many defensive precautions Rosamund would let him add to the house. 'Welcome home,' she'd said. Well, if this was his home now, he was going to protect everyone in it to the best of his ability. "I don't want to be a burden to you" went both ways.

Leo exited back through the small gate and headed towards the stables, where Rosamund had—his mind shied away from the thought, but he stopped and forced himself to look it in the face. Where Rosamund nearly got herself trampled trying to save her people.

He shook himself, unnerved. The important thing was that she was fine. Or at least mostly fine. She'd taken a bit of a knock to the head, but she seemed to have all her faculties intact. Though she also hadn't mentioned petting him and talking about his shirts . . . or calling him by her dead husband's name . . . so either she didn't remember (possible) or had decided never to speak of it (likely).

The grooms were in a state of barely controlled chaos, cleaning anything and everything so that the horses wouldn't spook when they were returned to their stalls later in the day. The fire had been set some distance behind the building, but the burned branches that made a trail towards it spoke of some forethought, not to mention a desire for multiple cascading disasters. It might even be an indication of some spite, Leo thought wryly to himself, that the arsonist had bothered to set yet another fire as he fled Charlotte's chamber pot onslaught.

His circuit around the stables complete, Leo climbed the stairs to the outer wall again and let the summer breeze cool him, trying to look on the bright side. If this was to be his home for the next few years at least, that certainly posed no hardship. The house itself was huge, and the haunting call of the caladrius birds, anxious for their second meal of the day, echoed within the inner ward. The outer walls were sturdy; the forest he'd ridden through the night before had been well-managed; notwithstanding the security situation, it seemed a pleasant place to live.

In addition, he wasn't going to have to worry about money for some time yet. He was now Lady Rosamund's husband, and even if Edmund threw them both out as soon as he came of age, Leo anticipated five years of certainty. Far more than he'd ever had before. There was the issue of, well, *issue*, but Leo was certain that while Rosamund might have put him in what he had initially taken to be her bedroom, she probably didn't intend him to do anything other than sleep there. Perhaps it wasn't her room after all, merely a place reserved for someone who needed medical attention?

He shook his head. Sleeping arrangements weren't important right now, and he couldn't afford to get distracted. By his count Queen Eudosia would be arriving tomorrow, and King Roland too. And then would come the Feast of Remembrance, where Baron Mabry would undoubtedly make his play for Rosamund's estates. Among other things.

The unbidden image brought a spike of rage: nasally, gaunt, pug-faced Mabry smugly extending an offer to Rosamund. Leo drew a long breath, his grip tightening on the stones of the wall. Rosamund was his wife. That meant Mabry couldn't touch her. Literally or figuratively. Which was fine. Good, even.

Leo took one last look at the surrounding countryside, intending to go downstairs and make himself useful, when a horse crested the rise and galloped towards the house, a very familiar figure on its back.

Robin.

Chapter 16

ROBIN ARRIVED WITHIN SIGHT of the estate at that awkward time between meals, worse luck. On the upside, Leo met him some distance out from the gate. 'No time for chit-chat!' Robin declared as soon as the man was in earshot. He dismounted and threw Willow's reins to his friend. 'There's an entire squad of Mabry's soldiers arriving soon, with Mabry himself in the lead.'

'How far behind?'

Robin shrugged, relaxing just a little as they made it to the outer gate. 'They'll probably be here before dinner.' He sniffed the air. 'Can you smell burning?'

'It's been quite a day,' said Leo dryly before shouting, 'Shut the gates!' There was a short pause and an undercurrent of whispered conversation, but the creak of oak and iron as they passed through the archway was unmistakable.

Robin grinned, though he was so weary that even his face hurt. 'They're already dancing to your tune, I see?'

Leo didn't answer. Instead, he handed Willow's reins to a groom—one who raised her eyebrows at the sudden return of her mistress's horse and its rider both, but said nothing—and strode off towards the house. Robin jogged to keep up.

They found Rosamund in the sitting room off the small hall. She looked up from the ledger she was poring over when they hurried in, and Robin was gratified to catch her whispered 'He made it,' when she saw him. Though it wasn't nearly as gratifying as the softness on her face when Leo strode forward to speak with her.

Together they turned towards him as Robin made his way across the room. Rosamund raised an eyebrow in question, and he filled them in on all that had happened since they'd last seen one another before she did the same for him. 'So,' Robin said grimly, 'Mabry's planning to arrive in the aftermath of an arson attack and make himself at home.'

'That's a flimsy pretext by anyone's reckoning,' Rosamund said, and he shrugged.

'I doubt he cares. Ever heard that expression about possession?'

Rosamund wrinkled her nose. 'We need to close the gates.'

'Already done,' said Leo, and Rosamund gave him a grateful smile.

'I'll alert the servants,' she said. 'They've been preparing accommodations for the feast anyway. We'll just be receiving guests a little earlier than expected.'

Duty done, Robin flopped into a chair. 'If you let him know that the queen's arrival is imminent, that should stop him from trying anything clever tonight.' He frowned. 'But that still leaves other options on the table. Not to mention that if Mabry finds out you've remarried before the feast, he'll have time to make alternative plans. And if any of his soldiers recognise my face, or Leo's . . .' Robin stood up again, though he'd really have preferred not to. 'We need to stay out of sight. Where's the most out-of-the-way spot in the house?'

'The Rose Room,' Rosamund replied immediately, then bit her lip, glancing up at Leo.

Leo just smiled at her, his expression nothing but concern. 'If you stay with the children—'

'—in the same room, for safety's sake,' Robin interrupted.

'Then Robin and I can stay up in the Rose Room until the feast.'

'Is that all right?' Rosamund sounded concerned. Robin didn't take offence at the suggestion that he was a bad roommate.

'Of course, my lady,' said Leo. Rosamund tutted but didn't comment as he went on. 'Don't worry. If he snores too loudly, I'll just smother him with a pillow again.'

Rosamund's face broke into a grin. 'I am going to need the story of why that is an "again" at some point, sir.'

'Any time you like.'

Robin rolled his eyes. He did *not* snore. All evidence to the contrary was clearly manufactured.

Rosamund took charge. 'Both of you need to get upstairs now. I'll have Charlotte bring up some food, and I'll deal with the baron.' She glanced at Leo. 'Supper with the family is off the table, it seems. But at least you don't have to have dinner with Mabry.'

Robin watched Leo with some concern as the implications of leaving Rosamund alone with her late husband's murderer flitted across his face. But whatever his misgivings, he kept them to himself as he and Robin took their leave of Rosamund and made for the stairs.

✕

'Ah, such a shame you won't be able to share a room with your new husband for the next few nights,' Caroline offered, playing with the curtain fabric rather than meeting her heroine's eyes.

'I . . . suppose?' Rosamund couldn't help but feel that she'd missed something. 'Should I be worried, Caroline? Are you planning something else?'

'Planning something?' Caroline dropped a green tassel and looked up. 'I think you have higher priorities at the moment than my aspirations for your romantic subplot.'

That was undeniable. Rosamund's legal obligations would keep for a few days, but Mabry was about to land on her doorstep. She needed to move.

×

Half an hour later Robin had settled into the Rose Room. He was warm, comfortable, clean, and waiting for Leo to return from the garderobe when there was a gentle knock at the door.

'Leo? That was quick.'

'No, Uncle Robin,' came the voice of his favourite not-actually-niece. 'It's me.'

Uncle Robin had arrived. Charlotte knew this because Captain What's-His-Name had brought him into the sitting room to talk to Mother. She was not eavesdropping, thank you, she just happened to be passing by during that part of the conversation.

Well, if Uncle Robin was here, he would know what was going on, and Charlotte had complete confidence that he could sort out all of this legal stuff in five minutes flat. Then the strange man who had followed Mother home like a lost puppy could leave. 'Robin and I can stay up in the Rose Room until the feast,' Captain Thingy had said. That was fine by Charlotte. She didn't even object when her mother asked her to take a tray up for the two men; she was headed there anyway, though she didn't tell Mother that.

And her luck was in. Just as she neared the foot of the stairs, she heard Captain Whoever open the door of the solar, presumably making for the garderobe. Charlotte knew she didn't have long. She scurried upstairs into the solar, set the tray on the table, and knocked on the door of the bedchamber.

'Leo? That was quick.'

'No, Uncle Robin,' she said quickly. 'It's me.'

There was a short pause, and then the door opened, and Uncle Robin smiled down at her before engulfing her in a hug. 'Lottie!' he cried, a picture of cheer. 'How are you? I'm sorry that I probably won't be of much use in the uncle department at the moment; I'm stopping in here for the foreseeable on your mother's orders. But I'm delighted to see you. How are you doing?' He sat down at the table, surveying the tray with unparalleled enthusiasm.

Charlotte took a deep breath. 'Mother's married this Captain So-and-So for some . . . stupid legal reason and I want to know when he's leaving.'

Robin, mouth full of nuts and cheddar, gestured for her to sit down next to him. 'Well, we have a few minutes until Captain So-and-So returns,' he told her, 'so let's talk about it now.'

'Why did she have to get married to some man we've never met?'

Robin started to butter a slice of bread. 'What did your mother say about it?'

Charlotte snorted derisively. 'That it was something to do with Father's will and some contract, or—she did explain about the will before, but she said she was going to try and ask the queen to sort it out, or something. And then she went to the palace, but instead of her coming home, we just got a letter saying, "I'm going on a trip, when I come back Queen Eudosia is coming to visit and so is King Roland, please make sure there's plenty of food in the house and that all the rooms are clean!" Then someone tried to set fire to the house and we were all trying to put it out and then she came running through the gate in a ballgown at five o'clock in the morning and then she was trying to open the stable door and she got knocked down and I thought she was dead!'

Then the tears came in earnest, and her not-actually-uncle moved to kneel in front of her chair, letting her sob on his shoulder until she got control of herself again.

'Charlotte?'

She sniffed. 'What?'

'There were some problems sorting out your father's will.'

'Yes,' she said impatiently, 'I know—'

'No,' he said gently, 'I don't think you do. It's very complicated, and we probably don't have time to go into the details at this moment, but trust me when I say that your mother marrying Captain Collins was actually a very elegant solution.'

Charlotte sniffed again, pulling a handkerchief from her sleeve. 'I don't want him here.'

'I know. But Captain Collins is a friend of mine, and he's a good man. He's not going to be a bother to you. I wouldn't have let your mother marry him if he was.' He winked at her conspiratorially, but she pretended not to see.

'He's staying till Ed comes of age. Do you know how long that is?'

'Yes.'

'So you think I should just—' She gave him her best glare. '—Put up with him for the next few years?'

'I think,' said Robin, 'that for now you can just pretend he isn't here. And in less than a month you'll be back at school, so it won't matter that he's here. And if he's still a problem when you come home for the winter, you can write to me, and I'll come and deal with him.'

She stared at him very solemnly. 'Promise?'

Uncle Robin returned her solemn look. 'Promise. But for now, he's keeping me and your mother safe, so you might want to make yourself scarce before he gets back. Unless you'd like to talk to him too? He's not a bad listener.'

This was clearly nonsense, so Charlotte gave her honorary uncle a final hug and left the room.

×

The door squeaked on its hinges as Caroline's line manager entered her office. 'Caroline?'

She sounded anxious. Annabel often sounded anxious, but her darting eyes and hunted expression were new and worrying developments. 'Good morning!' Caroline attempted cheeriness, hoping against hope that the cause of Annabel's nervousness was her unnamed, useless boyfriend (whom Caroline strongly suspected of being married).

It wasn't.

'Well—' Annabel didn't seem to know quite where to begin. 'I looked into the issues you raised with me, and I wanted to thank you for flagging your concerns.' The words might have been encouraging, but Annabel's facial expression didn't match them at all. 'While it's always better to overreact than underreact in these kinds of situations, I've had a look myself. There were a few minor issues, which

I've fixed, but overall, there's absolutely nothing to worry about. I've revoked your access again —' Caroline started, and Annabel gave her an insincere smile. '— For security reasons, obviously. You're quite right, it's important that only employees with a real need are able to access sensitive data, and it isn't part of your remit, is it?'

Nor is being tech support for bullying executives, Caroline thought bitterly. *Nor is potentially being party to criminal behaviour!*

But Annabel hadn't finished. 'With your performance review coming up next month, I wouldn't want to distract you from getting your projects finished. After all —' She gave a tinkly little laugh. 'You're a DBA! We need to see evidence of you, well, administrating databases. In these tricky economic times, we've all got to pull our weight, darling, because otherwise we'll find ourselves out the door!'

If that wasn't a veiled threat, then Caroline was a triceratops. Stunned into silence, she could only nod blankly and try not to panic as she listened to the door click shut behind Annabel. Her mind was racing, but one thought stuck out in particular: *Rosamund wouldn't stand for this.*

Caroline nodded sharply, anger shoving her fear aside. It was time to invoke a higher authority.

✕

Robin tucked into his chicken as Leo poured himself some wine, and for the next few minutes the silence in the Rose Room's solar stretched out comfortably. Once Robin had taken the worst edge off his hunger, his thoughts turned to Leo and Rosamund's previous interactions. They'd been polite enough to each other, but Rosamund, soft looks aside, had been a little too quick to hand her sleeping quarters over to the men. That didn't bode well for the state of marital relations.

Still, Robin Waverley prided himself on impeccable comic timing. Which was why he waited until Leo had taken a large mouthful of wine before asking, 'So, has Rosy deflowered you yet?'

The wine went *everywhere*. Robin, satisfied that he hadn't lost his touch, waited patiently while his friend finished aspirating his drink. He even mopped up some of the spillage with his own napkin. Just to be helpful.

Eventually Leo managed to choke out, 'What part of "marriage of political convenience" escaped you?'

Robin frowned. 'The part where you're still required to consummate it, obviously.'

Leo's head snapped up. 'Wait. What?'

Robin shook his head and smiled ruefully. 'You know, I sometimes forget you're not a . . . a . . .'

'Posh boy like you?' Leo grunted.

'Posh boy like me,' Robin agreed affably. 'Leo, there are . . . contractual obligations. The marriage isn't valid until it's consummated. Didn't you read what you were signing?'

There was a very long silence. 'I read the extra clauses.'

'Not the standard portion?'

'We were in a hurry. I skimmed it.'

This was very unlike Leo, but Robin decided not to mention it. 'Of course, officially speaking, consummation only needs to occur by the summer solstice—'

'That was last month.'

'*Next* year, Collins, next year. But while it's unlikely that anyone is going to call on you at midsummer to vow before witnesses that you've done the deed,' he shrugged and started in on a second chicken leg, 'technically you aren't actually married until you do.' Then he paused, suddenly awkward. 'And since Rosy is absolutely, completely, and scrupulously honest, she's . . . not going to see a reason to wait.'

Leo said nothing. The silence was now a good deal less comfortable.

Robin sighed. 'Having done my supremely awkward duty and informed you of this — be kind to her, please? Judging from how she was when we conferred at the river, I don't think she's coping terribly well with the news that Hugo was murdered. She's not thinking very clearly, and it worries me, given her tendency to jump in feet-first. This' — he waved the hand holding the chicken leg, gesturing at the general situation — 'would not have been my solution to her legal problems. I grant you that it's elegant, I grant you that it's efficient, but I don't trust her to think about herself at the moment. Which means that you're going to have to do it for her.'

He fell silent, chewing. Leo sipped his wine. Carefully.

'She . . .' Leo trailed off.

Robin schooled himself to patience. Captain Collins, he knew from experience, liked to take his time with words. Sometimes you just had to hold your tongue until he thought through what to say.

'She still recites the Litany for the Dead for Hugo,' Leo mumbled finally. His gaze dropped to the floor. 'Every day. And I've heard her in the middle of the night sometimes when she can't sleep.'

Robin grimaced in sympathy.

Leo set the wine aside and scrubbed his hands through his hair. 'This is a mess.'

'Do you love her?' Robin enquired, then grinned when Leo's head snapped up. 'Actually, don't bother to answer that, Captain Collins; it's all over your face. Well,' and the look he gave Leo was suggestive, 'at least I can rely on you to try and make her happy?'

Leo groaned and buried his head in his hands.

'And I'd wager she has warm fuzzy feelings for you, deep down.'

Leo's head shot back up. 'Robin, I just said—'

'I heard what you said.' Robin settled himself back in his chair, ignoring Leo's anger. 'But I've seen how she looks at you. She might not be in love with you yet, but she cares about you enough to ask you to marry her, with all that entails.'

That appeared to give Leo food for thought. Robin pressed on. 'So the fact that you're painfully in love with her'—he held up a hand—'and please don't insult my intelligence by denying it—is ideal from my perspective.'

'Why?'

'Because you married her, idiot, which solves at least some of her problems in the short to medium term. But your love is worthwhile in itself. She deserves someone in her corner. That's now your job. So make her happy.' Robin gave an easy smirk, but there was an edge to it. 'That's, "Make her happy or else", by the way.'

Silence once again greeted this proclamation. Robin allowed a suitable interval to hammer the point home, then glanced around the room, stifling a yawn. 'I take it we're in here for the duration?'

Leo roused himself from his thoughts. 'I can't promise you a great variety of views, but this seems to be the furthest room from everything. So as long as someone remembers to feed and water us, we're not going to be spotted. And now that we're in Bevoria, we probably can't be arrested.'

'Ah, how I've missed your indefatigable optimism, Captain Collins.' Robin stood up and headed for the bed-chamber. 'Wake me if the world ends, won't you? It's been a long day.' He thought he heard a stifled sigh behind him, but he ignored it. He'd done his best. Leo and Rosamund would just have to work the rest out between them.

Chapter 17

IT GAVE ROSAMUND no small amount of satisfaction to see the look on Baron Mabry's face when she received him in the Cavell Room: of all the contingencies he had planned for upon his arrival at Hawkhurst, finding the gates locked had evidently not been among them.

'Lady . . . ah . . . Lady Rosamund!'

Rosamund gave him a formal Bevorian bow, sternly reminding herself as she did so that she must not murder him on the spot. 'I fear you will find us a little unprepared for your arrival, sir,' she said, affecting cheerfulness, 'since we weren't expecting guests for the Feast of Remembrance to start arriving until tomorrow at the earliest. But for our liege lord, I daresay we can expedite.'

The baron nodded, still off-balance, and eyed the pair of Hawkhurst guards who had accompanied him into the room. Guards complete with crossbows.

Rosamund followed his gaze. 'There were fires on the grounds last night, my lord. We suspect' — she dropped her voice — 'they were deliberate.'

The baron's mouth dropped open.

'Therefore,' said Rosamund, doing her best not to bare her teeth, 'I must insist that your soldiers relinquish their weapons. It seems very unreasonable, I know,' she continued, holding up a hand to prevent his interrupting, 'but with the queen's arrival imminent, we cannot take any chances.'

Mabry looked very much as though he would like to argue. Instead, he narrowed his eyes, offered her a cloying smirk, and nodded. Rosamund returned the expression in kind and gestured for the baron to precede her out of the room, her guards — and their crossbows — close behind her.

All things considered, Leo had shared quarters with worse roommates, and it was a reasonably quiet night. True, Waverley had hogged the bed and woken him twice by dropping an arm over his face, but the thump Robin had made when he hit the floor had been very gratifying. However, Leo did a double take the next morning when he answered a knock at the door to find Rosamund holding a breakfast tray, and he didn't need eyes in the back of his head to know that Robin smirked at his reaction.

Rosamund set the tray down in the solar and perched on a chair at the head of the table. 'Queen Eudosia's party plans to arrive today,' she told them, 'and of course you will wish to report directly to her once she's settled, but until then, please stay here. Is there anything you need?'

'Paper and pens, if you'd be so kind,' said Robin around a mouthful of bread. 'Also Edmund, if possible.'

Rosamund and Leo both looked at him. 'Paper, pens, and . . . Edmund?' Rosamund said carefully.

'Yes. Please.'

Leo had spent a lot of time in The Honourable Robin Waverley's company in the past year, but sometimes his thought processes were still opaque. He shared a glance with Rosamund, who looked equally bewildered, but she shrugged.

'I'll ask Ed to deliver your supplies. Whether or not he stays longer is his decision.'

As soon as Edmund knocked on the door of the Rose Room, Robin hauled him inside.

'Edmund Hawkhurst, Leo Collins. Leo, Edmund.'

'We've met,' Edmund and Leo said simultaneously, then exchanged an awkward, mutually confused glance.

Edmund moved away to deposit his handful of quills on the table. 'What was that for, Uncle Robin? Why are you whispering?'

Robin waggled his eyebrows in what he hoped was a sufficiently mysterious fashion. 'Eddie, we need your help.'

Edmund slapped the paper down on the table and turned to leave. 'I have work to do.'

'Please?'

Edmund treated his honorary uncle to an unimpressed look, and his expression so closely resembled his mother that Robin winced. Fifteen-year-old Rosamund had also been skinny and flame-haired and shy; on the other hand, she hadn't been haunted by grief and worried over a parent who had turned up on the doorstep with a new spouse and very little in the way of explanation.

'No, there's too much to do.' Edmund glanced pointedly at Leo. He didn't have to say, 'Why aren't *you* helping?' for Robin to hear it loud and clear.

'Captain Collins has been ordered by your mother to stick with me for the moment.' Robin tried his most charming smile. 'Pretty please, Ed?'

Edmund grunted. 'What is it you need my help with?'

'A map of the Hawkhurst estates. Nobody else here can actually draw. Well,' Robin amended, 'your mother does an

acceptable watercolour, the benefits of an expensive education, but I need a plan that's at least vaguely to scale.'

Edmund scowled at Leo. 'Why should I hand tactical
information to a complete stranger?'

Robin grinned. 'Excellent question! You shouldn't.
But Captain Collins is your new stepfather' — Edmund and
Leo both winced and looked away from each other — 'which
means he's staying here for the next little while. You'd do
well to make use of his expertise.' Robin paused, unsure of
how much he should say. 'It's clear from the fires that the
house isn't as secure as it could be, and more people will be
arriving soon for the feast. We have a responsibility to keep
them and everyone else safe. And we can't do that without
accurate information.'

Robin held his breath as Edmund considered this. He
was particularly proud of how he had worked the word
"responsibility" into his impromptu speech. That had always
been the best angle of attack when persuading Rosamund,
and he hoped it would work on her eldest too.

'Fine.' Edmund looked between the two men, his
expression sulky but a little intrigued. 'Half an hour. Then
I have to get back to work.'

'Thank you,' said Leo quietly, and Edmund sniffed.

'Don't get used to it, *sir*. But you're welcome.'

Queen Eudosia arrived at eleven of the clock, precisely on
schedule. Before her came the blue-clad messenger, riding
ahead to ensure that all was prepared for Her Majesty, then
fifteen of the Queen's Guard on foot, plus that many again
on horseback, every animal's coat groomed to a mirror
shine. Two identical carriages glided through the middle
of this procession, one of which would contain Queen

Eudosia herself. Perhaps the other contained the crown prince, but Rosamund doubted it. Too many royals in one place made the guards antsy.

She was proved correct when several of Eudosia's ministers emerged from the second carriage, blinking in the late morning sunlight. Some of them looked like they didn't get out much. While Hawkhurst had received word some days ago that the worst of the fever had now passed in the capital, Rosamund was relieved that the queen's retinue did seem smaller than usual. She just hoped they had enough room in the hastily restored stables for all the horses.

The formal greetings necessitated an exercise in things unsaid. As the queen stepped down from her carriage, Rosamund offered a deep bow: 'Your Majesty, be welcome in our halls.'

Eudosia answered, with apparent sincerity, 'An amiable welcome gladdens the heart,' but then came the rigmarole of allocating her entourage their rooms and allowing the aristocrats to refresh themselves and dress for the midday meal. Every guest arriving that day turned out in the Great Hall promptly at twelve, as much to be present for the gossip as for luncheon. Rosamund, trying not to stare too obviously at certain members of the assembly, wished for Leo at her back. And then was ashamed of herself.

Eudosia took her place at the high table. 'I visit Hawkhurst on an occasion of sorrow and joy intermingled,' she began. 'An occasion of solemn remembrance for Sir Hugo, but also an occasion of hope for our country. We anticipate the near arrival of King Roland of Abrenia to discuss an extension of our truce and the construction of a more lasting peace.' She paused as the crowd muttered its surprise. 'And therefore we extend our most gracious thanks to Lady Rosamund Hawkhurst, without whom this would not have come to pass.'

Rosamund bit down a self-satisfied smile at Baron Mabry's barely concealed glower. All the same, she was relieved when she could slip back upstairs to knock on the door of the solar. Eudosia had been unusually warm towards her, perhaps, but seeing her again had brought back the sting of fear and hopelessness Rosamund had felt when she'd first been given her mission. Perhaps the queen was on her side. Or perhaps Rosamund had merely found herself on Eudosia's.

As she reached the top of the stairs, sweating a little in her formal court attire, Rosamund was startled to hear her son's voice through the door. He hadn't been there to receive the queen, but she'd sent him up hours ago; surely he wasn't still—

'Enter!' Robin called, and Rosamund made her way into the room to discover Edmund deep in discussion with Captain Collins, both of them poring over a large sheet of her best parchment.

'Those trees are a nightmare from a tactical standpoint,' Leo was saying, pointing at something on the paper. Edmund hummed an acknowledgement—then looked up guiltily when he spotted his mother.

Robin, as ever, was perfectly at ease. 'Rosy! As you can see, we're getting on famously.' He lowered his voice. 'Edmund has been such a help to his new stepfather.'

Edmund and Leo looked abashed. Rosamund decided not to mention it. 'Her Majesty Queen Eudosia has arrived, gentlemen.'

Robin nodded. 'I'm sure you can continue this

discussion later, chaps. Come on, Leo. Don't keep Her Majesty waiting!'

When they had gone, Rosamund sidled over to the parchment half covering the wooden table. A plan of the Hawkhurst estate spread out before her in black ink, supplemented with reds and blues for important elements. 'Impressive work, sweetheart.'

Edmund looked sheepish. 'Sorry, I should've been there to—'

'It's fine,' Rosamund said quickly, 'but we do need you now. If the queen noticed your absence, she hasn't mentioned it, but I'll seat you near her at dinner to make sure she knows she's not being snubbed.'

Edmund grunted but didn't object. 'I still don't think you should have gone to court.'

She didn't trust herself not to turn that statement into the start of an argument. 'I know,' she said carefully.

'You didn't have to get married,' Edmund pressed.

Rosamund closed her eyes, giving herself a moment to find calm. He would be Hawkhurst, and this whole estate would be his. Maybe not now, but soon. *He needs to know I trust him with it.* That would start with him knowing that she valued his opinion. 'Do you think it was the wrong decision?' she asked finally.

There was a long pause. 'I don't know.' Another silence. 'Maybe. But he did bring you home. I'm glad you're home.'

Rosamund blinked back ready tears. 'Me too, sweetheart.'

Edmund hesitated for a moment, then put an arm around her shoulders and squeezed hard. 'It's going to be all right, you know.'

Throat too tight to speak, Rosamund wrapped him into a hug instead. It was more difficult now that he was taller than her. When had that happened? *And when did it become his job to reassure me?* 'I'm proud of you, Ed.'

He made an uncomfortable noise but hugged her back. After a while he said, 'Should I go downstairs and make socially acceptable chitchat with our guests?'

She let go. 'Probably.'

After Edmund left, Rosamund lingered for a moment on the estate plan. She noted a couple of places where a careful, unfamiliar hand had made notes like "concealing trees" and "needs reinforcement". Turning to leave at last, she stepped on something that rustled and picked up a scrap piece of paper that read, "Ask Lady R. how many household guards in total".

Rosamund placed the paper scrap back on the table, picked a quill from the ink jar, and wrote the answer underneath. After another moment's consideration, she signed it "Lady R" with a flourish.

×

'Are you going to add a kiss to the parchment?' Caroline enquired.

'Not sure that's historically accurate,' said Rosamund, smiling. 'What would Henry say?'

×

Caroline took a deep breath and knocked on the door.

'Come in!'

The CEO's office was even nicer than she had supposed. In place of the four cheap desks her own office held, there was one very expensive desk. Real plants sat on the shelf by the window, and, as a concession to the unreasonable top-floor heat, there were several stylish fans humming away.

Caroline had heard that George was allergic to lilies, but she counted at least three of them in the room. *Are these here to ward off the CFO? Is he as disliked by the executives as he is by his subordinates?* One could only hope.

Eunice Wood looked surprised to see Caroline, but that was to be expected; it was July, and a full third of the company was on holiday before the late-summer rush started. The holidaymakers included Eunice's assistant Poppy, normally the CEO's fiercest gatekeeper against time-wasters. Something Caroline had been counting on.

'It's . . . Cara, isn't it? You fixed something at a board meeting a while ago?'

Caroline was surprised Eunice remembered that much. 'It's Caroline, Ms. Wood. I'm one of the DBAs.' Her hand was bunched into a fist, her knuckles white. Caroline forced herself to relax her fingers.

'My mistake, Caroline.' Eunice gestured to a seat in front of the desk—one far nicer than Caroline's office chair, naturally. Caroline edged forward and sat down. 'You can call me Eunice, though. What brings you to my office on this absurdly hot day?'

'I . . .' And just like that, Caroline's mouth went dry.

She'd had a whole speech prepared, and she'd waited twelve nail-biting days for a time when the CEO would be onsite and neither George nor Annabel would be in the office. Caroline opened and closed her mouth several times, willing the words to come, but nothing happened. *What if I'm . . . wrong?*

This was the thought that shook Caroline out of her daze. She *wasn't* wrong. She *wasn't* overreacting. She was quite good at her job, and she knew very well what was going on. She just didn't quite know where to start.

What would Rosamund do?

There it was. Start with the most important thing. 'Would you mind lending me your computer for a moment?'

Eunice blinked. 'Excuse me?'

Caroline gathered her courage. 'There's something you need to see.'

×

Leo and Robin's report to Queen Eudosia seemed to intrigue and concern her by turns. But when they reached the part of the tale where Rosamund had asked Leo to marry her, the queen laughed so hard that she had to be fetched a glass of wine. Leo felt that he was being made fun of to an unfair degree, but that wasn't something you could say to your monarch. He also wished he could put a stop to Robin's sniggering.

'She persuaded you to wed her?' Queen Eudosia repeated, dabbing her eyes with a handkerchief. 'I have clearly been underestimating her negotiation skills.'

Leo looked down at the floor. What could he say? That he'd married a virtual stranger and put himself in danger because she'd *asked him nicely*? The queen must think him a fool.

And then a new, unpleasant thought hit him: what if Her Majesty wanted him to continue working as a clandestine operative? How would Rosamund feel if he disappeared on dangerous missions after . . . after what had happened to Hugo? He hadn't thought it through. Rosamund had wanted him to marry her, so he had.

No wonder the queen had laughed. It wasn't like him at all. Leo had always been careful not to form any attachments due to the nature of his work, and the few women

233

who thought it worthwhile to seek his attention in recent years had received a cold reception. Her Majesty had even joked that he was by far the most prudent choice to escort Lady Rosamund to Abrenia, given the notoriously easy charm of some of the royal guard.

What had changed him so abruptly? Leo found he didn't know.

He was brought back to himself when Queen Eudosia cleared her throat, apparently taking pity on him. 'And then what happened?' she said. Her smile disappeared completely as Leo detailed the events surrounding the house fire and Baron Mabry's subsequent early arrival, and she addressed herself to Robin next. 'Tell me this gives us enough evidence to convict Mabry of a crime.'

Robin shook his head. 'Not quite, Your Majesty. But we're close.'

The queen huffed but nodded. 'True enough. You have supplied me with ample information to anticipate his next move, which, I must say, Captain Collins here has done some sterling work in heading off.'

Leo's face warmed, and the heat spread up to his ears when Eudosia turned a wicked grin his way.

'If we can unbalance the baron further, he may tip his hand. And if you'll kindly fetch me your wife, Collins, I know just how to do it.'

King Roland arrived that evening to general consternation. It was one thing, apparently, to expect the arrival of a foreign monarch, but quite another to actually see one. Rosamund hadn't been feeling too sanguine about it herself. Explaining the events of the past few days to her sister's husband would have been mortifying enough without him also being King of Abrenia. But Roland took the news that he was now related to a man he had arrested less than a week prior in stride. He was more concerned about the fire.

'I sincerely hope you've plugged the holes in your security, Lady Rosamund,' he said severely. 'The quantity of royal guards should keep us all safe in the meantime, but Baron Mabry will clearly stop at nothing to claim this estate. Be careful.'

So saying, he pulled a letter from Catherine from his pocket. She had apparently written it just after Rosamund fled Quayforth on horseback.

> *Hope you're safe, that the boys are looking after you, and that you are letting people look after you, Rosy. Come back soon (under less dire circumstances, if you'd be so kind).*
> *Cat*

Roland passed Rosamund a handkerchief and pretended to be very interested in a rather bewildered-looking caladrius that had just perched on the windowsill.

The remaining days before the Feast of Remembrance were a blur of constant motion, and Rosamund counted herself fortunate that the sheer amount of physical work required meant that she was too tired to remember her dreams, or possibly even to dream at all. She concluded that any dreams she'd had hadn't been nightmarish, at least; Ed and Charlotte would have woken her otherwise.

Baron Mabry had so far been contained in one of the guest wings, aside from the unfortunate necessity of feeding him multiple times a day, but Rosamund was still on edge. His snide digs, first about her widowed status, then regarding the vulnerability of her house and children, made her long to stab him in the throat—and the fact that this would be frowned upon only grated further on her nerves.

While Mabry himself remained content to stay within his chambers outside of mealtimes, there had been more than one occasion when one of the staff found a member of his guard wandering far from their assigned rooms. Luckily, despite retaining their suspicions of Leo, Edmund and Charlotte held no more fondness for Mabry than their mother and were very much on board with preventing problems for Uncle Robin.

When a lone soldier made it as far as the landing outside the Rose Room, Charlotte, who had assigned herself a post there, grabbed him by the hands and said, 'Have you come to show me the horses?' She promptly dragged him down the tower stairs to the stables, ignoring all his stammering denials. When Edmund spotted another of Mabry's men at the base of the stairs leading up to where the king and queen remained closeted with their advisers, the boy had loudly insisted the guard join him on the training ground to demonstrate his sword work.

On a third occasion, Rosamund herself had been descending the tower steps just as a pair of soldiers started their climb. A simple 'Are you lost?' was sufficient to send them scurrying away, but Rosamund narrowed her eyes at their backs and checked her sleeve for its hidden knife.

She reported these incidents to Leo and Robin the next time she was able to steal away. 'Mabry may consider himself above skulking in dark corners, but he has more than enough men to do it for him. We've been keeping a sharp eye on the royals, and on you.' Robin scoffed at the idea that Mabry would have any reason to snoop near the Rose Room, but Leo, at least, seemed comforted by her vigilance.

The rest of the invited guests arrived the day before the Feast of Remembrance. When Elinor Waverley arrived, she was escorted straight to Rosamund for an explanation of, in Elinor's words, 'Whatever idiot thing my husband has done now.' But when Rosamund gave her the gist of what had happened, Elinor just laughed, shook her head ruefully, and asked how she could help.

'Honestly, there's not much to do,' Rosamund said. 'Shall I take you upstairs? He's been doing a sterling job keeping Leo company, but I'm sure he'd rather stay with you tonight.'

Upon the women's entry, Robin seized the opportunity to greet his wife with a noisy and demonstrative kiss. Rosamund might have accused him of doing it on purpose just to provoke her embarrassment or envy (if so, it was working) had it not been for Elinor's reciprocal enthusiasm. It didn't help when Rosamund sneaked a sideways glance at Leo only to find him doing likewise. She looked away, her face hot. *Will we ever be so much at ease with each other?*

The feeling of uncertainty that thought produced was a sharp, unexpected pain. Rosamund hurried off as soon as was polite, citing work needing to be done downstairs.

The morning of the Feast of Remembrance dawned clear and dry. After a frantic few hours of last-minute preparations, Rosamund went to dress for the feast itself. Her black gown was drearily familiar at this point; she had been required to don it on the first day of every month since Hugo's death. But this was the last day of the official mourning period, and she fervently hoped never to have to wear the thing again.

For now, though, she still had to observe the forms. Rosamund focused on pinning pearls into her hair, then searched her wardrobe for a white scarf. The only thing she could find was the veil she had used for her wedding to Leo.

She wondered, just for a moment, if the pain in her chest would split her right down the centre. *Hugo's widow. Leo's wife.* But her heart kept beating, and the figure in the mirror merely looked appropriately solemn rather than about to tear apart at the seams.

She wrapped the lace around her neck, hugged her arms across her chest, and closed her eyes.

It was time.

Chapter 18

IT WAS ALMOST MIDDAY when Rosamund made her way downstairs, and she could hear the murmur and bustle of the multitude of guests well before she entered the Great Hall. The room was filled to the brim with the bright jewel tones of court dress: crimson and verdant green, sapphire blue and gold, but she saw all of it as though filtered through thick glass. The rich, heavy smell of roasted meat turned her stomach, and she drew shallow breaths through her mouth as she strode through the middle of the long tables, the crowd quieting as they took note of the lone, silent figure in black.

To her left she could see Robin and Elinor offering her sympathetic smiles and pointedly ignoring Lord Stanley's attempts to continue their conversation. Mabry, seated nearby in purple court dress, smirked obsequiously at Rosamund as she ascended the steps. She ignored him, focusing on the high table. Six places were set, and four of them filled: Eudosia in royal blue and Roland in burgundy, Edmund and Charlotte between them in green and black, all four faces identically solemn. Two seats at the centre of the table stood empty: one for the deceased, the other waiting for her. But she couldn't sit down yet.

Complete silence fell as Rosamund bowed and curtseyed in turn to the seated monarchs, then took her place in front of the high table, opened her book, and began the recitation.

Baron Mabry fell away. The royals fell away. The hall disappeared. Her children, close at hand, registered only dimly. All that mattered were the words. The last thing she would do for Hugo would be perfect.

'Though we perish to darkness and decay,' she intoned, 'we will rise to Light that makes the sun itself seem a mere candle. Let us remember Sir Hugo Hawkhurst, who a year ago today walked into that Light.' Her voice was steady as a rock, though she heard it only vaguely, as though she stood some way apart from herself.

'We remember,' the crowd responded.

'Though the Wisdoms give us life, our days are surely numbered. Deliver us from darkness, that we may rise to Light.'

'Deliver us.'

She heard Charlotte sniffing behind her and almost stumbled over, 'Comfort in our sorrow those of us who remain,' but she made it through to conclude, 'that we may meet the days to come with thankfulness and joy.'

'Comfort us,' came the response.

'Guide us in all wisdom and truth.'

'Guide us.'

'In hope, and Light, and love, we remember Sir Hugo Hawkhurst.'

'We remember,' the hall intoned, and Rosamund blinked. It was done. She closed the book, trying not to notice how her hands shook, bowed and curtseyed again, and took her seat, raising her goblet to signal the start of the feast. The gathered nobility began to chatter again immediately; she was grateful for the hubbub as she choked down a sob, reaching to serve herself food she couldn't stomach eating.

Queen Eudosia, seated to the left of Charlotte, leaned over as Rosamund arranged her napkin in her lap. 'Thank you for your hospitality, Lady Rosamund. I am conscious that it must have been an extra difficulty at a trying time.'

'You are always welcome, Your Majesty.' Rosamund glanced up, trying to show proper respect, but the sympathy on the queen's face proved too much to bear. Thankfully, Eudosia did not appear to take offence. She turned to address Charlotte on the subject of an ailment besetting one of the royal horses, and Rosamund's youngest was only too happy to converse.

After a short time, Queen Eudosia leaned slightly over Charlotte's head to address Rosamund again. 'I am pleased to inform you, Lady Rosamund, that the peace treaty is being finalised as we speak. We should be able to sign it by the end of the day.'

Rosamund's heart leapt. 'Indeed!'

The queen nodded, a satisfied smile playing across her face. 'King Roland and I will both dispatch messengers to relay the news of it throughout Abrenia and Bevoria on the morrow. Of course, the details regarding rights around the river took a great deal of finessing, but Bevoria has agreed to cede land on the north side of the Grenalla in exchange for certain other concessions in matters of trade.'

For a moment Rosamund couldn't speak. 'It . . . I . . . fast work, Your Majesties.'

✕

'Remarkable what can be accomplished when third parties aren't interfering,' Caroline offered.

Rosamund just barely refrained from rolling her eyes. 'Isn't it.'

✕

King Roland, seated to Edmund's right, had smiled at Rosamund when she sat down, though he said little during the meal itself. But perhaps, she thought to herself, it was just that the Page sisters tended towards the silent types. At least Edmund managed to engage the king in a discussion on falconry during the main course.

When the last of the dishes had been cleared away, Queen Eudosia rose and requested the honour of reading the inheritance lines. 'Of course, Your Majesty,' Rosamund murmured. She clapped her hands for the papers to be brought forth.

Hugo's last will and testament was mercifully short and to the point. The queen read swiftly through the details of the lesser bequests to Charlotte and Rosamund. While nothing in them came as a surprise, Eudosia still paused for a moment when the clause bequeathing Hugo's favoured brood mare to Charlotte elicited a dry sob. Rosamund reached over to squeeze her daughter's hand, noting the softness on Eudosia's face as she dabbed gently at Charlotte's welling tears.

The queen had just begun to read the bequest to Edmund when a familiar and unwelcome voice interrupted. 'A point of law, Your Majesty.'

'Here we go,' Rosamund mumbled under her breath.

✕

The annual company picnic was not an occasion Caroline typically anticipated with joy. For a start, she was a pale, freckly redhead, so a sunny day spent outdoors required the kind of outfit that made her look like a Coco Chanel knockoff, complete with a large hat, prescription sunglasses, long sleeves, and long trousers. Second, she was deeply suspicious of the concept of "team bonding". Not that she didn't *like* her colleagues, generally speaking, but enforced jollity always seemed a bit much.

Then again, it meant she got paid to get some fresh air and eat picnic food for three hours on a Friday afternoon, so she wasn't complaining. And it wasn't as if she could refuse the CEO when Eunice specially requested her attendance.

As the sandwiches and salads were cleared away, Ms. Wood stood and clapped her hands for silence. 'I won't keep you from the food for more than a minute,' she began, and everyone laughed politely, though Caroline knew they doubted it. 'But there's a little housekeeping to take care of. I'm delighted to announce that Caroline Lindley, who I'm sure many of you know, has agreed to take charge of Cyber Threat Detection. Stand up, Caroline!'

Caroline did, suddenly thankful for the inscrutability of her sunglasses. Several people clapped half-heartedly, but while Caroline's head was turned towards Eunice, her eyes slid off towards George, who looked thunderstruck.

'So,' Eunice continued, favouring the crowd with a toothy smile, 'if any of you have been downloading things you shouldn't at work, you'll be answering to her!'

That statement produced a full-body flinch from the CFO. Annabel laid a hand on his arm and whispered urgently into his ear as he made to stand. Caroline, still pretending not to be watching them, resisted the urge to turn and glare.

'Now then, let's get on to the important stuff: dessert! Tuck in, everyone, thank you all again for coming, and enjoy the rest of your day,' Eunice concluded. Caroline sat back down to the sound of slightly more enthusiastic clapping as people returned to their food. Then she watched from beneath the brim of her hat as Eunice glided between picnicking employees to stop by George's chair, where she leaned down and murmured something.

Caroline helped herself to a slice of strawberry tart and tried unsuccessfully to smother her grin.

×

Baron Mabry rose from his seat. 'Lady Hawkhurst's marriage contract stipulates that she retains her Abrenian citizenship. Thus, upon the cessation of the Period of Remembrance, she is returned to her status as a foreigner who is ineligible to administer the estate until her son's majority.'

'Excuse me —' Rosamund began, moderately politely.

Mabry ignored her. 'Is that not so, Your Majesty?'

Queen Eudosia's face was thoughtful. 'That would be the strict interpretation of the law, yes,' she said slowly. 'But it would be hard-hearted indeed to throw Sir Hugo's widow out of her home on the anniversary of her husband's death. Particularly given her service to the Crown in the matter of the peace treaty.'

'Of course, Your Majesty,' replied the baron through obviously gritted teeth. Then he rallied. 'Mercifully, there is an alternative.'

'That being?'

'Marriage to an eligible Bevorian citizen, Your Majesty. It may perhaps be unprecedented,' he conceded smoothly, 'but given the appropriate oversight and swift, ah, execution, I am certain the Crown would not have an issue?'

There were a few murmurs of agreement, Lord Stanley's among them. Elinor, at his elbow, stared straight at Rosamund, her dark eyes fierce. Robin looked like he was trying very hard not to laugh.

'A novel solution, Baron,' Eudosia responded pleasantly. 'Have you some suggestion as to who Lady Rosamund's new husband should be?'

'*Me, obviously,*' Rosamund muttered nasally under her breath, even as the baron offered his florid answer in kind. Charlotte looked up at her sharply. Rosamund shook her head slightly to reassure her daughter. *Wait.*

'And why, Weston, should it be you in particular?' Queen Eudosia enquired, with the air of one who has seen a very obvious loophole. 'The country—indeed, this very room—is full of eligible Bevorian men.'

'As her feudal liege, I have the responsibility of ensuring her safety. Particularly since I was not able to do the same for her dear departed lord.' Rosamund nearly leapt out of her chair, but a sixth sense pulled her gaze to Eudosia, who subtly motioned for her to remain calm. 'And since the death of my own dear wife some years ago . . .' At this, Rosamund's brain short-circuited completely. *Your own dear wife? The one you loathed so much you lived in separate buildings? The one who died tragically under mysterious circumstances? That wife?*

Reeling from the gall of his lies, it took her a moment to start listening again, and then she wished she hadn't. '—Who would not be taken with the lady's fiery nature, her dislike of smoke and mirrors, and her care for her children . . .'

He's threatening me. In front of an audience of her peers. And the queen, *and* King Roland. In her own house. *On the anniversary of Hugo's murder.*

She was going to kill him.

Rosamund gripped the hilt of her knife tightly under her skirt, her breath quickening. Charlotte was tugging her sleeve and whispering, and Rosamund distantly noted that Ed had come to stand on the other side of her. But a red mist was descending, rage rising up in her chest until she thought she might choke on it.

Over Charlotte's head, Eudosia lifted a thoughtful, calculating brow, and then winked.

The shock of it rooted Rosamund to the spot for just long enough. *No. I can't come apart, not now.*

She let out a long, slow breath, and when her vision cleared, she saw Charlotte peering up worriedly at her, and she felt Ed's large, firm hand on her shoulder.

Tears clouded her eyes. She let the knife slide back into its sheath.

I can do this. We can do this.

Finally, Mabry stopped talking. Elinor's eyes were still locked on Rosamund. Robin had disappeared.

Rosamund took to her feet. Her hands no longer shook, and her voice was clear and firm. 'As generous as your offer is, my lord' — and here she bared her teeth in what could charitably be called a smile — 'I fear my new husband would be disinclined to share.'

General consternation ensued. The official period in which remarriage was discouraged had passed months ago, but it was well known that Lady Hawkhurst had shunned both the hospitality of court and several offers of marriage. *Who is this new husband?* The murmur raced through the room. *And where is he?*

Right on cue, the doors of the Great Hall opened. Rosamund almost missed the entirely too pleased expression on the queen's face as Leo strode in, impeccably groomed and attired in court dress of a deep midnight blue with a sash of Hawkhurst green.

The sight of him coming to her defense and the overwhelming sense of triumph as Weston Mabry sputtered impotently flooded Rosamund with warmth. It was, she admitted, a better feeling than her recent contemplations of murder. If she indulged herself a little by fluttering her eyelashes down the hall at her new husband, that was really no one's business but her own. 'Good evening, my lord.'

Wisdoms, if that wasn't the broadest smile she'd ever seen him wear.

The chatter dramatically intensified. Leo marched down the hall, ignoring numerous pointed remarks until Queen Eudosia was forced to call for silence. Elinor caught Rosamund's eye once more and beamed. Rosamund couldn't help grinning back.

Edmund stepped back from her and returned to his seat as Leo took his place at Rosamund's side. Somehow, it didn't bother her that the chair he would occupy was the one traditionally left vacant for the deceased.

Hugo's widow. Leo's wife. Somehow, she felt Hugo wouldn't mind too much.

'My lord — *who*?' Mabry was practically apoplectic; Rosamund revelled in it. Lord Stanley was tugging frantically at his cloak, but Mabry ignored him. 'I've never met this man! He's not a Bevorian knight; surely he can't — oh, what *is* it, Stanley?'

'I believe Lord Stanley may have met *Viscount* Collins before,' Rosamund suggested, idly wondering if this might lead both noblemen to drop dead on the spot. One could only hope.

'Indeed!' Queen Eudosia broke in. 'Lord Stanley must have been introduced to him while you were travelling to Abrenia.'

The lord in question sat down, hard, and appeared to preoccupy himself with fighting off a fit. Mabry remained standing, though Rosamund was unsure whether fear or rage prompted the pallor on his face.

The queen now took the opportunity to explain to the assembly how formerly-Captain Collins and his new wife Lady Rosamund had been rewarded with a viscountcy for their aid in brokering peace. The gathering again broke into hissing whispers, and Rosamund felt Roland's eyes on them. When she looked his way—was that a wink?

Out of the corner of her eye she could see Edmund's ill-concealed expression of triumph, and Charlotte wasn't even bothering to hide her delight. Robin, having returned to his place as mysteriously as he left it, preened like a cat. Leo took Rosamund's hand, and she allowed herself a smile that was only slightly vicious as she turned to face Mabry.

The baron, for once, was at a loss for words. He had gone from red to white to a nasty greenish colour in a matter of minutes, and the sight gave Rosamund no little satisfaction. 'So you see, my lord,' she concluded, still smiling, 'I am well taken care of, but I do so appreciate your efforts to keep us on the right side of the law.'

It wasn't even a lie. If he hadn't stood up and made such a fool of himself, she'd have been robbed of the joy of slapping him down in public.

And she was sure Hugo would have appreciated it.

> **HBWalker:** I see you decided on a little audience-inferior storytelling here?
>
> ----
>
> **CSLindley:** Well, I did write a scene where Leo and Rosamund found out about their elevation, but I didn't feel like it had the same dramatic satisfaction.

✕

Five minutes after she'd written the comment, Caroline's phone buzzed in her pocket.

> **Henry**
> How did Leo take his sudden ascent to the aristocracy?

She beamed.

> **Caroline**
> Poorly, as it happens. Would you like to see?

> **Henry**
> Always.

> **Caroline**
> Tough :P

> **Henry**
> Tease :P

Caroline, still high on adrenaline in the wake of the picnic, wrote:

> **Caroline**
> you love me really ;)

And sent it before she could change her mind.

✕

'Well, since Viscountess Hawkhurst Collins has already taken the baron's excellent advice to marry a Bevorian citizen — and a viscount, no less,' said the queen, her expression serene, 'that takes care of that particular point.' She scanned the crowd once more, but the warmth in her tone did not reach her eyes. 'Would anyone else like to raise an objection?'

Absolute silence reigned. The queen's manner defrosted slightly, and the room filled with a collective sigh of relief.

The feast drew to a close without further incident. Afterwards, Rosamund took her place by the doors of the Great Hall to bid a formal farewell to each and every guest — every guest, that is, except for Weston Mabry. The baron had disappeared from the hall without fanfare during the cheese course; when Rosamund asked Eudosia about it, she merely smiled.

Leo assumed his post just behind Rosamund, a solid and reassuring presence, politely nodding to each of the guests but letting her do the talking. Upon later reflection, Rosamund was quite certain that his attendance upon her had prevented several incidents; a few of her more difficult neighbours found their words drying up in their throats when faced with his flat, appraising stare. 'Goodnight, Your Ladyship,' they said instead, and, 'A beautiful recitation, my lady.' Rosamund bowed acknowledgement, and, at length, the hall was almost empty.

'Goodbye, Rosy,' said Roland, pulling her into a hug. 'I won't be staying. We can get back into Abrenia tonight if we depart as soon as we're ready, and I think that would be wisest. But I'll make sure to tell Cat all about what happened. You're certain to receive an extremely impractical wedding gift very soon.' He lowered his voice. 'And do please throw your wedding ball post haste. She's desperate to visit.'

✕

'It's not going to be a masquerade,' Rosamund said out of the corner of her mouth. Caroline pouted.

'Spoilsport.'

×

Leo, to whom the words "wedding ball" came as something of a shock, bowed to—

To his new brother-in-law.

While he'd been assured that King Roland was willing to forget the incident at the masquerade ball (not to mention the two royal horses recovered at Oakbridge—a detail Leo hoped would never get back to his wife), it was still deeply strange to think of royalty as family.

As if being married to Rosamund wasn't strange enough.

As if being—*viscounted*—wasn't strange enough.

But he studied the relief on his wife's face as she waved King Roland off, and he decided that maybe this aristocracy business wasn't so bad. Even if Queen Eudosia did smirk at him on her way out. She would stay for another night at least while the viscountcy paperwork was finalised, and Leo wasn't going to object to extra friendly guards in the house.

As the staff began clearing plates, he took his leave of Rosamund and went to find a room with a desk where he could look out over the inner ward. He had occupied a quarter of an hour writing notes on the aristocrats he had just met (and their reactions to Rosamund's sudden ascendancy) when Edmund and Charlotte appeared on either side of him. He tried not to jump and quickly folded his notes out of sight. He must be slipping.

'Good evening, Viscount Collins,' said Charlotte.

'Can I . . . help you?'

'You were a soldier,' said Edmund, and Leo turned to look at him.

'You know how to fight,' said Charlotte, and his head swivelled back around.

'You could teach us,' Edmund finished.

Is this deliberate? If so, it was working. Leo swallowed and tried not to grip the arm of his chair too tightly. *Couldn't one high-stakes encounter have been enough for today?* He *could* teach them, but what would their mother say? Leo closed his eyes for a moment before directing his response straight ahead instead of at one child or the other: 'Don't you have a regular instructor?'

Edmund shrugged. 'Father taught us. And Mother. Uncle Robin when he's here. Martin, sometimes. School. But I'd like to know what you can teach us.'

'Why?'

'There are three Mabry children at school, which means we have to spend six months of the year with them. And Charlotte is in the same year as the youngest boy, and he's a nasty little sh—' Edmund cut himself off.

Leo grinned. 'Since I was, as you pointed out, a soldier, I can cope with a little undiplomatic language.'

'Will you *please* teach us to fight?' said Charlotte, and she lowered her voice conspiratorially. 'You know. The *useful* stuff.'

Did he really have a choice? '. . . Yes.'

Charlotte cheered and hugged him. Edmund just nodded. 'We appreciate it, Leo. Thanks.' They hurried off together, leaving him to uncrumple the single page he still held in his fist.

Well. That was a start. Now he just had to sort out what to tell Rosamund, and when.

One crisis at a time.

Not all of the guests left at the same time as King Roland and his retinue, but enough of them did that the house seemed almost tolerably uncrowded. After a few hours of desperately needed idleness and a light repast taken in her regular quarters, Rosamund went to say goodnight to Edmund and Charlotte, who still shared a room, much to Edmund's chagrin—one now warded by two of Eudosia's guard, no less—and would until everyone had departed.

'Will you stay for a while?' Charlotte said sleepily.

Rosamund sank into the chair between their beds, unwinding the white veil from around her neck and letting it drape down her front. 'I was so proud of you both today, you know. And your father would have been proud of you too.'

They settled into a comfortable silence.

'I'm glad you got that awful man off your back,' Edmund said eventually.

'Yes. We have Captain—excuse me, *Viscount* Collins to thank for that.'

'Leo's not so bad.' Charlotte mumbled, turning onto her back. 'He made Baron Mabry look like a complete—'

'Charlotte—' Rosamund began.

'—fool, Mum.' Charlotte's face was all wide-eyed innocence. 'What did you think I was going to say?'

Rosamund raised an eyebrow, but she poked her daughter's shoulder playfully. 'Never mind. It's been a long day. Lock the door behind me, and go to sleep.'

✕

'Where are you going?' Caroline asked as Rosamund descended the stairs.

'The chapel.'

'Why?'

'To count my blessings.'

Chapter 19

THE CHAPEL WAS DARK when Rosamund slipped through the door. She navigated between the rows of benches to the dais on the far side more by memory than by the light of her candle, and it was the work of a moment to light the half-dozen wicks on the high table's candelabra and wash the limestone walls and forest-hued tapestries with gold.

She stepped back, blew out her taper, and knelt on a pad set a little back from the dais, closing her eyes. She would have to return to the house soon. To the Rose Room. To her new husband.

It would be fine. He was . . . she opened her eyes, frowning. *Nice.* He was a good man. Trustworthy. Dependable. Handsome, too, which didn't hurt.

She just needed to be alone. To be Hugo's widow for a few minutes more. Then she'd dry her eyes and face her future.

×

Caroline sat down beside her.

'I know it's not over yet,' Rosamund murmured (to whom, Caroline wasn't sure), 'but thank you.'

'Um. Rosamund?'

Rosamund looked over, her expression distantly polite, her face pale. 'Good evening, Caroline. Did you need something?'

'It's been a very emotional day for you,' Caroline began, feeling her way through. 'You don't have to do anything you don't want to.' She moved over to put her hand on her heroine's shoulder. 'You're allowed to need more time, Rosy.'

'I don't need time.'

Caroline was reminded that while her characters couldn't deliberately deceive her, that didn't seem to count for much when they were lying to themselves.

She tried again. 'You're allowed to need things in general—'

'I've done nothing but *need*!' Rosamund snapped, pulling out of Caroline's grasp and beginning to tick things off on her fingers. 'Need the inheritance settled and Baron Mabry dealt with. Need help in a fight. Need pulled out of a river. Need my hair brushed, need to be held like a frightened child after a nightmare, need to—' She stopped and gulped, before adding more softly, 'Need to beg forgiveness.' She sniffed and continued more energetically, 'Need to get married. Need to be carried up the stairs after I knock myself senseless. Need a dramatic entrance from my new husband at my murdered husband's remembrance feast . . . !' Rosamund turned around, leaning back on the dais steps. 'I've done nothing but need things,' she repeated. 'And *I'm* the one who asked Leo to marry *me*.' She looked down at her as-yet-uncounted tenth finger. 'I made a vow, and I will keep it. I merely require a moment to . . . collect myself, that's all.' She was starting to tremble.

'But—'

'Leave me alone, Caroline.'

×

Leo was examining one of the accounting ledgers he'd found in the bookcase of the Rose Room's solar when the sound of someone whistling filtered through the door.

The someone knocked.

'Come in?' Leo ventured, and Robin poked his head around the door, frowning.

'It's ten of the clock—do you know where your wife is?' Robin demanded.

Leo shrugged.

Robin threw the door open, marched over to the table where Leo sat, and glowered down at him. Leo looked up for a moment, but Robin said nothing further, so Leo returned to the ledger. A second later, the ledger was slammed shut, and Robin's face was a handsbreadth from Leo's. 'Why don't you know where she is?'

Leo scowled, pulling his fingers out of the book where Robin had trapped them. 'Why would I know where she is?'

'Because you won!' said Robin, exasperated. 'The pair of you—with a little help, of course,' he added, without a trace of modesty, 'have made it very difficult for Baron Mabry to move against you without starting an open revolt. You *won.* You should be turning cartwheels!'

'We won,' Leo pointed out, trying to keep his voice even, 'on the anniversary of her husband's *murder.* If she wants to be alone, I'm not going to bother her.'

'Right attitude, wrong conclusion, my young friend,' Robin replied, throwing himself into the adjacent chair and clamping an arm around Leo's shoulder. 'Have I ever shared my Three Rules of Marriage with you?'

'No.'

Robin tutted. 'Clearly I'm slipping. Now, pay attention. Rule One: work out if there is a problem. If there isn't, everything is fabulous, sunshine and roses, gambolling lambs and frolicking puppies and all that sort of thing.'

Leo snorted.

'If there is a problem, we move on to Rule Two: work out what the problem is.' Robin wagged the index finger of his free hand at Leo. 'Important to find out what needs fixing before starting to fix it. Then we move to Rule Three: determine if the problem can be fixed, and if so, how. So: what's the problem, and can you fix it?'

Leo shrugged Robin's arm off his shoulder. 'Why do you think there's a problem?'

Robin rolled his eyes. 'Because you're looking at accounting ledgers and arguing with me instead of being with your wife.'

'You could leave.'

Robin gave him a look that was half sympathy, half pity.

'The problem,' Leo snapped, goaded, 'is that she's sad that her husband was murdered. I can't bring Hugo back; therefore, the problem is not solvable. Stop meddling and leave her alone.'

Robin sighed. 'If she wants to be on her own—and, granted, she might, she's an odd duck—then you should give her the opportunity to say so. If she doesn't want to be alone, she'll have wandered off and isolated herself anyway because she doesn't want to bother anyone. Honestly, you're as bad as each other.'

'I assumed she'd be staying with the children.'

'Why? You don't have to share with me anymore. Ellie's room is perfectly nice; I just came up to collect a few things I'd forgotten. I no longer need to keep tactfully out of sight, so you can bet I'm not going to pass up a night with my wife.' He poked Leo's shoulder. 'Rosamund should be here'—*poke*—'with you'—*poke*—'but she's not. Aren't you even slightly concerned?'

Leo grabbed Robin's hand before he could prod him again. 'Stop that.'

'Make me.'

Leo rolled his eyes. It was clear he would get no peace until Robin left. And Robin, he knew from experience, wouldn't leave until he'd got what he wanted. 'Where do you think she is?'

'No idea,' Robin replied, apparently content that this part of it was not his problem. 'But she won't have gone far.'

×

Her Friday triumph notwithstanding, Caroline didn't sleep at all well that weekend; instead, she worried that George would somehow wriggle out of trouble while in the meantime her new managerial role would land her in more of the same. Even the celebratory phone call from her mother hadn't done much to cheer her up.

'Congratulations on your promotion!'

'Thanks, Mum.'

'Are you sickening for something? You don't sound well. Is everything all right?'

There was a moment where Caroline almost said *I'm fine* and carried on.

'You know you can always talk to me, Carrie.'

For a long moment she couldn't speak at all, then everything came tumbling out. Caroline's mother, whom she had often seen panicking under the most minor of circumstances, listened without interruption while Caroline poured out her woes regarding George, work, her book, George, and (albeit obliquely) Henry. Her mother's initial advice, when Caroline finally ran out of steam, was well-meaning but typically unhelpful.

'Well, you'll just have to wait and see what happens with George.'

'Yes, Mum, I am aware,' Caroline said dryly.

'I wouldn't worry too much about it, though. They gave you that new job, didn't they? And that lady in charge seems to like you. Emma? Alice?'

'Eunice.'

'And Henry sounds like he has his head screwed on,' her mother continued, but (most unusually) refused to opine further than, 'Just make sure he's the sort of man who's not too good to do the dishes.'

This feedback duly received, Caroline said goodnight and did her best to snatch a few hours' unconsciousness before stumbling zombie-like into work on Monday morning. Still, when she sat down in her George-free office, she did finally feel that she had room to breathe. And think. And work.

This feeling was short-lived, however. Caroline had acquired a team now: actual people who had to work with her, but even though she knew them all, she'd never really collaborated with any of them and hadn't talked to most of them in months. And her previous experiences with management hadn't exactly left her with a positive example to follow.

How To Be a Manager for Absolute Beginners hadn't been a lot of help, either. It did advise her to call a meeting with all three people in her department, which she duly did. But she was only met with the noncommittal diplomacy of people wondering if they were meeting the new boss, same as the old boss.

Her lingering anxiety over George refused to dissipate, and the catastrophising part of her brain felt fully justified when the auditors turned up on Wednesday, determined to uncover financial shenanigans. Office gossip claimed that Annabel had resigned rather than deal with them, and Caroline could understand why. Caroline's first run-in with them was sympathetic, which unnerved her, but she provided names, dates, times, facts—everything she could, to the best of her ability, and hoped that would be the end of it. But the second meeting was a grilling she hadn't experienced since school debate club. They spent over an hour making her sweat before the woman in the severe black suit concluded, 'We'll be following all of this up with your current and former colleagues, of course. Please don't talk to any of them about it in the meantime.'

Getting thrown straight back into a terrible situation over which she still had no control and being reliant on people whose goodwill she had no reason to trust was not her most relaxing experience ever. Caroline called her mother again that night.

'You used to get on well with your work friends, Carrie. What changed?'

'I don't know any of them!'

'You met that nice boy Ali when you were on that training course last year.'

'Yes! For two days!'

'And Pippa came to your birthday party two years ago. She brought you a lovely plant. We had a nice chat about how to grow lavender.'

Caroline stared at her phone. 'I didn't even remember that. How do you remember these things?'

'And I don't think I've met your other friend, was it Christian?'

'Christos.'

'But he gave you a lift home once, didn't he, when you missed the bus because of George?'

Confronted with this litany of well-wishing acquaintances-turned-subordinates, Caroline could only stammer out, '. . . Yes?'

'Well then,' her mother concluded, 'I don't think you have much to worry about. Do try and get an early night, dear, and look out for a parcel in the next couple of days. I found another one of those stripy shirts you like so much.'

Caroline, who now owned eight different striped work shirts and had given up arguing about it, just said, 'Thanks, Mum,' and then tried to take her advice.

Sleep came very slowly indeed that night—but now it was because her mind, comforted by the thought that she probably had at least a few people in her corner, had gone back to Rosamund. And by the morning, Caroline had worked out exactly what it was that her heroine needed. Rosamund wasn't going to like it. But it would all work out in the end.

✕

Rosamund dried her face on the sleeve of her black mourning dress, but her eyes still hurt. The gardens, scorched earth notwithstanding, would be green and cool after sundown; perhaps a stroll through them would aid her recovery. She made her way down one of the carefully laid-out paths towards the main house, her slippered feet crunching a little on the gravel. As she passed under the bower marking the entrance to the ornamental portion, she thought she saw someone ahead of her, his back towards her, just by the maze with its chest-high bushes. 'Leo?'

No, not someone—*two* someones. One carefully creeping up behind the other, using the hedge for cover.

'Leo, look out!' she screamed and started to run. *This can't be happening. Not again. Not now!*

Leo turned just as the stalker sprang. A blade flashed in the moonlight, and then they were both on the ground, scrambling for leverage, Leo underneath.

Rosamund was still running, but now there was a knife in her hand. 'Get away from him!'

✕

'How many knives do you routinely carry on your person?' said Caroline, incredulous.

'Clearly not enough!' Rosamund panted, and kept running.

×

Rosamund lunged, driving her knife into the attacker's side, and he screamed. It was a high, tearing sound, and she flinched even as he twisted towards her, off-balance, dagger in hand, and slashed at her. Fire streaked across her hip and stomach, and she screamed too, falling backwards onto the grass.

Through a haze of pain she saw Leo throw the man off. The cloaked figure cried out again as he hit the ground, struggling to get up but collapsing when the weight of Leo's knee hit his back. 'Guards!' he bellowed.

Rosamund braced herself and tried to scramble upright too. She had just made it to a sitting position when she saw the man's face, and the shock knocked the breath from her all over again. The second bandit from the road. *The one that got away.*

By now Hawkhurst guards on the wall had piled into the gardens, but ultimately it was the Queen's Guard who took the would-be assassin into custody. Rosamund lost sight of Leo as he was swarmed with questioners. There was a lot of shouting. So much shouting. The man on the ground was screaming about Baron Mabry, about the queen, about fire and birds and cheeseboards and . . . Rosamund tried to keep track. It wasn't working terribly well. She decided that she needed to take charge, but all that came out of her mouth was, 'Ow . . .'

That wasn't what she'd meant to say.

She closed her eyes and heard rapid footsteps over gravel and grass, followed by Leo's voice. 'Are you all right, my lady?'

That's not important. Why did he think that was important? Rosamund opened her eyes again, trying to focus past the pain. 'He might not have been alone,' she ground out. 'Please go and check on the children!'

Leo frowned, hesitating, but after a heartbeat he called for a guardsman to accompany him, and they ran off in the direction of the house.

Rosamund winced, set her palms flat on the ground to steady herself, and tried to clear her vision enough to make sense of her surroundings. The assailant, still howling, was being hauled upright by two more guards, and Martin, now outside in his nightshirt, was directing them to the prison tower. It hadn't been used for its intended purpose for two years at least, but it would still be secure.

Everything hurt. Her formal clothing had proved surprisingly slash-resistant, as evidenced by all her organs remaining inside her body, but as the initial shock receded, the pain came in waves that made her want to be sick.

She had to get up. Rosamund drew a ragged breath, pushed herself onto her knees—and bit back a scream. This caught the attention of two Hawkhurst guards, who ran over to her.

'My lady! Can we assist you?'

She took a deep breath and prayed she wouln't faint. 'Take me to my children. At once.'

Together they made their way into the house. Lamps were being lit everywhere; guests were coming out of their rooms and staring; the building was filled with noise. Rosamund ignored all of it, hands on her stomach, and concentrated on the stairs, a guard at each elbow. *One stair at a time. Just one at a time.* She could do this.

They gained the landing to the family quarters right as Leo stepped through the door from the children's room. He blanched. 'My lady! Are you all right?'

'Mother?' came Edmund's voice from behind him. 'What happened?'

Leo looked sharply at her, then pulled the door the rest of the way shut. Rosamund rallied with an effort. 'I'm fine, sweetheart. I got cut—the perils of knife fighting—but I'll be fine. As you can hear'—she tried to keep the strain from her voice—'I am walking, talking, and climbing stairs. Look after your sister, please. I'll see you in the morning.'

'Lottie's asleep, and no one is coming in here,' Edmund promised, and Rosamund heard him throw the bolt. She nodded, though he couldn't see her through the door.

'Good boy.'

Abruptly reminded that she hadn't been the only one in the fight, she turned to Leo, who hovered anxiously at her side.

'I'm sorry, Capt—my lord, are you all right?' She was starting to shiver. That wasn't helpful. She felt the guards' grip on her arms tighten.

'Yes, my lady, thanks to you.' His eyes raked up and down her, panic bubbling under the surface of his expression. Rosamund was suddenly acutely conscious of how she must look. They stared at each other a moment longer, and then, very carefully, Leo said, 'Would you like some help?'

The response was automatic. 'I . . .' *I'm fine.*

Maybe, she thought, shivering and bleeding outside her children's room in the dark of the night, *I am not, in fact, fine.* 'Yes, please.'

Leo took charge. 'Sit down,' he said, guiding her to a chair. Then he addressed the guards. 'Stand watch over Lady Rosamund and the children until I return with medical supplies.' And he set off at a run.

> **HBWalker:** Good to see Rosamund getting into the habit of letting people help her.
>
> ---
>
> **CSLindley:** Character growth!

Chapter 20

THE FIRST THING LEO DID when he returned from the kitchen with the medicine bag was hand Rosamund a small, curiously shaped grey stone. She focused on it with an effort, then sighed. 'A bezoar? Really?'

'Yes.'

She put the stone in her mouth, shifting it into her cheek and looking up at him. 'You think the knife might have been poisoned?'

'Maybe.' He handed her a cloth to press against her wound.

She winced as she did so. 'At least the blood is slowing down.'

Pleased to note that his hands were only shaking a little, Leo held out the painkilling draught he had mixed. Rosamund removed the stone from her mouth, took the mug, and gulped down the draught in three swallows, grimacing.

'Thank you.'

Leo nodded and offered her his arm. Rosamund took it, stifling a groan as she eased back onto her feet. Leo directed one of the guards to remain behind outside the children's door, and he and Rosamund began to make their way to the Rose Room, the other guard preceding them.

'That was good thinking, with the bezoar,' Rosamund said slowly when they were halfway up the tower steps. 'Did you bring one for yourself?'

There had only been a single stone in the drawer that a hand Leo recognised as Rosamund's had labelled *Bezoar: poison antidote.* 'No.'

'Hm.' Rosamund considered him for a long moment before tucking the compress under her arm, then pulling the stone out of her pocket with her freed hand and waving it at him. 'Here you go.' Leo hesitated, and she frowned. 'Honestly, rinse it in water if you're that fastidious, but please, take it.'

'I—'

'Please? You might have been scratched by that knife.'

He *had* been scratched, and his left arm was bleeding, so he supposed she was right. *But I was lucky.* Rosamund had shouted a warning in time. He was alive and, admittedly, rather hoping to remain so. Leo took the bezoar and slipped it into his cheek.

Rosamund hummed with satisfaction, then frowned. 'I think I should have asked if you'd been hurt before ordering you to run around earlier. I'm sorry.'

She was slurring her words a little. Leo realised that he normally mixed painkillers for large men, not small women. He might have overdone it a bit. 'You didn't order, you asked. And I'm fine.' Mostly, anyway.

'I can't actually order you around any more, you know,' she told him as they reached the landing, her tone confidential, 'because you're a viscount. Even if I'm a viscountess, by Bevorian law, you outrank me.'

'I'll bear that in mind.' While the guard assumed a position at the top of the stairs, Leo opened the door for her, and Rosamund stumbled through. Even though the fire still burned in the grate, he could see goosebumps on her forearms. *She's shivering. Not good.*

No unwanted guests lurked under the bed or behind the curtains. Leo locked the door to the solar, grabbed the kettle, and joined his wife in the bedchamber, locking that door behind him for good measure. He took up a light to put by the bed as Rosamund clumsily started to pull off her previously white scarf.

Her wedding veil.

He wasn't going to think about it.

'That veil made a lovely scarf,' Rosamund muttered, oblivious, as she dropped the white lace on the ground. 'And now it's all torn and . . .' She blinked, searching for the word. 'Bloodstained.'

Leo rolled his eyes, comforted that she was still coherent enough to mourn her wardrobe, and set the bezoar on the dresser, grimacing a little at the aftertaste. 'We'll get you a new one, my lady.' He started to unpack the satchel of medicines, wondering why it contained so many things that were entirely useless to him right now.

Rosamund started to unlace the bodice of her mourning dress, frowning in concentration. Once she had worked it loose enough, she pushed the garment off her shoulders, and there was a muffled *clank* as the various knives concealed in it hit the ground. But Leo didn't notice this so much as the amount of blood on her underdress, and he fought down another spike of panic as he busied himself with fetching old blankets from the wardrobe to stop her from getting blood everywhere.

He spread a ragged wool counterpane over the bed and Rosamund levered herself onto it. There was another dull *clunk* as a stray knife, apparently hidden in the linen shift, thumped against the wooden frame. As carefully as he could, Leo peeled the slashed fabric back from her skin and wiped the blood away, praying that the wound was superficial. Its limits were revealed as he dabbed with a damp cloth, and he sighed with relief. The cut was long, starting on her hip and crossing most of her stomach, but it wasn't deep. The bruises would be impressive, but she should be all right.

He poured vinegar into a bowl. 'I still say you should have had the queen's physician—'

'You know she's working on the assassin,' Rosamund grunted, a little woozily, 'and if he can give evidence that gets Baron Mabry locked up for the rest of his life—or better yet, executed—then I will not begrudge him the help. Even if he did nearly kill you.'

'Have you forgotten he nearly killed *you*?' Leo snapped before he could help himself. 'Why did you come charging in? Why didn't you just use one of your throwing knives?'

Rosamund struggled to sit up, offended. 'It was dark and I was too far away. I couldn't risk hitting you!'

'So you decided to get yourself stabbed with a potentially poisoned blade instead?'

'I did what I had to do!'

> **HBWalker:** Nice callback.
>
> ---
>
> **CSLindley:** Thank you, I worked very hard on it.

Leo scowled. 'You shouldn't have put yourself in danger! Your children need you!'

'*You* needed me!' Rosamund shouted.

'We didn't spend all this time and effort getting you home for you to throw your life away!'

Rosamund's mouth fell open. 'I saved your life! You're welcome!'

'Be sensible, my lady, your life is much more valuable than mine!'

'Really? By whose reckoning, *my lord?*'

'By *mine!*'

There was a long silence. Neither of them looked at each other.

Eventually, Rosamund said quietly, 'I'm fine.' She lay back down again gingerly, grimacing. 'Am I going to need stitches?'

'Not if you've got caladrius glue somewhere in this bag,' he said, making an effort to keep his voice light. He tried to examine the wound more thoroughly, but it was no use; he needed to push the shift aside entirely. He gestured helplessly at her hemline. 'May I?'

Rosamund blinked at him, brows creased in confusion.

'Your shift,' he said softly. 'I need to move it out of the way.'

She shrugged, seemingly unconcerned, but he noticed her hands tighten on the blanket. Leo lifted her underdress up over her hips as gently as he could and tucked another blanket over her lower half before he surveyed the wound again. The wound to his leg had been deeper; she had patched that with caladrius glue, and it hadn't bothered him at all for the last week. If he did this right, she should be fine. 'If you can rest for the next few days, I don't think stitches will be necessary.'

She relaxed a little and attempted to smile at him. 'No more foiling assassins for me.'

He smiled back in spite of himself and reached for a fresh cloth. 'Best avoided, my lady.'

She frowned in his general direction. 'My name is Rosamund, you know,' she said, with the careful over-enunciation of someone who is not entirely in control of all their faculties. 'I tried to get you to stop calling me "my lady", and you won't. But you *can* call me Rosamund. I think we're friends.' Leo's hands stuttered, and he nearly dropped the bowl. 'And you did marry me.' She considered him through eyes that were struggling to stay open. 'You can probably call me Rosy. I won't mind.'

Part of Leo thought that was the shock and the pain-killer talking. But the greater part of him was unaccountably warmed by the fact that *his own wife* thought that they were friends. She'd accepted his help. She'd trusted him with her children's safety. And she'd saved his life. Violently. Again.

She might not love him, but Leo was suddenly a lot more confident that she trusted him. And that made a lot of difference.

'I'm . . . not in the habit, my lady,' he admitted, wring-ing out the cloth.

'Well, *Leopold*,' Rosamund retorted, and there was a jolt in his stomach at the use of his full first name, 'you never will be if you don't start.'

Leo gave up. He was in love with a lunatic. He was mar-ried to a lunatic. What was worse, he didn't seem to care. 'An excellent point. *Rosamund.*'

She smiled at him. 'Better.' He took advantage of her distraction to sweep the vinegar straight across her stomach.

'*Ow!*' She started to roll away by reflex, but Leo put a hand on her shoulder to push her back down.

'Stay still. I know it hurts. I'm sorry.'

Their heads were now very close together, which meant he had an excellent view when Rosamund made a somewhat cross-eyed face at him. 'You're not really sorry,' she huffed, settling down onto the pillow, 'you're getting your revenge for being called Leopold.'

Leo shrugged, released her shoulder, and returned to his ministrations. 'I understand the legal necessity during the wedding service, but honestly, I'd have preferred Landon.'

She laughed but cut off abruptly, wincing. 'I'll bear that in mind, my lord.'

'Now who's being overly formal with their spouse, my—Rosamund?'

Rosamund smiled again, though it was a little strained. 'Takes one to know one.'

The subsequent silence was a lot more comfortable than the previous one had been. Once Leo had finished cleaning the wound, he picked up the jar of glue (which he had indeed found in the bottom of the bag)—and hesitated.

Rosamund tipped her head to the side. 'Do you know how to use that?'

He shook his head.

'Then let me expand your education.'

It didn't take long to stir up the mixture and spread it over the wound, though it felt strange to leave her stomach so exposed while it dried. Rosamund had stared blankly at the canopy of the bed while he applied the adhesive, but at least she wasn't shivering any more. Her breathing had slowed too.

Once the caladrius glue was no longer sticky to the touch, Leo lifted Rosamund to a sitting position so that he could bandage her stomach. As she eased back onto the mattress, he gathered up the supplies strewn across the bed and contemplated the relative merits of offering to help her change compared to the merits of just letting her fall asleep, half-dressed in bloodied rags.

He had just decided that simplicity was the order of the day when Rosamund inhaled sharply and opened her eyes. 'I need to get changed.'

'Right.'

'I'd appreciate some help.'

Ah. 'Where are your nightclothes?'

She jerked her chin at a dresser. 'Second drawer.'

It was a feat of finesse to get her ready for bed without disturbing her bandages, but they managed it eventually. Leo tucked her carefully under the counterpane and bundled the bloodied cloths into a corner. He had just gone to retrieve his own nightclothes and snuffed the candles when he stopped and hesitated. *I should probably find somewhere else to sleep.*

Rosamund seemed to know what he was thinking. 'Stay. Please.'

He could hardly refuse.

He lay down beside her as she pulled the ribbon out of her hair, letting the plaits fall about her. Then she leant her head on his shoulder. 'I'm not dying,' she mumbled.

'I'm glad.'

'I'm not sorry for saving your life.'

Leo sighed. 'I wouldn't have expected you to be. Go to sleep.'

His eyes slowly adjusted to the gloom, and a little while later, he felt her limbs relax. A patch of moonlight marched over the floorboards while the minutes slipped by, and it gradually became clear to Leo that he would be unable to take his own advice. He lay staring up into the darkness of the canopy, listening to Rosamund breathe (and occasionally snuffle) in her sleep — but every creak and groan of the building, every bird call, every crackle from the hearth made his tension worse.

He had almost died.

And worse, Rosamund had almost died trying to protect him.

This was getting untenable.

✕

Leo closed his eyes and concentrated. 'Caroline? A word. *Now.*'

A violently clashing vision appeared: Caroline in a purple dressing gown and tartan pyjamas. She was foaming at the mouth while a small wand in her hand buzzed. Was she rabid? Trying to cure herself with magic?

Caroline took the instrument (*toothbrush*, his mind supplied, albeit belatedly) out of her mouth and silenced its buzzing before stabbing it at him. 'Excuse me? Did you just . . . whistle me up like the genie of the lamp?'

Leo ignored this, waving a hand at Rosamund. 'How could you do this to her? Hasn't she suffered enough?'

Caroline bridled. 'Excuse me?' she said again. 'Do you have any idea how long I spent working out an injury that would allow you to patch her up by yourself and still keep her off her feet for a few days? I went through five iterations before I hit on one that would get past my editor! You're welcome!'

Leo growled deep in his throat, and Caroline beamed at him. 'You should do the growling thing more often in-story, you know, it's —' She broke off at his look. 'Sorry. But really, Leo. Who do you think made Robin share your room? Me! Who tried to talk Rosamund out of a marriage of convenience? Also me! And —' Here she slammed the toothbrush down and marched over to the bed, her posture one of wounded dignity. 'Who do you think has been trying to keep the pair of you out of the same bed until she's ready to deal with her feelings? *That was me as well!* It hasn't been easy, let me tell you, but I couldn't . . .' Caroline sighed. 'I wasn't going to let her jump into bed with you out of duty.'

Leo was taken aback. Who knew Caroline Lindley was capable of a sudden attack of conscience?

'If for no other reason than because sudden crying jags aren't very attractive.'

Ah. Never mind.

But she wasn't finished. 'This was supposed to be an enemies-to-lovers story, you know. Sidelong glances, heated banter, physical altercations that end in almost-kisses — "Oh no, I nearly had a feeling!" All of that! And what do I get instead?' Caroline flung her arms wide, the gesture encompassing both him and Rosamund. 'Two people too noble and — and *sensible* to pick fights! You weren't even proper enemies.' She glared at him. 'You forgave her for the masquerade in a second when she looked remorseful. She got you thrown in *prison*! She didn't hesitate to rat you out to the highest possible authority on the slightest suspicion!'

Caroline flopped down on the chair next to the bed. 'And yet, somehow, entirely against my outline and my tropes, you've managed to build something that could be a functional relationship.' She smiled in spite of herself. 'Even Lady I-Make-My-Own-Decisions-And-Don't-Deserve-Help seems to have worked that out by this point.' Caroline looked back over at Leo. 'And you. You're going to declare your love for her outright at some point, aren't you? No mystique about it at all.'

Leo rolled his eyes back up to the canopy. Perhaps this hadn't been one of his better ideas.

'Please don't bother telling me you're not head over heels for her. I'm your author; you can't actually lie to me, I can hear what you're thinking.'

'She doesn't need me intruding,' Leo ground out through his teeth. 'And you know she doesn't feel the same.'

'Really?'

'Gratitude is not love. Nor is loneliness. Nor is grief!'

'I'm not going to convince you of this, am I?'

Leo said nothing.

'Fine. She'll do it herself, I'm sure.' Before Leo could ask what she meant by this, Caroline stood up. 'I'm going now. Don't call me up like this again. Not even Rosamund does that. Not even *Robin* does that. I'm not sure I like it.'

Leo sighed. 'I make no promises.'

Caroline rolled her eyes. 'Pleasant dreams, Leo. Conventions of the medium mean you're about to spend a while watching her sleep before having a very good night's rest yourself. Enjoy.'

×

Leo jumped as a hand laced itself into his. Rosamund gave him a sleepy smile, barely visible in the firelight.

'Go to sleep, Leo.'

He squeezed her fingers. 'I will.'

Chapter 21

THE PROBLEM with an injured Rosamund wasn't patching her up. It was preventing her from immediately un-patching herself.

'Stop that,' Leo said the next morning when she got out of bed and attempted to open a drawer. 'You're going to hurt yourself.'

She gave him a flat look. 'I need to—'

'You need to go back to bed,' he said, trying not to roll his eyes. 'I am going to ask the royal surgeon to attend you while I fetch the physician from town.' She still looked mutinous, so he added, 'If you reopen your wound and get an infection and—and *die*, you are never going to know the outcome of the interrogation. Don't you want to be alive when Weston Mabry is stripped of his titles and executed for treason?'

Rosamund digested this for a few moments before muttering something that her priest wouldn't have approved of and sliding back under the blankets.

Luckily for Leo, both Hawkhurst's local physician and the queen's personal surgeon were on his side regarding the importance of rest and recovery. He had just come back from collecting Edmund and Charlotte after their late breakfast only for them all to arrive outside the bed-chamber door to overhear, 'Yes, Lady Rosamund, the glue seems to be holding well, and no, I don't think there will be any lasting negative effects from your injury. However, you need to stay in bed, and I'm prescribing you a phoenix-blood draught for the next three days at least.'

'But—' Rosamund did not sound impressed.

'No *buts*, Your Ladyship,' Dora said severely. 'You have pushed consistently beyond your limits, as I have often warned you against, and if you refuse to rest now, you will do yourself permanent damage.'

'There is work to do,' Rosamund replied with great dignity, 'that cannot be done if I am whiling the hours away in bed!'

Edmund and Charlotte shared a resigned look.

'If you don't take the draughts and remain reclined as much as possible, you will be stuck in here much longer, my lady. The phoenix blood will hasten the healing process, for all that it will also make you—'

'Useless.'

'Less mobile, and only temporarily. I'm sure your husband would prefer you to be well, given the pressing matters demanding your attention.'

'I would,' he said from outside the room. Charlotte clapped a hand to her mouth to stifle a giggle. Edmund, not bothering to hide his smirk, opened the door.

Rosamund snorted. 'Eavesdropping is rude, you know.'

Leo strode to her bedside. 'Disobeying the physician is also rude. Rest. Please.'

Rosamund mumbled something he didn't catch, then huffed. 'Fine.'

Mistress Dora rose and collected her things. 'I'll visit again in three days, my lady, at which point—provided Viscount Collins can attest that you have followed my orders to the letter—I might be willing to let you go outside.' She gestured at a pouch on the dresser; Leo picked it up and loosed the drawstring to reveal a fine, golden-red powder. 'Mix a spoonful of the dried blood into a cup of wine for her once a day. No arguments.' Dora shot him a parting glare. 'And no *excitement*.'

Robin had spent the rest of the previous night entirely occupied with chasing down Baron Mabry. Though the baron had taken leave of no one, the Hawkhurst staff reported that he had discreetly departed around the same time as most of the other guests. After the assassination attempt, Queen Eudosia had been adamant. 'I don't care if you have to drag him by the collar from the threshold of his door, Robin Waverley: get him back here. Now.'

Only the prospect of apprehending the baron could make up for losing an evening with Elinor. Robin had raced through the forest with thirty of the Queen's Guard, catching up with their target at last on the outskirts of the Mabry estate. All the work he'd done establishing his foppish persona was worth it to see the dumbstruck look on Weston's face when Robin had drawn his sword.

'Waverley!'

'Weston! No, please don't move,' he added, as Mabry's hand twitched towards his own sword. 'I don't think you'd enjoy the consequences. Best just to come along with me and these fine gentlemen. They have some questions about missing caladrius salve. Oh,' he continued lazily, 'and assassinations.'

Mabry spluttered something about preposterous allegations and untrustworthy Abrenians besmirching his good name. Robin tutted.

'I don't think Her Majesty will see it that way, Weston. After all, Roland and Eudosia signed a peace treaty only yesterday, so some trustworthiness must be assumed. But regardless of the side you're on, stealing medical supplies from your own troops and selling them to the highest bidder just isn't the done thing.'

The triumph might have been sweeter were it not for the incessant, nasal whines of their prisoner all the way back to Hawkhurst.

They returned in the early hours of the morning. Robin instructed the soldiers to deposit the baron within the prison tower so that Mabry and his subordinate might compare notes. But when Robin had gone to enquire after his friends, the watch outside the Rose Room informed him that their lady and lord were within, that they had taken medical supplies with them, and that under no circumstances would anyone else be permitted to enter until they stirred. His worries alleviated along multiple lines, Robin reconvened with his wife in their room, where she stroked his hair and let him talk out his exploits until they both fell asleep around sunrise.

Phoenix-blood-induced sleep lasted for hours at a time, so once Rosamund had taken her draught, Leo took himself off on an inspection of the grounds. The assassination attempt had horrified Queen Eudosia, and already at breakfast that morning she had made a substantial amount of noise about better guard rotas and where to find reliable soldiers. Leo was in the middle of canvassing blind corners in the formal gardens when a noise from behind one of the bushes made him pause. His spike of panic subsided when he caught a glimpse of a bright yellow dress through the leaves.

Charlotte.

He sat down nonchalantly on the dry grass, catching sight of his boots as he did so. The brown leather was covered in dust. *Is it someone else's job to clean them now?* 'Good afternoon, Miss Hawkhurst.'

There was a squeak from behind the bush, and Charlotte appeared. She looked at him suspiciously. 'How did you know it was me?'

'Your dress is quite distinctive.'

She narrowed her eyes. 'Uncle Robin said you were a spy. Is seeing through bushes a spy trick?'

Uncle Robin needs to learn to hold his tongue, thought Leo, but instead he said, 'He does like to exaggerate.'

'So you're not a spy?'

'Apparently I'm a viscount, Miss Hawkhurst.'

She snorted. 'That's what they call me at school. "Charlotte" will be quite satisfactory, thank you.'

'Leo, then.' He held out his hand.

Charlotte considered him for a moment longer, then sat down on the grass a little distance away, plucking a few daisies and twisting them into a bracelet. 'Is Mum going to be all right?'

Leo dropped his hand. 'Yes.'

'Uncle Robin says you saved her life.'

Uncle Robin, Leo thought grimly, *needs a talking-to.* 'Yes,' he said, because it was no more than the truth, 'but she also saved mine.'

'How?'

She threw a knife straight into the throat of the man trying to kill me; she married me so I could get out of Abrenia; she attacked my assassin with no thought for her own safety . . . 'You'd have to ask her, Miss — Charlotte.' What was it with Hawkhurst women and their insistence on first names, anyway?

But Charlotte had something else on her mind. 'Have you seen the tree, Leo?'

'Which tree?'

'The hiding tree.' The girl lowered her voice. 'I think that's where the man who attacked Mother was staying, because look.' She gestured at the largest tree in the gardens. Leo had noticed the collection of yews previously and marked them on the map as a potential problem. With so many servants and tradesfolk coming and going to prepare for a royal visit, anywhere that weapons or people could be secreted away was a risk. He stood up and walked over, Charlotte trailing behind him.

Viewed from far away, the yew was a dense mass of branches, but as Leo drew closer, he could see signs that the grass around it had been trampled. One of the caladrius birds was absently pecking at the trunk.

Leo drew his knife. 'Get behind me.'

Charlotte didn't move. 'There's no one there *now*, silly, or George wouldn't be there. He's very stupid, but not *that* stupid.'

Leo kept his eyes on the tree. 'George?'

'The caladrius.'

'The bird is called *George*?'

Charlotte sniffed. 'What else would you call him?'

Leo had no answer to that, but as he approached the tree, he could see that Charlotte was right twice over. No one currently occupied it, but there were several large hollows in the trunk, and someone had carved out extra space by discreetly removing a few branches.

"Concealing trees" was how he'd marked the yews on the map Edmund had drawn for him. He'd been more right than he'd known. 'Charlotte?'

'Yes?'

'Where can I get an axe?'

> **HBWalker:** I was about to ask how you were going to handwave a bunch of fires and an assassination attempt.
>
> --
>
> **CSLindley:** It's all in hand! Sort of?

Rosamund was just succumbing to the draught when she heard the noise.

Thunk.

Thunk.

She pushed herself upright, frowning, and then levered herself out of bed to look out the window, clutching the sill to ensure she stayed upright under the influence of the phoenix blood. A small crowd had gathered by the largest tree in the gardens. She could see Charlotte's bright dress and Edmund's red hair among them. Leo was at the centre of it all, wielding an axe.

Thunk.

Thunk.

He wiped his face on his sleeve, turning around as Edmund said something to him. They spoke briefly, then Leo handed Edmund the axe and stepped back.

Thunk.

What on earth are they doing? Rosamund considered going down to find out, but the thought of navigating all the stairs in her current state was not appealing. Besides, by the time she got down there, they'd probably have felled it already. Perhaps it was dead, or rotten.

She'd ask later.

Leo returned to the Rose Room at the dinner hour to check on Rosamund. He had expected to find her asleep, but he heard her stir as soon as he lifted the latch.

'I see you and Edmund decided to take up logging this morning. Was that some kind of bonding exercise, or do you have a secret passion for gardening of which I was previously unaware?'

He sighed — *leave it to Rosamund to out-will a phoenix* — and explained. She closed her eyes, blowing out a breath. 'I had wondered. Though, of course, that seems to be far from the only hole in our security.' She looked up again, expression sharpening. 'Any news on the assassin?'

'He's not dead. And he's proving . . . talkative.'

Rosamund's smile had no warmth in it. 'Good.' But then, unexpectedly, she reached for Leo's hand. 'Thank you for coming to visit me.'

He smiled. 'How do you know I didn't just want a nap after all my hard work?'

'Well, don't let me stop you,' said Rosamund, yawning, 'though you should probably take your boots off first.'

'Certainly, my — uhh . . . I will.'

The queen left the next day, with one would-be assassin dragged in irons after her and one highly-suspect baron chained hand and foot in a coach with half a dozen of her guards. Rosamund was just glad to get them all out of the house. The tension of keeping both her first husband's murderer and the attempted murderer of her second husband under her roof had meant that while she still slept, the nightmares had got steadily worse. Leo had been instructed by the physician not to wake her from them, but given the frequency with which she found herself sobbing in his arms at midnight, she was doing a good enough job of that all by herself.

Still, the memory of the dreams faded more quickly with him there, and she often fell back to sleep with her head on his shoulder.

When Dora returned as promised on the third day, she pronounced Rosamund "improved" — but she also ordered the doses of phoenix blood to continue for two more days. Rosamund groaned and buried her face in the counterpane. After the physician left, Leo sent Charlotte and Edmund to fetch Rosamund some breakfast. She looked around at them and nibbled bits of egg and toast, perfectly at ease. 'I feel much better today.'

Leo raised his eyebrows. 'Should I padlock my horse, or will you promise to behave yourself?'

Rosamund wasn't quite sure if he was holding on to that for entertainment value or because he was genuinely still cross about it. 'I promise to refrain from horse theft,' she said solemnly, 'if the rest of you promise to stop coddling me and tell me what we're doing to secure the house against further attacks! After which' — she grimaced, leaning back into the pillows again — 'we'll get to all our other problems.'

'Coddling?' said Leo. 'You think *this* is coddling?'

'Well . . . yes,' said Rosamund, 'of course. All this staying in bed and being waited on business. Clearly coddling.'

'Then no.'

'*No*, my lord?' Rosamund repeated.

Edmund and Charlotte exchanged a glance: *this is going to be good.* The adults ignored them.

'No, we will not stop coddling you.'

Rosamund stared at him flatly, but despite her best efforts, her mouth twitched.

'We'll consult you about securing the house, of course. Edmund had some excellent suggestions, and I have a few of my own. But the coddling is non-negotiable.'

Rosamund looked between the three of them. 'I see. Am I permitted to leave the bed while this consultation occurs?'

'Yes. But Mistress Dora says no horse riding, running, lifting, or . . .' Leo stopped, an awkward look crossing his face.

'Or what?' Charlotte piped up.

The grin Rosamund flashed him was wicked. 'Yes, Leo. Or what?'

'Err . . . working too hard.'

Edmund, sitting beside his sister, looked between his mother and stepfather with growing comprehension and made a disgusted face.

Rosamund sighed dramatically. 'I suppose climbing the caladrius loft ladders is also out of the question?'

'Yes.' Leo and Edmund said simultaneously.

She pouted. 'But I was so looking forward to introducing you to them.'

'I can do that, Mum!' said Charlotte.

Edmund gave her the practiced stare of a disbelieving elder brother, but Rosamund's face lit up. 'That could work, thank you. Maybe after dinner?' She turned to Leo. 'If that suits you?'

Leo looked uncertain, but . . . 'Thank you, Miss— Charlotte,' he said. 'I'd appreciate your insight.'

Prior to Leo's visit to the lofts, Rosamund insisted that they all go downstairs so they could talk about security somewhere with a bigger table. Leo, for his part, insisted on carrying her, and though she considered protesting, she contented herself with the single victory. The staff were pleased to see their lady out of bed, albeit still in her nightclothes and dressing gown. Edmund brought the map down and spread it over the table, and the next two hours were filled with vigorous discussion—Leo and Edmund leading the exposition, with Charlotte providing an ample supply of questions. Rosamund considered every one of Leo's suggestions in turn, and they spent a good three-quarters of an hour arguing passionately about what was feasible.

It was . . . pleasant.

Eventually, somewhere during the third exchange over whether the southwest corner of the outer wall should be reinforced, Charlotte and Edmund wandered off to the kitchen. Leo had just conceded that the project might wait until the following spring when Rosamund said, in a somewhat chagrined tone, 'I'm afraid you haven't married into the safest of families.'

'It has its compensations,' he offered, taking her hand across the table. When she blushed, he added, 'The food is excellent.'

She burst out laughing, which made him smile until she winced and gasped. 'Ow, don't make me laugh!'

It was almost the dinner hour by the time they had a rough plan sketched out, and Leo could see Rosamund was flagging a little; her shoulders had begun to droop.

'Let me bring your dinner upstairs,' he said quietly. She nodded, and when he lifted her from her seat, she rested her head on his chest like she had the night of the fire.

On our wedding night.

Not that he was thinking about their wedding night at this moment.

Well.

Maybe.

He made her take the medicine before he gave her food, and she scowled at him. 'Coddling will continue until morale improves,' he said, taking a mouthful of cheese.

'If you say so, sir. Now eat up, you have an important engagement with some gorgeous birds.'

He choked, and she cackled, victorious.

✕

'I have a question,' said Leo.

Charlotte had completed his tour of the caladrius loft only to start begging and wheedling for a sword-fighting lesson before supper. 'You taught Ed how to fell a tree, and I just taught you how to feed the birds without losing an eye. When do *I* get to learn anything good?' Now she completed her practice strike and looked up at him. 'What is it?'

'Why do the caladrius like you so much?'

Charlotte grinned, swinging at him again. 'At least four reasons. They prefer women, though not pregnant ones; they don't like sudden movement; they like quiet people, but not silence; and I'm wearing a lot of lavender oil.'

That was a lot to take in. Leo considered it in order. 'They don't like pregnant women?'

Charlotte adjusted her stance and gave the new technique a third try. 'No one's sure why, but the caladrius will fight to keep them out of the enclosure until a few weeks after the baby is born. We always know about babies months in advance.'

Leo put this thought aside for later. 'And the lavender?' Rosamund always smelled of lavender, but he'd never really wondered why. The oil she put in her hair was perfumed with lavender, and there were bags of lavender tucked into the corners of all the dressers and closets in the Rose Room. He probably smelled of lavender himself at this point.

'They build lavender into their nests. They're also absolutely obsessive about lavender cheese.'

Leo held up his sword by way of demonstration. 'Angle your wrists this way more.' She copied him. 'That's it. Try again. But you were joking about the cheese.'

'No!' Charlotte frowned at him. 'The males hoard cheese to present to the females when it's mating season. Only . . . they don't always remember where they put it.' She wrinkled her nose. 'I found some inside the chapel once, up on the rafters, much too high for a person to have left it there. It reeked.'

They practiced for another quarter-hour before supper, but for the rest of the evening Leo was still stuck on birds eating cheese and infiltrating the chapel. Though he supposed it wasn't a stretch for the residents of Hawkhurst to take at least the latter in their stride. The caladrius made themselves at home literally everywhere on the estate, to the extent that the evening before Robin and Elinor left with Eudosia's retinue, they had found one in their bed. That incident had demonstrated how well the birds combined great beauty with the temperamental moodiness and imaginatively destructive tendencies of three-year-old children.

Rosamund, chagrined, had given them her own previous room in the family wing, but Elinor had just laughed and hugged her gently. 'You've thwarted enough renegades for a lifetime. Take care of yourself, Rosy, and get some rest.'

Robin, naturally, was incorrigible. 'For a noblewoman who prefers life on her estate to courtly politics, you must admit, Viscountess Lady Rosamund Hawkhurst Collins, that you're nonetheless a magnet for drama.'

✕

Caroline was prodding her soggy cheese sandwich in a desultory fashion when Eunice knocked on her office door. 'Afternoon!' said Caroline, trying to look casual. 'How are you?'

'George Radley has been arrested.'

The shock of it hit her like a bucket of cold water. 'Because of me?' Caroline squeaked. 'Because of the things we found out?'

'Not . . . exactly.'

The auditors had been working non-stop for days to determine what had been done and by whom. George, it transpired, had tried for months to pay off the people who had infected his laptop with ransomware, which would have been quite sufficient by itself to land him on the wrong side of the law, given how much sensitive information it contained. But when the auditors seized his personal laptop (and the shouting match at his avant-garde eight-bedroom mansion had been *intense*), Eunice had taken one look at the file names and called the police.

The CEO did not elaborate on the nature of George's personal files, and Caroline didn't ask. Eunice gave her a small, thoughtful smile and said, 'So, all that to say — good work, Caroline. Keep it up,' and let herself out.

Caroline floated some distance above herself, disconnected, through the rest of her day and on the bus home. Halfway through her dinner of reheated beef stew, she started crying, and it took her some time to stop.

She wanted, so much, to call Henry. She didn't.
But she did call her mother.

×

When Leo returned from his visit to the caladrius loft (and impromptu sword fighting lesson), Rosamund was standing in the solar, holding a letter and staring blankly into the fireplace.

Leo moved closer. 'Rosamund?'

She looked up at him, her eyes wet, and passed him the sheets of paper with a shaking hand.

'"Further to the attempt on the life of Viscount Collins, and following interrogation of the assassin . . . Baron Mabry has been found to have in his possession . . ."' Leo's eyes widened at the list that followed, and he turned to the next page. '"And after interrogation, has confessed to . . . "' He took in another long list, incredulous. 'Conspiracy to commit murder. Smuggling. War profiteering. Wait, *tax evasion?*' He settled himself on a stool in front of the fire and continued reading. '"The Crown has therefore decided . . . Hawkhurst will now swear fealty to the Collins viscountcy!"' Leo looked up, beaming.

Rosamund said nothing. She was still shaking. Maybe she was just in shock. Tentatively, Leo took her hand. 'Rosamund, this is wonderful! Even if he avoids execution, Mabry no longer holds your fealty. You're *free.* You delivered the declaration, you made it home, and you can do whatever you want. You don't even need—' *Me*, he thought with a start.

Rosamund looked at him sharply when he stopped speaking. Perhaps she'd guessed what he had been about to say. Leo shoved down the pang of loss in his stomach. 'You don't need me here at all. Even if I'm in charge of Hawkhurst on paper, I can move to the Collins estate.' This, per the letter, was currently a lot of unclaimed land, but that wasn't the point. 'You'll only have to see me at official functions. If you want me to, I will.'

Rosamund opened her mouth, but no sound came out.

Heart sinking, Leo stood and took a step back. 'I'll just . . .'

'Stay,' she whispered. Then, more strongly, 'Please.'

'I really need to stop weeping on you,' Rosamund said some time later. 'You're going to run out of shirts.'

'Don't worry. It's the same shirt.'

×

Caroline cleared her throat, and her heroine looked up as Leo froze in place. 'What is it now?'

'I was rather expecting some kind of . . . declaration of love?' Caroline ventured.

'From me? Why?'

'Because—he loves you! You love him! Or—you mean a lot to each other, at least?'

Rosamund wiped her face on her sleeve and said nothing.

Caroline tried again. 'You've just had the thing that's been preoccupying you for the last year resolved! Mabry is no longer a danger, and he could very well be executed. You won! I even had you injured in a non-lethal way specifically to give you some time to process your feelings. How have you not managed it yet?'

'Not now, Caroline,' Rosamund whispered.

'But—'

'Not. Right. Now. Isn't that what you always say?' She mimicked Caroline's accent: '"I can't possibly tell Henry how I'm feeling! What if something bad happens?"'

Caroline bridled. 'How dare you? This is my *life*, you know! There are consequences to my actions!'

'And there are none to mine?'

Caroline nearly shouted "No!"—and realised she couldn't.

'Do you think I've forgotten what happened to Hugo? I loved him, and he died. What if it . . . What if . . . I can't do it again, Caroline. I'm not strong enough.'

Caroline chewed on her lip, wondering what to say, but Rosamund wasn't finished. 'What are *you* so afraid of? You've written books! Got promoted! George has even been—arrested . . .' She trailed off. 'Hold on. Have you been basing the plot of this story on—'

'That's not important right now!' Caroline interrupted, eyes firmly on the floor.

'It's important to *me*. But fine. What is important right now?'

'That I *am* afraid. No one's going to die, no one's in actual danger, and I'm still afraid. I'm a coward. Happy?'

Rosamund sighed, disentangled herself from Leo, and put an arm around Caroline. 'What are you afraid of, Carrie?'

'What if I tell him how I feel and he doesn't feel the same?' Caroline covered her face with her hands, pushing her glasses askew. 'How awkward is it going to be when he turns me down? How embarrassing is it going to be when I have to get a new editor because I made a pass at the previous one, and what if he *tells people*? I don't—I can't—he—it . . .'

'What if he says yes?'

'He lives in Birmingham! For pity's sake, I live in *Canterbury*! Do you have any idea how long that takes on a train?'

Rosamund snorted. 'Really? That's your excuse? That in a world with trains, planes, and automobiles, not to mention video calls and remote working, he *lives too far away?*'

Caroline sniffed. 'You think I'm being silly.'

'I think that maybe the reason you made me so insanely decisive is that you're afraid to make decisions in your own life. But I *am* you, Caroline. At least a little bit. Trust yourself. You know he's been flirting with you.' Rosamund gave her a gentle nudge. 'Take the risk.'

'I . . . I'll think about it.'

×

'So how are you doing?' said Henry, and Caroline frowned at him before she realised she hadn't meant to frown at him.

'Well, I'm going to get to writing the final scenes soon, but overall, I think I'm on track. The revisions are going to be a nightmare, but the story is —'

'No, Carrie,' Henry said softly, and she froze. 'I mean how are *you* doing? You told me a few weeks ago that there were problems at work, but you've been radio silent on it since then. Is everything all right now?'

She looked away, uncomfortable. The stress of it all had lessened somewhat after a few weeks' adjustment, but her inadvertent defeat of a white collar criminal still felt a little too close for comfort. Her throat threatened to close, and she coughed to try and clear it. 'I've been left an absolute mess to sort out, but everyone is being, um, very helpful.' More helpful than she would ever have guessed. It was a little overwhelming.

'I'm glad.' There was a pause. 'For what it's worth, I agree. You're on the right track.' Twenty minutes, and a good-natured argument on the appropriate number of ellipses to have per page later, Henry checked his watch. 'We're almost out of time, but do you have a date in mind for another meeting?'

Caroline braced herself. *What would Rosamund do?* Nothing that would work in this situation, she concluded wryly. The real question was: what was she going to do?

'Well, I'm free, umm . . .' Caroline took a deep breath. 'Actually, Henry, I was going to ask you something else.'

'Mm?'

Now or never. 'I'm going to visit family at the weekend, and I'll be passing near you on my way up on Saturday. Since they're not expecting me till dinner, would you . . . umm . . .' She could do this. She could do this. '. . . Would you like to meet up in person? I feel like we talk all the time,' she rushed on, 'but I never really get to ask about you, and how you are, and what you're doing, and—'

'I'd love to.'

'—it's not a problem if you're busy, but—' Caroline checked herself. 'Wait, what?'

Henry was smiling. 'I'd love to. Did you have a time in mind?'

She did, as a matter of fact.

'Perfect.' Henry grimaced as he looked at his watch again. 'I'm sorry, but I really have to go.' Then the smile broke through again, and she didn't care that it was a cliché, it really was like the sun coming out from behind the clouds. 'See you on Saturday.'

'Bye!' Caroline chirped and cut the connection. Then she very carefully shut down her laptop.

She allowed herself thirty seconds of squealing before she called her cousin. 'Jenny? Yes, I'd love to come up and see you and Dave this weekend . . .'

Chapter 22

'ER . . . ROSAMUND?'

Rosamund finished her bite of pastry and looked over at her husband. They were alone at the table. Edmund and Charlotte had returned to school a week ago, and the house was still too quiet without them. What concerned her most at the moment, though, was the way Leo was twisting a napkin in his hands, his breakfast only half eaten. She frowned. 'Yes?'

'You sent out the messengers to announce the wedding ball in a fortnight?'

'Correct.'

'Are—' Leo looked away, cleared his throat, and tried again. 'I mean . . . am I going to have to dance?'

Ah. Stage fright. But then . . . 'Do you mean to tell me,' Rosamund began, trying not to smile, 'that you offered to escort me to a masquerade at the *Abrenian court*, a place where hundreds of eyes would have been scrutinising your every move—and you *don't like to dance*?' The silence that followed spoke volumes. 'I will tell you honestly, Leo, that may present a problem. Part of the tradition is that we lead the volta.'

Leo's forehead creased in confusion. 'The what?'

'The volta. The first of the four dances?'

Leo's face paled. 'But I . . .' He swallowed, and she waited for him to form the words. 'I don't know how to dance.'

Worse than stage fright, then. *Well, we'll see about that.*
Rosamund laced a hand into Leo's, pulling him to his feet.
'Then let me expand your education once more.'

✕

'Do you actually know how to dance the volta?' Henry asked as they
wandered through central Birmingham on a surprisingly sunny
Saturday. He'd promised to take Caroline to his favourite restaurant, but she had been so nervous about missing her connection
that she'd told him to book it for much later than she planned to
arrive. This left them with a couple of hours to kill in a place that
wasn't exactly known for its plethora of beautiful sights. Still, it
didn't do too badly, though the life-size plastic giraffe had been a bit
of a surprise.

Caroline shook her head. 'I watched a couple of videos where
people in fancy dresses performed it, but I was just going to look the
details up when I got to the second draft.'

Henry laughed. 'Planning ahead? You?' He ostentatiously checked
his watch. 'Ah yes, I see. *Ad kalendas Graecas*. That explains it.'

Caroline's mouth twitched. At another time she might have been
offended by his laughter, but his expression was warm, and he didn't
seem able to stop smiling. She could relate. In a fit of boldness she
tucked her arm into his. He didn't look unhappy about it. 'I'll have you
know that I am an *excellent* planner,' she said, mock-stern.

'Whatever you say, my lady.'

She tried to shove him into the canal. He was unmoved. But he
did buy her an ice cream before lunch.

✕

Leo followed his wife into the Rose Room's solar, where
she promptly set her back against the wooden table and
started to push. He assumed an expression of exaggerated

patience, gestured for her to stop, and moved it into the corner himself. 'No heavy lifting, remember?'

Rosamund raised her eyebrows innocently and closed the door before beckoning him to the centre of the room. 'Not a problem. Assuming you don't object, I can teach you the volta right now. Which means the heavy lifting is going to be your job.'

He had no idea what she meant. Mercifully, she saw the look on his face and continued.

'The volta has two parts. The first part is just like the galliard –'

'I think I've heard of that one,' he interjected.

' – which merely requires you to know your left from your right and be able to count to six.'

'Right.'

Rosamund kirtled up her skirts – 'So you can tell what my legs are doing, you see' – and demonstrated the footwork. Leo, standing next to her, did his best to copy the movements, feeling clumsy as a newborn calf. It wasn't a difficult sequence, but all he could think about was stepping on Rosamund's feet, getting tangled in her skirts, tripping her, exposing her to ridicule in front of her – their – peers . . .

'Relax,' she said softly after the third run-through. 'You're thinking too much. I can see it on your face.'

'I don't want to trample you.'

'You won't.'

'How do you know that?'

'Because I know where you are,' she answered easily. 'I'm not going to put my feet in your way.'

His wife took his hand, and they began again. Leo felt fortunate that he retained vague memories of the galliard from his teenage years, and after a quarter of an hour, he was a lot more confident. It helped that they were dancing hand-in-hand rather than facing each other; if he blundered, it wouldn't cause Rosamund difficulty.

And she seemed to be enjoying herself. As the steps came back, it occurred to him that the quiet, solemn-faced lady with whom he'd spent so many hours on the way to Quayforth was rarely to be seen any more. Returning home to her children and finding herself safe at last from the baron had turned Rosamund into a woman Leo had only glimpsed during their travels. This new Rosamund smiled like she meant it. She laughed, joked . . . and touched him. *All the time.*

When he held her after her nightmare in Abrenia, she had melted into him and clung to him like she was drowning. But she had been desperate, and he had been the only person available; he'd tried not to read into it too deeply.

But now she took his arm when they walked outside. She held his hand in public, though less so around the children. When he had returned from his first session teaching Edmund and Charlotte, soaked with sweat and covered in bruises, she had closed her arms around him with infinite gentleness and whispered, 'Thank you,' in his ear.

But she hasn't kissed me again. He'd told himself not to push. Her nightmares persisted, and Rosamund had cried in his arms more than once since Mabry's arrest. Sometimes, too, Leo caught a twist of sadness in her expression that he had to assume related to Hugo.

She married me to keep her children safe. She misses her husband. He needed to remember that.

But sometimes . . . sometimes, Leo caught Rosamund looking at him. She'd been doing it for at least the last week, perhaps ever since Ed and Charlotte had gone back to school. He'd catch her out of the corner of his eye, just watching him, a faint crease of concentration on her brow. He tried not to let her know that he'd noticed, especially because he couldn't work out what was going on in her head. Or rather, he didn't like to speculate.

Particularly because he knew as well as she did that the marriage wasn't valid yet.

He had decided not to dwell on that. Rosamund had explicitly asked him to stay; she clearly welcomed his presence; they had time. Till midsummer, at least, and autumn had barely begun.

She'd saved his life. She'd married him. If she needed more time, then she could have it.

He realised Rosamund had just said something while he'd been woolgathering. 'I'm sorry, what was that?'

'I said: the second part is a little more tricky, but I swear to you, it can be learned.'

Leo braced himself.

'You don't need to look so scared, sir,' she said brightly. 'I'm not going to hurt you.'

That remains to be seen. 'How many knives must I try not to dislodge?'

She considered this, looking slightly abashed, and stepped back to the table, where she withdrew from her garments . . . a *half-dozen* blades?

Including one from the top of her hose.

'Your safety now assured,' she continued, returning to face him, 'we will require a change of positioning.' She reached for his right hand. Leo expected her to hold it, or maybe put it in the correct place. He was not expecting her to kiss the back of it, her eyes on his.

Heart thundering in his ears, he tried — and, Wisdoms help him, probably failed — to keep his feelings from showing on his face.

Rosamund, for her part, merely beamed at him, her eyes alight. She placed his hand high on her waist. 'Normally you'd have your hand a little lower, but allowances must be made for those of us who are convalescing.' She repeated the process — kiss and all — with his left hand. 'Ready?'

Leo, who could feel her ribs through the fabric of her butter-yellow dress, had never felt less ready in his life.

His wife was *flirting* with him.

'Where do your hands go?' he asked.

'My left holds my dress,' said Rosamund, bending to do so, 'and the right goes on your shoulder. Now —'

Rosamund stopped abruptly as he caught her hand, kissed it, and placed it on his shoulder. He thought she might be blushing.

He *definitely* was.

'The second part of the volta,' said Rosamund, and he thought the calm in her voice sounded a little too practiced, 'is a lift and three-quarter turn. I jump. You lift.' She dropped her skirts for a moment to make a circling motion with her hand. 'And turn, thus. You also lift your left knee, but we'll come to that later.'

Leo wondered if he'd misunderstood. 'I put my hands around your waist and lift you into the air?'

'Yes. In time to the music, of course.' She tipped her head to the side. 'You have a question?'

He did, but . . .

Rosamund was having none of it. 'Come, sir,' she said, and her smile was very gentle, 'there are no silly questions in this room.'

Leo took a deep breath and said, 'Is it usual for formal dances to be this . . . handsy?'

He was rewarded for his boldness with a delighted cackle. 'Courtly ballgowns have a lot more structure to them than this.' Rosamund gestured down at the overdress she had laced over her chemise. 'So it's a little more difficult to paw your lady partner.' Her eyes sparkled with mirth. 'That said, I would be very upset if you danced the volta with anyone but me.' She stepped in closer, which meant she had to tip her chin quite far up to look him in the eye.

Leo could see the pulse fluttering in her throat.

'I can imagine,' he choked out. Should his heart beat this quickly? His chest felt tight. Why was it so hard to breathe?

'Would you like to try the lift without the turn first? I'll jump up and you can support me.'

He wanted to say yes. He very much wanted to say yes. But panic was clawing its way up his throat, so he shook his head instead.

Rosamund's expression softened. 'Do you want to stop for a minute?'

Leo nodded, letting go of her. She studied him for a moment, then went and poured two cups of water from the ewer. He joined her at the table, and they sat down together. Rosamund leaned her chin on her hand and waited.

When he felt he had his breath back, Leo spoke. 'I don't want to let you down.'

Rosamund said nothing, and the sympathy on her face was more than he could bear. 'What use am I to you?' he burst out. 'You're an aristocrat! You *fit*. People respect you. You don't need a husband who'll tarnish your reputation and make people gossip about you behind your back!'

Rosamund took his hand, studying it rather than meeting his eyes. For a long time neither of them spoke.

'Leo Collins,' she said finally, 'you have saved my life on more than one occasion. Without you, my children and I would be entirely in Mabry's power at best, and dead at worst.' She poked—*poked!*—the end of his nose with her free hand. 'You have, over and over again, proved yourself to be a man of honour and integrity. If you want to divorce me'—she held up her hand as Leo opened his mouth to interrupt—'then you can. But I am more grateful to you than I could ever possibly express in words. You will always have a place here, and you *will not let me down.*'

He was gripping her hand more tightly than he'd realised. Leo let out a breath and tried to relax. 'What should I do?'

Rosamund leaned in to kiss him gently on the cheek. 'As I said before. Stay . . . please.'

Leo nodded, throat tight. 'I'd . . . be honoured.'

They lingered there for a moment longer. Rosamund's thumb was now stroking the back of his hand. Her eyes were warm, and he suddenly noticed the room had grown uncomfortably hot.

'Will you dance with me, Leo?' The grin she gave him made his heart pound in his ears again, but . . . differently, somehow.

He nodded again and stood up before he could say anything stupid. They took their positions in the middle of the room.

'Let's review what we've done so far,' Rosamund told him, and Leo soon found himself dancing around the solar less clumsily than before. 'You see?' she said cheerily, 'It's all just practice. You've learned more complicated foot-work for sword fighting. I knew you'd pick it up quickly.'

They danced a little longer until Rosamund called a halt for refreshments. But she insisted that they weren't finished. 'You really must try the lift,' she said. 'It's only scaring you because you haven't done it yet.'

Leo, more confident now that he wasn't tripping over his own feet every ten steps, agreed. However, they moved away from the wall and the tabletop full of knives. Just in case.

Rosamund positioned his hands at her waist again, and he tried to remember any of the things she'd explained a short while ago. Lift—spin? Three-quarters? Or was it two-thirds?

'On three then,' Rosamund said briskly. 'One, two, three!'

Leo braced himself and lifted his wife into the air. Halfway up, he recalled there was supposed to be a knee-raising part, and both his hands slid up into her armpits, but he didn't stumble while turning in place and lowered her safely to the ground.

Rosamund shook her head, but she was smiling. 'Not a bad beginning, Viscount Collins, but you're too far away.' She stepped in closer. 'There we are, that's better.'

By now, Leo supposed, he was *almost* used to Rosamund hugging him, taking his arm, even lying next to him. But getting to touch her himself was intoxicating, and it was made worse, or perhaps better, by how happy she seemed to be about it. Part of him was overwhelmed by his good fortune. Another, smaller part was still terrified that he was going to do something to mess it up.

An opportunity to do just that came mere moments later when his fourth lift went awry. His grip slipped halfway into the turn. Rosamund, caught off-balance, squeaked in surprise as they both tumbled to the floor, Leo desperately trying to hold her up. She landed on his chest, his hands still around her waist. After a complicated moment in which Leo forgot to breathe— *What if I hurt her? What if her wound reopened?*—she started to laugh.

He stammered an apology and wondered if Mistress Dora was going to shout at him, but Rosamund reached out a hand to stroke his cheek with her forefinger.

'Are you hurt?'

He shook his head.

'All to the good, then.'

'I'm sorry, it was my fault, I—'

She shushed him. 'Accidents happen.'

'Are you all right?'

'Quite comfortable, thank you.'

His wife was very definitely lying on top of him—and grinning. Leo swallowed.

'And you needn't worry,' Rosamund continued, 'you're doing a marvellous job with the dancing.' She leaned over to whisper in his ear. 'I'm terribly impressed.'

Leo decided it was time to take charge of the situation. 'Er . . .' That wouldn't work. Too hesitant. 'Ahh . . .'

Rosamund blinked down at him, a flash of vulnerability in her expression that made his heart twist in his chest.

Talking had never been his strength. He raised a hand and cupped her face, stroking her cheek with his thumb. Rosamund leaned into the gesture, closing her eyes. Leo hardly dared to breathe, but she seemed quite content.

After a minute or so, Rosamund opened her eyes again. 'Leo?'

'Yes?'

'You're lying on a wooden floor with a full-grown woman on top of you.'

He couldn't deny it.

'I fear you must be very uncomfortable.'

'Do you think we should swap places?' he said innocently.

Rosamund burst out laughing. 'Perhaps a change of location might work better?'

Leo pushed himself into a sitting position, Rosamund in his lap, and kissed her hand. 'I think so, my lady. I wouldn't want to risk crushing you.'

Rosamund leaned in, starting to kiss her way up his neck. '"My lady", Captain?'

Leo groaned. He felt her smile against his cheek as she began to trail feather-light kisses down his jaw. '*Rosy* . . .'

'Much better,' she murmured, and pressed her lips to his.

✕

Caroline, surveying her screen with undisguised satisfaction and not a little relief, decided that it was time to tactfully fade to black.

She was sure the fanfic writers could take it from there.

Chapter 23

THE NEXT WEEKEND Henry did the travelling, and Caroline met him in her favourite tea room: the place she went when she got completely stuck on a draft and needed to get out of the house. The red and cream walls, dark furniture, and cheerful fire in the colder months made her feel like she was stepping back in time. And the scones were amazing.

Caroline had emailed Henry to say that she needed a chat about various story-related details when he came to visit, and he hadn't even sat down at the table in Peace and Tranquilitea when he threw down his opening gambit: 'So what are you going to do with Rosamund and Leo?'

He never had been much for small talk. Caroline hid her smile behind her menu before setting it down to consider the question properly. 'Well, to begin with, I thought I'd write them a nice epilogue,' she said. 'Something that has a hook for a future sequel if I feel like writing one, while also making it clear that things are a lot more settled now.'

'An epilogue?' said Henry. Was that a twinkle she saw in his eye? 'Controversial. Are you going to have a prologue as well?'

'You know how I feel about those. No.'

✕

Viscount Leo Collins, formerly Captain Collins, considered that his life had become very strange. Marrying a noble-woman and joining the ranks of the nobility himself all in the space of a few days would have been quite enough to be going on with, but it hadn't stopped there. He had also danced with his wife at their wedding ball in front of hundreds of people—and hadn't minded at all, even when Robin had wolf-whistled. There were also his new stepchildren, who had returned from school for the midwinter holiday without deciding to hate him again in the interim.

And then there was the day that he walked into the kitchen to ask for a suppertime snack only to find his wife pulling bandages out of one of the neatly labelled boxes. Leo hurried forward. 'You're bleeding!'

Rosamund turned her hands over. There were several long scratches running down her forearms, and blood was starting to drip onto the pale flagstones. 'That is an accurate statement, yes.'

'What did you do?'

Rosamund grimaced. 'The caladrius were being difficult. Again. Blood was spilled, most of it mine.'

'Again?'

She shrugged. 'It's happened twice in the last week. I . . .' She trailed off. 'Wait. Umm. Have I . . . explained the particular quirks of the caladrius to you?'

A memory stirred. *'They don't like pregnant women?'* . . . *'The caladrius will fight to keep them out of the enclosure until a few weeks after the baby is born.'*

'Rosy—a *baby*?'

'Seems that way,' she began, but the rest of her reply was lost in his embrace.

✕

'Well!' said Caroline. 'That would explain why you've been feeling—'

'Like I've been knocked down by a cart?' Rosamund mumbled, her bleeding arms still wrapped gingerly around her husband.

Caroline snorted. 'I don't think "down" is the direction you've been knocked, Rosamund Hawkhurst Collins.' But then she smiled. 'Congratulations.'

'Thanks,' muttered Leo, hugging his wife more tightly.

Both women stared at him.

'You're welcome,' said Caroline, and promptly made herself scarce as Rosamund yelled, 'Wait, you talk to Leo too?'

✕

'So then, what about after the epilogue?' said Henry, who had listened with careful attention to the general sketch of her idea while afternoon tea was served. He glanced longingly down at the sandwiches, scones, and cake arrayed on the china plates but waited until Caroline had poured them both tea before starting to serve himself. 'Are you going back to the Moonbeans Coffee Shop?'

Caroline shrugged and picked up a scone. 'Turns out I quite enjoyed my foray into the fantasy genre.' She added a slice of lemon to her cup of Earl Grey. 'So in the spirit of trying new things, I thought I might have a go at writing a sci-fi romance.' She took a sip of her tea. *Perfect.* 'You know, a proven set of romance tropes — but in space!'

Henry shook his head, but he was grinning. 'Two people who don't like or trust each other have to undertake a long journey alone?'

'Oh dear,' said Caroline, grinning back. 'The StarSeeker drive is only functioning at ten percent capacity, so that light-speed trip that should have taken a day is now going to take three weeks!'

'Good thing they have emergency rations,' Henry noted, taking a couple more sandwiches from the platter.

'Isn't it fortunate? But will they make it to the end of the trip without killing each other?' Caroline considered a moment longer. 'And there have to be robots,' she said decisively. 'One of whom should be called Steve.'

'Do I even want to know who Steve is?'

Caroline shrugged. 'No one in particular. I just think it's a good name for a malfunctioning Roomba.'

'Never change, Carrie.'

'Wasn't planning to. But—' Caroline's smile was wry. 'I need to revise this story first.'

'Yes, well, I had some notes about the politics—'

'Of course you did.'

Acknowledgements

THE FIRST PERSON TO THANK is obviously you, for getting so far as to read the acknowledgements. Really, who does that? I hope it's because you enjoyed the rest of the book so much that you don't want it to end, and not because you're looking for the other people responsible for this mess.

Thank you to every member of my family and every friend who listened to me complain about writing this book. I'm pretty sure that's all of you at this point, but I appreciated every single one of you, and also the tea, prayer, and sympathy you provided.

Thank you to the people who helped me put this book together on a technical level: everyone who gave me feedback on a draft; my editors Stephanie Eagleson, Annie Percik, and Bella Woods (Steph probably still has nightmares about correcting all my wonky ellipses); my proofreaders; my typesetter Libris Simas Ferraz, who made my words look fabulous; and my cover artist Scott Perry, who gave me something far more beautiful than I could ever have envisioned, let alone made myself.

Thank you to the real Nick, without whom Caroline's job would have been even more vague, and who spent more time than was really necessary trying to come up with a plausible acronym for the KNIFE program.

Thank you to my Patrons and channel members, whose support meant I didn't have to worry about not making a proper video for months because I could still pay the bills. Without you, this book would not exist, and I am more grateful than you know.

And lastly, thank you again, reader, for not only starting to read the acknowledgements but also finishing them. You are very thorough, and I respect that. I hope I made it worth your while.

About the Author

JILL BEARUP is an Actor Combatant who has turned her hobby of pretending to hit people with swords on stage into a full-time job as a YouTuber. In 2022 she made a video series about an author and her recalcitrant fantasy heroine. The videos have been viewed over 20M times on YouTube and TikTok, and *Just Stab Me Now*, her debut novel, is the result. Jill was born in Northern Ireland but currently lives in England with her husband, daughter, two cats, and nine swords.